WILDCAT

REIJUL SACHDEV

INDIA • SINGAPORE • MALAYSIA

ISBN 979-8-88975-977-5

Dedication

I would like to dedicate this book to IIIT-Bangalore, my alma mater (and current employer!) for all the wonderful experiences that have shaped me and moulded me into the person I am today – well, at least the good parts! I would particularly like to thank my college ex-Director Professor Sadagopan and current Director Professor Das, as well as all the Professors for inspiring me and making me feel so comfortable there.

I would also like to dedicate this book to Ananth Murthy – for sharing my burdens, lightening my mood with his bad jokes and helping me through the twists and turns of college life. I couldn't ask for a better friend.

ACKNOWLEDGEMENTS

I would like to acknowledge everyone (from our esteemed Professors to our amazing administrative staff) in my college for their support and guidance. But naming everybody would involve writing an entirely new book! However, my gratitude to all my Professors is boundless. If any of you recognise them in these pages, I hope that you realise that most of what I've written is exaggerated and fictionalised, except for the good bits which they truly possess.

I would also like to thank all my batchmates in college and my juniors. Some of my closest friends, including Rahul, Kartik, Sanat, Chandan, Yashvanth, Sankalp, Srikrishna, Tanmayee, Kevin, Prerit, Lucky and Tarun play pivotal roles, or have made guest appearances, in this book. Many thanks to everyone who believed in me and stood by my side when I developed schizophrenia. You guys deserve the credit for this book.

Finally, I would like to thank my parents for helping me polish, edit and publish this book and my grandparents who continue to inspire me (from even beyond the grave).

PROLOGUE

The clouds rumbled ominously overhead. The sky blazed with lightning. As drops of rain fell on my brow, I wondered why I was getting wet in the rain and where the hell the roof was! My mind was fuzzy with the drug with which I had been injected. I knew I wasn't thinking clearly. All I knew was that I was in college. In the distance, I could hear my mother's shouts, or at least something that sounded like them. But were they real or just a figment of my imagination? My consciousness seemed to ooze out of my body. As I blacked out, I felt a sudden rush of memories about this place and everything that had happened here.

You're probably wondering why I had chosen to come here. After all, most people in their right minds would never join a college whose campus was considered by many to be either a parking lot or a wildlife sanctuary!

Well, it's a long story...

CHAPTER 1

Amrish and I were sitting intently in the auditorium packed with people. Not Amrish Puri, unfortunately, though Mogambo (from the movie *Mr. India*) would probably have loved the tension in the air. All around the hall, parents and children sat side by side, as though awaiting judgement in a court. However, all that was going to happen here was a college sales pitch.

Now most people wouldn't understand why a sales pitch by the Principal of a college could be so intimidating. However, I have till now withheld 3 important facts – the country was India, the college was an engineering college and this wasn't an IIT! If you have grown up in India, then you know that there are 3 classes of children – engineers, doctors and rebels. It's also imprinted in all children's minds that if they don't get into an IIT and still pursue engineering, then they are failures, a blight on the family name and a blemish on society in general. However, even that is preferable to pursuing (Heaven forbid!) a Bachelor of Arts degree, anywhere in India.

Now, I was something of an oddity. I came from a family with liberal parents. Perhaps, that's why I had rebelled against being a rebel! I had first prepared for the law entrance exams. But, thanks to the fact that I had studied in such a conservative school, I had changed my mind midway through 12th grade and decided to pursue Physics at St. Stephen's College. But, while awaiting my

CBSE results, my friends and teachers persuaded me to sit for JEE-Mains. By then, I had concluded that if I couldn't be an engineer, then I had no future. I knew I didn't have the time or aptitude to qualify for JEE-Advanced and the IITs, so I decided that I might as well content myself with whatever scraps I could salvage. So, after a leisurely 2 weeks, I sat for the exam. In fact, Amrish (my best friend from high school) had been instrumental in convincing me to take the exam. He had spent a solid 2 years preparing for this exam and given me a bunch of useful tips. In the end, he had spent the last few nights before the exam constantly studying, while I had spent them watching movies, like Iron Man (in my defence, it had something to do with engineering!). So, the result was something of a shock to both of us.

He had ranked 6,000 and something, while I had beaten him and attained the (awe-inspiring!) rank of 5,999! In the meantime, I completed my interview for St. Stephen's and was eligible to study a Physics (Hons.) course there. Neither Amrish nor I qualified for the JEE-Advanced. Amrish was debating between BITS-Pilani and NIT-Surathkal. The thing was he loved Computer Science and didn't want to give it up just to study in a higher ranked institute. That's when he heard a name that would shape both our futures in ways we would never be able to imagine – ICSI.

I'm not sure how Amrish came to hear about ICSI – a fancy acronym for Indian Computer Science Institute. It wasn't even in the city limits. It was so far south of Bangalore that I felt pretty sure we were nearer Kanyakumari!

Anyway, Amrish had come to know about this place from one of his dubious engineering tuition friends, who was also keen on Computer Science and desperate for options. So, as usual, he convinced me to tag along. My parents believed that Amrish was an ideal student and all-round good guy whom I should try to emulate. So, the moment I hinted at ICSI, they were all for it.

Now, ICSI was a 20-year-old institute. But this year was the first time they were launching an undergraduate program (actually, a 5-year integrated BTech-MTech program) in Computer Science. This had generated a lot of interest among the non-IITians. Today was the Orientation, during which the Principal would address the institute's potential candidates, after which everyone would be treated to a vegetarian lunch. But I'm getting ahead of myself.

During the Principal's address, I tried to console myself with the thought of the appetising dishes which were no doubt being prepared. I toyed with the contents of the ICSI goody bag (T-shirt, mug and even a mouse pad) which we had all been gifted as we entered the hall. I noticed that most of the children were listening with rapt attention to what was no doubt a fascinating speech, but one I was barely paying attention to. I was busy checking out the other potential students. They all looked like they were getting last-minute tips for a final exam. I, on the other hand, was trying not to nod off. Finally, the Principal finished. My stomach leaped for joy, only to have its hopes dashed by the Principal's final words – "I now request all of the children to come up, introduce themselves and tell us whether they came to ICSI by choice...or by chance." I already knew there were 52 students in the hall. Yes, in my boredom, I had counted them all. That meant I was in for a long wait!

The students rose from their seats and formed a line, like well-built robots. They then proceeded to return to their seats after mumbling incoherently into the podium mic. All that changed when one enthu cutlet (already wearing his ICSI T-shirt) went up and said, "The fact that I am wearing this T-shirt proves that I came here by choice!" This was greeted by warm applause from around the hall. But, then again, this was someone who had been rejected by pretty much every other engineering college in India. So, his enthusiasm was born from desperation, since he had no other options. But, of course, no one knew that at the time. The only other entry in this one-horse race for brownie points was someone who clearly declared that he came here by chance. This was greeted by a few laughs as well.

Finally, it was my turn. I figured the audience had a sense of humour. So, I decided to tell the truth. "My name is Pranav Dasgupta and I came here for lunch!" For a minute or two there was pin-drop silence. I wondered if there was something sacred about Computer Science and lunch which I had defiled. But then, the Principal began laughing. The professors, students and parents visibly relaxed and started laughing too. I was greeted with scattered applause as I stepped down and took my seat. Thank gosh, the Principal could see the lighter side of things. Oh well, I was only there because of Amrish. Come tomorrow, I'd never have to see any of these people again. At least, that's what I thought...

CHAPTER 2

Generally, I'm not a morning person, especially on holidays. I literally spend only the wee hours of the morning awake and proceed to rouse myself from sleep at noon. I'm also a heavy sleeper – and when I say heavy, I mean it! In my childhood, my mom, dad and the usher at Rex cinema in Bangalore had simultaneously tried to shake me awake as I sat sleeping in our car, which was parked outside Rex. Unfortunately for Rex cinema, they had all spectacularly failed and we had missed watching *George of the Jungle*.

But today, my mom had applied her steely resolve to get me out of bed. She literally tugged me out of bed and deposited me in a lump on the floor. "Okay, Ma. I'm awake, I'm awake!" I exclaimed groggily as I struggled to unwrap the blanket around me and figure out which way was up. "Good, your father and I want to talk to you. It's a serious matter," she said calmly and left the room, as if pulling her son out of bed was the most casual thing in the world.

I glanced at the clock. It was only 7 a.m.! What in the world could be so important at this hour?! Then, with a sense of foreboding, I knew. I quickly showered and changed. I walked out to meet my fate head-on in the dining room. Both my parents were already seated there.

I sat down quietly. Just as my father began, I interrupted, "I think I know what you're going to say and I'm okay with it." My parents shot each other a surprised glance and looked solemnly at me. I wished they could just get on with it and not pretend someone was about to die! "You are?" my father finally asked me. Of course, I was. I wasn't so innocent that I didn't know the way the world worked. I was an adult now. Besides, it wasn't that big a deal for me. I'd watched enough TV to know that plenty of kids went through this.

"So...you understand the full ramifications of this?" my dad asked tentatively. "Of course," I replied promptly. "However," I continued, "I do want to know whether it was mutual or not." My mom replied, "Yes, it was. But we weren't sure whether you'd believe us." I nodded my head in assent. "Then, I guess there's nothing left to say. If money isn't an issue, I hope I get to keep all my stuff?" I asked. I didn't want to part with any of my books or the bookshelves which held them. See, I'm a bookworm at heart, so that's the first thing that popped into my mind. "Of course. Your needs always come before any money issues," my dad replied instantly. "But I'll take some time to make up my mind. After all, for me, money comes first," I said cheekily. "We understand that. But we want you to be happy as well. That's why the choice is up to you," my mom said with a forced smile on her face. "We just thought you'd like to meet him once."

Huh? What was *that* supposed to mean? "Meet whom?" I asked curiously (note how I said "whom" and not "who" – I'm a stickler for grammar). "The Dean, of course," they replied in unison. What on earth was going on? Were they talking about some Dean at St. Stephen's? And what did he/she have to do with this?! Was Dean some sort of codeword? I was totally lost! "Which Dean?" I asked hesitantly, dreading another riddle. "The Dean of Admissions at ICSI, of course. Didn't you say you knew what we were talking about?" my mom asked, looking confused.

"But-but..." I spluttered. "What about the *divorce*?" I finally demanded. "Whose divorce?" my father asked, looking amused. "Your divorce!" I exclaimed, "What have you 2 been talking about all this time?" My mom answered glibly, "Your education and future career, of course." She said it like it was the most obvious thing in the world. "So, what about all that stuff about money and mutual consent?" I asked, totally confused. "Well, the fees at ICSI are much higher. But we didn't want that to worry you. And we mutually agreed that you should speak to him. Did you know that he and Commodore Abhimanyu are college friends? Yesterday, we spoke to the Commodore and he showed us the error of our ways," my dad finally stopped for breath. "Error of our ways"? Seriously? Who spoke like that anymore? Of course, the answer was staring me in the face – Commodore Abhimanyu!

My mom continued the narration. "We met him yesterday and he told us to take ICSI seriously. That's exactly what we're doing now. We think meeting the Dean will be an eye-opener. We're only sorry we didn't guide you properly sooner." Great! So much for being liberals. My parents had turned out to be just as conservative as the rest.

"So, why did you wake me up so early?" I asked furiously. "Oh, that. Well, you're supposed to meet the Dean of Admissions at 10 a.m. So, get dressed fast!" my mom replied, trying desperately to keep a straight face.

Then, they both burst out laughing. I was left staring like the idiot I am. I gritted my teeth in frustration. Commodore Abhimanyu – I should have known.

I should probably back up a little and better explain the situation. Let me start with Commodore Abhimanyu Singh. Imagine a patriotic, retired army officer, who is upright and has served his country devotedly for many years. Imagine he now acts as a security consultant for several companies and has adjusted to civilian life. Finally, imagine he is a gentleman who is concerned about the youth of the nation. You have now imagined the exact opposite of Commodore Abhimanyu!

He is a cranky, old man who drinks heavily and spends most of the day asleep. I have never seen him attend a flag hoisting on Independence or Republic Day. His patriotism seems to have been left behind with his career in the army, but his tendency to bark out orders at people certainly has not! He can't hold on to any job for a reasonable length of time and he loves to reminisce about the "good old days" with anyone who cares to listen.

The only thing which is true is that he *is* concerned about the youth of the nation. His "concern" shows itself in a very odd way. He basically goes around warning parents of how children have lost their innocence completely and how only engineers and doctors can save the future. He is the kind of man (and I speak from experience!) who would cross the road to intercept you and then stop dead in his tracks and claim that you were blocking his path!

The best part of all is that he happens to be my next-door neighbour. Now, my parents aren't as cynical as me. So, while I ignore him completely, they cling to his every pronouncement like it's the gospel truth. And this man had set up a meeting for me with the Dean of Admissions at ICSI. Clearly, it was going to be a *long* day!

I cautiously knocked on the door marked 'Dean of Admissions' and waited expectantly. I continued waiting there for a while before a voice addressed me from the other side of the door. "Come in!" it commanded sternly. I entered and faced a woman holding a steaming cup of coffee in her hand. "I'm Sir's secretary. I like to be addressed by students as Smriti Ma'am. Now, open the door behind me and go in to meet Sir," she said, smiling at me. I pushed through the glass door that led to the Dean's office.

Inside, I got a good look at him for the first time. I mean, I had seen him a week before, but from the last row of a very crowded auditorium. Up close, he didn't look quite so imposing. He was wearing a white bush shirt with a pair of black pants. His shirt shone so brightly that I was surprised he hadn't starred in a Surf Excel ad. He had a bushy, grey beard and moustache. He looked like a typical Tamilian Brahmin, which is exactly what he was.

I assumed he would be laid-back, but his energy surprised me! He jumped up from behind his desk and gestured vigorously for me to come closer. I did so nervously. When I was close enough, he grabbed hold of my hand and shook it so hard that I thought it might fall off!

"Hullo! Welcome to ICSI! I always love meeting new students early in the morning. All of you with your *frush* young minds! The only thing that compares is *frush* filter coffee." His accent was a bad mix of Tamil and American English. "Would you like some coffee?" he finally asked. I shook my head uncertainly. I'm not too fond of coffee in the mornings. Unfortunately, he wasn't the type of man who took "No" for an answer. Before I could say anything, he shouted, "Smriti, bring some coffee for our guest, please!" I hastily tried to stop him. "Sir, it's fine. I really don't need..." I began. But he cut me off, "Call me Professor Iyer. You know when I was in America, I used to tell Steve all the time about our filter coffee. American Starbucks can't compare!" I nodded, uncertainly. "Right, Professor Iyer," I said. I assumed Steve was some random friend of his from America. I was happy to let the matter drop, but he was in full flow.

"You know, I even warned Steve about all these *matlabi* (wily) women who were after him. Thankfully, Steve found Laurette," he continued. I was almost scared to ask, but I was curious. "Sir, by Steve do you mean Steve *Jobs*?" I asked. "Yaas! Of course," he replied. I sat there, not sure whether to be in awe of this man or whether to ask him about my non-existent love life! "You know, you must always beware of *matlabi* women," he finished. Okay, I was sure I wasn't studying at ICSI. I had barely met the guy and he was giving me advice about women!

Suddenly, he became serious and turned his eagle eyes upon me. I think the look he was going for was keen and penetrating, but he ended up looking grandfatherly. "You know Pranav, I know where you're coming from. I understand the different pressures. When I was your age, I also had to consider many different aspects of life before I chose my field. At ICSI, we want our new IMTech

(Integrated BTech and MTech) program to provide you with more than what a simple BTech from the IITs will give you," he said. While all that sounded well and good, I had my doubts. After all, in India, the idea that IITs are supreme is drilled into all our heads. But, hey! Who was I to argue with a man who was on a first-name basis with Steve Jobs?!

"I know how it is. When I was in Japan for some time, I used to have to eat their horrible 'octopushy'," he said, wriggling his fingers in front of his mouth. After some more wriggling, he continued, without breaking his stride, "But though it tastes bad, 'octopushy' is like bitter medicine you have to swallow – a bit like college." I nodded mutely, while he carried on, "Engineering might not seem like the most interesting choice, but it is one of the safest ones. Especially in a field like Computer Science, where you can easily make millions! On the other hand, if you are *frush* out of college with a B.A. or B.Sc. degree, nobody will want to employ you. I'm sure you want to buy a nice house, have a nice car, look after your parents, etc. ICSI will help you do that."

I continued nodding like a moron, until the full impact of his words hit me. He was basically telling me to forget studying at St. Stephen's and study at ICSI instead. "I know the difficulties of employment, Sir. But I'm considering further studies," I began, only to be cut off again, "Good, very good. But to get into the best institutes, an MTech will help you. It shows your commitment to research!" It was like he could read my mind and had an answer for everything I threw at him. I decided to try and blast a hole in his carefully laid plans for my future at ICSI. "Thank you for this talk, Sir. But as far as I know, the IMTech program is a mandatory residential one.

My diabetes might make living in a hostel problematic for me," I replied, surprised that he continued smiling. "Don't worry. I know all about it. Abhimanyu told me. For you, we are willing to make an exception. Think about it and I hope to see you on 1st August," he replied with a broad smile.

"Okay, Sir. Thank you, Sir," I said with a smile plastered all over my face. The smile was authentic. A happier day seemed to greet me as I walked out of the office, leaving behind an untouched cup of filter coffee, Professor Iyer and Smriti Ma'am. Then, I saw her...

She was loud, garrulous and seemed to possess a zest for sweeping floors. This was the cleaning lady. Then, she stepped aside and I again caught sight of the girl I had originally seen. The girl was a stunner and she knew it. She carried herself with an air of poise I imagined only models possess. Yes, I say "imagined" because I'm not really friends with any models, much to my regret. She had long, silky, jet-black hair which hung loose and luscious lips that seemed to promise a kiss. She was as beautiful as a sunset, as passionate as a sunrise, as...all right, you get the picture. I'm running out of similes here.

Naturally, I knew she was way out of my league. The last girl I had dated had more facial hair than me! But I was feeling pretty happy with myself for having survived Professor Iyer's meeting and my pending admission to St. Stephen's. So, with as much swagger as I could muster, I headed towards her.

A dozen lines crowded into my head – "How you doin'?", "Do you wanna grab a bite?", "What's a girl like you doing in a place like this?" and so on. You know, the usual corny pick-up lines that come from watching too many *masala* movies. She glanced briefly in my direction and then haughtily looked away. Clearly, I was not worth her attention. She was now tapping her foot on the freshly-swept floor.

Naturally, being the wordsmith that I am, I delivered the most casual ice-breaker I could think of. "Do you know where the Infosys office is?" I asked as coolly as I could. She looked at me like I was a moron. I was certainly acting like one! "It's just opposite the front gate," she replied frostily. "Oh, um, thanks," I cleverly replied. "No problem," was her less than enthusiastic response. I decided to go out on a limb. "Okay. So, are you like waiting for someone?" I finally asked after an awkward pause. "Did the foot-tapping give me away?" she countered.

Ouch! There is only so much a man can take. I was ready to admit defeat, turn and wander sadly home. Then, she smiled. No, it wasn't a 10,000-watt smile. But it was a cute, little smirk which said, "I'm just fooling around, having some fun. Don't take it personally." To my surprise, she answered, "I'm actually waiting for my brother. He's doing his MTech here and has to take some courses during the summer. Are you a student here?"

"No-yes, well, uh-um, I might be," I replied lamely. "You might be what? A student here? Shouldn't you know?" she laughed. It was the sweetest sound I had ever heard. "Um, yes. Exactly. I should, I guess," I managed to link words together, but I was still wondering what exactly I should say in reply to her question. Thankfully, she continued talking, "Well, I'm starting my architecture course at Synergy College. That's a little down the road. It's a 5-year program. So, see you around...maybe?" she asked, grinning like a Cheshire cat. It was all I could do to gulp nervously and nod mutely. She waved and walked towards someone behind me. I didn't turn to see who it was. I imagined it was her brother. I walked slowly out of the building, wondering if ICSI was such a bad option, after all.

CHAPTER 3

She was strolling down the lobby. The campus wasn't as big as many others, but it still had plenty of greenery and wildlife (and that's excluding the students!). She was enjoying her tour of the place. It seemed like a nice enough institute. Of course, she would never dream of studying here. Computer Science was a nightmare for her. Though it was the summer vacation, there were still a few students in the hostel. Some of them were doing summer courses, others were busy interning at various companies. She left the academic block and stepped out into the dappled sunlight. She made her way towards the basketball court. A few guys were playing, but most were just fooling around. Some of them were mildly good-looking, but she wasn't really interested in any of them. Some of them whistled as she walked by. She didn't bother to react. She was good-looking and she knew it. Some girls would have been offended, but she took it as a compliment.

Then, she decided to make her way back to the parking area. She'd seen enough of the college and her brother. At that moment, she spied someone coming out of the academic block. She only caught a quick glimpse of him before he turned away. But she liked what she saw. He wasn't handsome in a classical sense, but he had a nerdy, intellectual look about him that somehow managed to make him look distinguished. In a few years, she could imagine him as a college professor, charming his students.

Just then, she stopped to shake some stones out of her sandal when she saw it. It was a horrible, ugly centipede. It was fat and filled, no doubt, with all manner of disgusting juices. It crawled across the road on its filthy little legs. She could imagine it in her mind. The feel of the feet on her skin. The way her flesh crept at the very thought was enough. She couldn't bear the sight of it anymore. She quickly looked away and walked onwards. But not before she had done what needed to be done. She stepped deliberately with the heel of her sandal on the centre of the centipede and left it alive. It twitched in agony as it tried to move its severed midsection. She hadn't killed it, but the ants swarming over it would soon finish the job. The centipede writhed in agony as it was eaten alive.

She didn't bother to watch any of this. But she smiled inwardly. The Tigress had killed again and her hunger was sated – for now.

CHAPTER 4

So, there I was. Sitting ready with all my notebooks and pens packed in my school bag. Yes, I was there for my first day of class at ICSI. You're probably wondering how desperate I was to enrol in an institute for the sake of a girl's throwaway smile. I didn't even know her name or number, but I was determined to find out. Meanwhile, I figured I might as well join Amrish at ICSI. Before you dismiss me as a hopeless romantic, I should point out a few things.

My parents were thrilled to bits – so much for being liberal and open-minded! It seemed like Commodore Abhimanyu had brainwashed them into thinking engineering was my real calling. To be fair, I enjoyed Computer Science and I wasn't *that* determined to pursue Physics. Plus, the idea of financial independence appealed to me. I knew my parents were struggling to make ends meet and I was keen to help them out as soon as possible. Finally (and perhaps most importantly!), I would be able to live in Bangalore instead of Delhi. Delhi with its scorching summers, muggy monsoons and freezing winters was not a city I looked forward to returning to. I had spent a couple of years there while still in school. After those 2 years, I was more than happy to return to Bangalore's utopian weather.

In any case, I had finally decided to go to ICSI. Finding a chair, I sat down and put my bag on the table. Amrish was chatting with a group of boys. He had shifted into the hostel a few days ago and made some friends there already. I had no idea who anyone was and none of them knew me, except for Amrish of course. Amrsih waved me over, but just as I was about to go and meet his friends, a professor walked in.

He was short, by any standard. He wore a pair of spectacles and a grimace disguised as a smile. He wore a half-sleeved shirt and seemed fairly lean and fit. As all of us rose to greet him, I was wondering whether he was the P.E. coach. I half expected him to bark at us to stand at attention. Of course, I was wrong as usual. "Sit, sit, please," he said, waving his hands. As one, we sank back into our chairs, not knowing what to expect. He waited till everyone was seated, then he began, "For those of you who attended the Orientation and our Principal's address, welcome back to ICSI! As for those of you who are here for the first time, welcome! You can grab your ICSI merchandise from the reception. For those of you who have already received the ICSI T-shirts, I hope you noticed the message on the back – 'Can't live without IT!'. That's a little bit of ICSI humour. Since all of you will be studying Information Technology, or IT, you literally can't live without it!"

He paused, waiting for some reaction from the class. When his sad attempt at humour was met with pin-drop silence, he coughed and hurried on. I was beginning to like my batch-mates. They might not be great judges of good humour, but they certainly knew a poor joke when they heard one!

"In any case, I am your coordinator and will be responsible for your classes and schedules. My name is

Professor Swaminathan and I sit in a cabin on the ground floor. Do you have any questions before your classes commence?"

I should probably have kept my mouth shut, like the rest of the class, but I just couldn't help myself. I had listened to him drone on enough and I thought a joke (a good one!) would help break the ice. I raised my hand. "Yes?" he asked, looking at me. "What time is lunch, Sir?" I asked as innocently as I could. There were a few laughs from around the room. Professor Swaminathan gazed at me with an annoyed expression on his face. "Well, it depends," he finally said. "On what?" I asked, honestly curious now. "On how long your professors keep you! Now, I had best be off. Remember, in case you need anything, I'm downstairs in my cabin," so saying, he disappeared as quickly as he had arrived.

Amrish turned to me with a grin on his face and flashed me a thumbs-up, as the door shut after Professor Swaminathan's departure. However, the door opened just as suddenly and another professor walked in. I had already memorised the schedule, so I knew that our first class of the day was C-programming. Our ordeal had just begun.

I had already programmed in C++ in 11th and 12th grades. So, I figured I wouldn't have to waste too much time studying for this course. Boy, was I in for a surprise! As our professor walked towards the front of the class, I got a good look at him. He was reasonably tall and commanded attention. He was built like a mountain with forearms that were thicker than my body! He looked more like a bouncer at a pub than a professor! I suppose that's why we took to calling him "Bouncer" later on. But, once again, I'm getting ahead of myself. He had curly black hair with a nasty-looking bald patch. Everyone grew silent and waited for him to speak.

His voice, when he spoke, was surprisingly light. "Hi, guys. I'm Professor Scindia and I come from Alabama," he began. I was so tempted to cut him off and add, "With a banjo on my knee!" But one look at those arms assured me that this was not a man I wanted to tangle with! "I'll be teaching all of you C-programming this semester and Basic Electronics next semester. So, how many of you have programmed before?" he asked in a friendly tone of voice.

About half the class (including me) raised their hands. The rest looked intently at the bare floor, obviously embarrassed. Professor Scindia began counting the raised hands. I'm not entirely sure why. On top of that, he didn't count very fast and seemed to forget whether he had already counted a hand or not. By the time he was done, my hand was stiff from being raised straight up for so long!

As I massaged my stiff arm, he summed it up beautifully, "So around half the class has programmed before." I felt like screaming. A blind man could probably have surmised that faster! "Right, right! Now, let's head to the lab!" he exclaimed enthusiastically. Okay, to be fair to the guy, we were equally enthusiastic about heading to the lab at the time. It would be the first time we had actually entered any of the ICSI labs. In fact, the lab exceeded all our expectations. The lab had more than enough top-of-the-line desktops from HP. There was also a projector connected to a smart screen in the middle of the room. Plus, there were two massive LED TVs on both sides, so that everyone could watch what was written on the smart screen. The only thing that was missing was the air-conditioning. So, while we sweltered in the heat, Professor Scindia sent one of the students to call the electrician – an occurrence that would become all too common for all our lab classes!

"Right, right. Now we'll begin with a short introduction to your *favourite* programming language. Switch on your desktops and login as Guest. Then, open your *favourite* editor – vim," Professor Scindia carried on. He beamed broadly at 53 students who hurriedly set about implementing his instructions. I opened my desktop to a yellowish mauve colour scheme that I would soon come to hate. But I was still young and innocent. I was excited to be using a different operating system from Windows for the first time. Yes, unfortunately, I had never used a Mac before this. Judge me if you will. The operating system that was running on the desktops was Ubuntu – a newer version of LINUX (one of the oldest operating systems). I opened up a terminal and stared at the black screen with the white flashing cursor. I had seen plenty of movies in which programmers hacked into complicated systems with these ordinary looking terminals. But I had no idea what to actually do now that I had one open in front of me!

"Um, Sir, how exactly do you open and use vim?" I asked on behalf of the class. I could tell from the puzzled expressions around the room that everyone was as lost as I was. I suffered from no inhibitions! "Right, right.

So you have to type..." he droned on for the next 10 minutes about vim and how to compile and run a C program. For those of you who have no experience in C-programming in vim, consider yourselves lucky!

C is like the retarded older brother of C++. The similarity only lies in certain names used in both. How best to describe programming in C? It constantly causes your programs to crash with a message all programmers have seen at some time or the other – 'Segmentation Fault (core dumped)'. It displays bizarre error messages for a missing semicolon and has a tendency to enter infinite loops. Imagine driving in rush-hour traffic to reach a meeting which has already begun and then being held up by the stupidity of some other driver. This 'road rage' corresponds to the 'code rage' of programmers dealing with the idiocy of a computer.

By the time the class was done, we were all thoroughly fed up with C and its peculiarities. Professor Scindia had been droning on for a long time and I refocused my attention on him as he suddenly grinned like a maniac and said, "Ha-ha! I feel so evil right now. If only I had a cat to stroke, like one of those Bond movie villains. But survive this and you'll be ready for anything. Don't worry. Soon, this will be your *favourite* programming language." I wasn't so sure. The only thing that I was sure of was that his *favourite* word (pun intended!) was beginning to annoy me! But then he said something which cheered us all up.

"For the end of the semester, I want you to select your *favourite* batchmates and program an actual movable robot in C. Nothing is quite as much fun as that!" So saying, he strutted to the door and left the room.

There was an immediate buzz all over the room as students began assessing potential partners. But there wasn't much time to look around. It was time for our next class – English.

Where Professor Scindia was tall and muscular, our English professor was short and stout. She moved with an odd, duck-like waddling motion and looked severely around the room till the class had quietened down. Once she had everyone's attention, she introduced herself – "Myself Shanti Kasturba. I offer to teach you English here. I know you all don't think it's important, but I am here to tell it matters more than you know."

I think I was somewhere between a state of shock and a state of death by laughter! *This* lady was supposed to teach *us* English?! She spoke horribly accented English and what sort of person introduced themselves as "myself"? Thankfully, I managed to stifle my laughter. Amrish, however, made no attempt to hide his grin.

Almost immediately, Professor Kasturba fixed her eagle eyes (well, maybe she wasn't quite that penetrating) on him. "You think there's something funny here?" she demanded, almost daring him to answer. Now, Amrish is not the most tactful of people. He usually keeps his head down and stays out of trouble. But if he takes a dislike to someone, he goes out of his way to make life difficult for them. So, he slowly stood up and said, "Yes, Ma'am. I do think there is something funny here." Professor Kasturba immediately retorted, "And what's that?" Amrish continued, cool as a cucumber, "I think I'm overqualified for this class. I don't think there's much point in learning English from scratch all over again."

Professor Kasturba nearly choked on her next words. She swelled up to even larger proportions like a hot-air balloon! Her face turned a deep shade of red and I wondered if she was about to burst into flames! Frankly, she looked even funnier than before if that was possible. Finally, she seemed to settle down and spoke in a deceptively calm voice. "So, you know English very well? Then you come up and speak about your role model for a few minutes," she challenged Amrish.

Uh-oh! This could be a problem. Amrish was a nervous wreck on any public platform. While he always came up with good one-liners as a listener, his confidence deserted him as a speaker. Amrish seemed to realise that he had made a terrible mistake, but he had crossed the line. Professor Kasturba would force him to do this, even if he tried to back down now. He was stuck and he knew it. Besides, I knew Amrish would never back down from a challenge, even one as silly as this.

While Amrish hesitantly walked to the front of the class, Professor Kasturba plonked herself down in his now-empty chair. Amrish's hands were visibly shaking. It was clear that it took all his self-control not to run back to his seat. He fumbled and started, "My uh...role model is um...well, um...Narayana Murthy. He...um, well changed the way people thought of India. He uh..." His voice trailed away as he ran out of things to say. Meanwhile, Professor Kasturba was obviously taking great joy in humiliating poor Amrish. She suddenly stood up. "Um...uh...um – is that your English? I know your type. You think one or two words are good enough? That's why I offer to help," she mocked Amrish.

She resumed her place in front of the class, as Amrish shamefacedly slunk back to his chair. "Now, I need to know who can speak and who can't. So...I want each of you to take turns and come speak about your role model. Volunteers?" she asked, still looking annoyed. Everybody shrank back into their seats and tried to look as inconspicuous as possible. But I had had enough of this professor. Okay, Amrish was out of line. But a simple lecture would have been enough. There was no need to humiliate him in front of the entire class. Plus, I had thought of an apt quote and wanted to use it.

So, I decided to raise my hand. My hand was about half-way up, when Professor Kasturba noticed me. Now, make no mistake, I was no great orator. But I had participated in a few debates back at school when I was still interested in law. So, speaking to a crowd wasn't that big a deal for me. Professor Kasturba gestured for me to join her at the front of the class. I did so and looked around the room at my audience, hoping they would get my sarcasm and subtle humour. Meanwhile, Professor Kasturba occupied my chair and indicated that I should begin.

"My role model is the famous poet, playwright and novelist Oscar Wilde. I'd like to begin with a poem dedicated to him by Dorothy Parker:

When in literate society, I am

Impelled to try an epigram,

I never seek to take the credit

We all assume that Oscar said it."

I carried on about Wilde's life and works for a while, throwing in a few funny quotes of his to make the mood a little lighter. There were a few laughs from around the room. Finally, I decided to use a fictional anecdote about Wilde from a book by someone named Gyles Brandreth, who used Oscar Wilde's writings and turned them into stories starring Wilde as a detective. It was one of my favourite series of books and this anecdote came straight from one of the books. I was banking on the fact that no one else had read it. But that seemed like a safe assumption to make.

"I'd like to end my speech with an anecdote from Wilde's life. While once attending a party, Wilde was taken aside by his hostess who proceeded to give him advice on fashion. Now, Wilde was a proud man, especially about clothes. He certainly didn't like to be told how to dress. But he swallowed his pride and listened to her mindless talk. After some time, she said, 'I hope you don't mind my offering you this advice, Mr. Wilde.' Wilde replied, 'Ma'am, I find that people tend to give that which they themselves most need. I call this the depths of generosity'."

Yes, I was taking a dig at Professor Kasturba for her previous comment on her "offer to help" Amrish because he only knew a few words of English. Thankfully, she seemed to miss the sarcasm entirely, while the rest of the class seemed to get it. The room burst into applause and guffaws as I returned to my seat. Even Professor Kasturba was smiling. She waddled back to the front of the class.

"So, some of you can speak," she said, after the class had settled back down. "We'll hear more presentations next time. Meanwhile, I want you all to write a movie review of *Bend it like Beckham* by next class. Now, you can go for lunch." After she had left the room, a breath of fresh air seemed to fill the class and I was greeted by a lot of back-slapping and handshaking. Maybe ICSI wouldn't be so bad, after all...

CHAPTER 5

As I was heading towards the canteen, I saw something that stopped me in my tracks. It was her! The same girl I had met when I had come to ICSI to meet the Dean of Admissions. I was delighted to see her on my very first day! I told Amrish and his friends to carry on and assured them I'd join them soon. Then I turned and tried to swagger towards her with great style.

She was busy tacking a poster to one of our notice boards. So far, the only things on the notice boards were pictures of ducks with the caption 'Wildlife in ICSI'. All of us IMTech students would think of pinning pictures of our professors to the boards, but no one ever had the guts!

In any case, she was with a group of people who seemed to be our age. I guessed they were all from Synergy College. Unlike the nerds I had encountered in my batch (myself included), they seemed to be cooler and much more fashionable. She finished with the poster and suddenly noticed me. I tried to look cool and nonchalant. "What's wrong with your face? You look hopelessly lost! And why are you walking like that? Did you get a groin pull?" she asked with a mischievous smile on her lips.

So much for my jaunty walk and nonchalant look! I promised myself that I would practise both in front of a mirror every day. "Don't worry. Nothing permanently damaged, except my pride!" I declared with a smile. She tilted her head back and laughed. It was a full, throaty sound that seemed out of place, coming from someone so petite.

"So, was my irresistible charm the reason you're back here?" I teased gently. She laughed once again. "I'd have to be devoid of all 5 senses to call you charming!" she exclaimed. Ouch! I have to admit that stung. Then, she flashed that smile of hers and everything was right with the world again. "In that case, why are you here today? And what's up with your poster? Are you guys holding a fest or something?" I enquired, eager to steer clear of any potential jokes at my expense.

"Well, it's actually an inter-college debate competition. You have to come in teams of 2. One person speaks for the motion and one person against. It's being held in a month. Do you want to compete?" she asked, sounding (dare I say it?) hopeful. Yeah, right. Like I was going to embarrass myself in public while she looked on. "I don't think that's a great idea..." my voice trailed away as she smiled at me again. "Well, you could impress me if you win!" she said. "Don't be so shy. I'll protect you from the worst of it!" she exclaimed, egging me on. Now, I knew that I *had* to compete. Not just for her. I had competed in a similar-style debate in high school and ended up suffering a terrible defeat. This would give me a chance to retrieve some of my lost pride. All I really needed was a partner who was as motivated as I was. That's when I made one of the biggest mistakes of my life.

"Sounds like fun. I haven't exactly had a lot of practice lately, so you'll have to forgive me if I'm a little rusty!" I replied with a smile of my own. "Plus, I have to deal with college work," I continued. "But if I can survive a month in this place, I can probably survive anything!" I declared triumphantly. At that moment, it seemed like the world was laid out before me, waiting for me to conquer it. If only I had known then, what I know now. But perhaps that is the fate of all mortals – to live with regret. Listen to me, talking like a philosopher! Let's get back to where I left the story.

She replied, "Great! I'll catch up with you there!" She smiled and winked, turning back to her group of friends. A sudden thought occurred to me. "Oh! By the way, I never caught your name," I said casually, trying to be smooth. "Wow! Look at you. Smooth moves and everything!" she exclaimed, grinning wickedly. "My name is Naina. But if you want my number, you're going to have to win..."

CHAPTER 6

After meeting Naina, I headed in a state of general bliss towards the canteen. But since I had wasted the precious early minutes of lunch time, I found myself in a line at least 100 metres long. It was then that I realised that *everyone* in our college came to the same canteen. From the Principal to distinguished visitors to our support staff. Everyone had the same food. It was all well and good in the spirit of equality, but the food could certainly have been better!

I know what you're thinking. Every college student complains about canteen food, right? But not only was everything vegetarian (which for a hardcore Bengali like me was unthinkable!), but the food was so bad that even the most hardcore foodies (like Amrish) could only manage a few mouthfuls. And the worst part was that the menu never changed. For the entire semester, we had the same awful menu! Thankfully, I only ate lunch there. But Amrish later told me how bad breakfast was and dinner was as unappetising.

In any case, I loaded my plate with rice and water (pretending to be 'dal'). I also grabbed plenty of 'papads' and made my way over to join Amrish and his gang. Amrish had assembled quite a crew in a very short time. The first person he introduced me to was Ramesh, his roommate. Now I'm quite a heavy person, mostly due to my muscles and high-protein diet – just kidding! The sad truth is that I'm borderline overweight. But I'm also pretty tall, so it's not as though I have a paunch. Next to Ramesh, however, I looked positively anorexic! He was the big man in the room. Everything seemed to gravitate towards him. The funny thing was that he didn't look like some big mafia don. As a matter of fact, with his goofy spectacles and baby-fat, he looked like an overgrown child. So, I thought I'd get to know him better.

"How are you finding college?" I asked, after the introductions had been made. "Okay," he replied, trying to ignore me and focus on the plate piled high with rice in front of him. "Is Amrish making you clean the room and tidy up after him? Trust me, I know from school how he loves to dump his work on others and sit playing 'Call of Duty' or 'Counter-Strike'!" I tried to carry on the conversation. Amrish happened to overhear this last remark. He immediately replied, "You don't know this guy, *macha*. Before I moved in, my mom also gave me a lecture telling me to do some work and not exploit this fellow. But I'm literally not *allowed* to play anything until I've swept the room and cleaned up the bathroom! He's only sweet-looking from the outside. He's one proper don, *macha*!"

Ramesh smiled, gave a giggle and pushed his empty plate away. I looked at him in a new light. Anyone who could boss Amrish around like that demanded respect. "Is that true?" I asked him. He gave a strange half-smile and just uttered a single syllable – "Yeah."

After lunch, we were introduced to Professor Kumar and had our first class of Python programming. He was a short, stubby man, who peered at us from behind thick spectacles with a twinkle in his eye. His head was practically devoid of hair. But he made up for that with his luxuriant moustache, which we noticed that he loved to stroke. It was thick and white and looked completely out of place on his school-boyish face. As we got to know him, we found that he carried a lunchbox around his neck – that's how school-boyish he was! He had a funny kind of laugh which proceeded from the centre of his belly, making it jiggle madly, till it travelled up his throat and erupted from his mouth as a sort of roar.

Anyway, back to class. What can I say about Python? It is *way* better than C. But if you're trying to program polynomial multiplication on your first day, it can leave you with a headache. The thing about Professor Kumar was that he would not just give us challenging problems (which I can't solve till date), but would also give us extra credit for good-looking code rather than for ugly code which actually ran!

Professor Kumar found his favourite student on the first day. It was a boy named Dhanush, who had this annoying habit of bobbing his head up and down, like a floating cork. He couldn't get *any* code to run, but Professor Kumar loved his *style* of coding. Dhanush used long-sounding variable names and lots of spacing to make it readable. Now, even at the best of times, my code is what you'd call messy (and that's if you're being polite!). Coding styles are like handwriting. Some people have calligraphic handwriting and others (like me) might write something that doesn't look so great, but which would have some serious content concealed within.

By the end of class, I was totally exhausted after solving the problem. I presented it to Professor Kumar, convinced that no one could have done better. As usual, I was wrong. Professor Kumar quickly glanced at my code and muttered, "Make it more readable." He mumbled something along the same lines to everyone in class before finally reaching Dhanush. Seeing Dhanush's code, Professor Kumar started beaming. He then got Dhanush to stand up and announce his name to the class, before adding, "Guys, you should all try to code like Dhanush. Look how neat and tidy he is. He's a role model for all of you. Give him a round of applause!" There was some half-hearted applause which quickly faded away. Everyone, it seemed, was in a bad mood except for Dhanush.

Dhanush looked around shyly, then sank back into his seat. I couldn't believe that such a brilliant professor could like a student who couldn't even write running code. I turned to Amrish who was next to me. "Can you believe this? The 2 of us actually got running code and that Dhanush gets the credit! For all you know, Professor Kumar will start giving him gifts soon," I whined. Amrish nodded and agreed with me, "Too bad this is, *macha*. Die, die!" I was a little startled. "Well, I'm not sure we ought to be that harsh..." I began, but Amrish cut me off, "Not you, *macha*. I'm playing 'Call of Duty' online. Wanna join?" I was feeling frustrated, so I said, "Sure. Why not?" Losers can't be choosers, right? Besides, every time I killed someone, I imagined it was Dhanush with his bobbing head. Violent video games are so much better than therapy.

But one great thing we soon discovered was that Professor Kumar never picked on any students or tried to embarrass them. He was a jovial, easy-going type of guy. Whenever he gave us an assignment, he would try his best to act strict. He would say something like, "Okay, guys. This time you have one week for the assignment and no deadline extensions or anything of the sort." While the hardcore nerds would immediately start to program, Amrish and I (along with other cool guys) would wait till the deadline had almost arrived. We would then leisurely stroll over to Professor Kumar's cabin and try to look as shamefaced as possible. By then, even the sincerest students would have given up hope of getting their program to run correctly. So, naturally, they would join us.

He would come out of his cabin, trying (and failing!) to conceal a smile under his moustache. We would begin pitifully with something along the lines of "Sir, could we have just one more week...?" He would give an exaggerated sigh and say, "Guys, this is just not done. You must stick to deadlines." We would all reply, "Yes, Sir. But just this once..." Then, his belly would start jiggling and we would know we were in the clear. "Why does this happen *every* time?!" he would ask rhetorically. "All right guys. Take another 2 weeks." We would chuckle along with him and happily drift off till the cycle began again.

The last class of the first day of college was Real Analysis. Amrish and I quickly shut down our desktops and moved towards the safety of the back benches. Amrish was seated on my left and Soorya on my right. Soorya was another friend of Amrish's who I had been introduced to during lunch. How best to describe Soorya? If Ramesh looked like an overgrown baby, then Soorya looked like a weird little man-child. You know those guys who star in the 'Fair and Handsome' ads? Well, Soorya was the exact opposite. He was short and dark with nerdy-looking glasses and a youngish-looking face. His 'handsomeness' (if it ever existed!) was hidden behind a bushy black beard.

The professor who taught Real Analysis was curiously named Molecule Mukherjee! Yes, 'Molecule' really was his first name – not a nickname or anything of the sort. What kind of sadistic parents would name their child 'Molecule' and leave him to the mercy of a cruel world?! Professor Mukherjee was a colourful character. Though we didn't know it then, he was a fantastic table-tennis player. He had beaten most of my classmates before the first week was over.

He had a small, white Hitler-like moustache which never seemed to grow or shrink. We soon realised that he *always* wore a starched white shirt with white trousers and shoes to match. On top of this, he wore a white hat with a number of holes along the side, or as Professor Mukherjee called them, "AC vents". He had quite a bit of (you guessed the colour by now) white hair on his head. But he still chose to wear the hat. I saw him only once without it. With his sparkling clothes, short-cropped hair and moustache he looked like a cross between Hitler and Jeetendra!

On the first day, Professor Mukherjee started scribbling on the smart board and soon covered it with numbers and Greek symbols. After a while, my eyes glazed over and I drifted off. To stop myself from falling asleep, I spent most of the class looking at the sea of faces around me. Most people were daydreaming. A few had put their heads down and were openly sleeping. Every once in a while, an unfortunate student would be thrown a question by Professor Mukherjee. His/Her neighbours would then wake him/her up and for a time, the student would pay attention, before drifting off again. Even Dhanush seemed to be lost and had ceased his head-bobbing. But Soorya continued scribbling and asked Professor Mukherjee a few questions which clearly proved he understood every word.

After a while, I whispered to Soorya, "Are you getting this?" He whispered back, "Yeah...it's a proof by contraposition. You simply invoke the Trichotomy property of real numbers and then..." he carried on, explaining the rest of it to me. Not that I understood a word he said. He clearly saw that I was still lost. Finally, he added, "If you have any doubts, come to me after class. I'll explain everything."

Soorya was clearly a maths whizz. With an IQ like that, I was amazed that he had chosen to come here. Well, genius comes in different shapes and sizes. I had already decided that he was going to be my salvation for Real Analysis for the rest of the semester.

Professor Mukherjee, we later found out, was never strict about attendance or other administrative details. His only rule was that if you were in his class, you had to either be asking questions or answering them. On the first day, Soorya was the only one asking questions. Since I wanted to do as little work as possible, I soon began questioning every step of Professor Mukherjee's proofs and results. This kept him in a good mood. However, occasionally he would compare us to his ex-students at IIT-Kanpur. This, naturally, cast us in a rather unfavourable light. All non-IIT engineers will know what I'm talking about. But what won him popularity points was that he let us sit for plenty of retests as and when needed. And they were needed a lot!

CHAPTER 7

By the end of the first week, we had to choose an elective – Biology or Chemistry. For Amrish and me, it was a no-brainer. We had ditched Biology in Grade 11 and opted for Computer Science. We were in a college that specialised in Computer Science. So, why would we want to study Biology again? I assumed the Biology classes would bombard me with a host of unfamiliar terms and I would be asked to prepare slides in the lab (and I don't mean the PowerPoint variety!). So, I had my speech prepared for our coordinator as to why I wanted to study Chemistry. Amrish and I had agreed to visit our coordinator together. But you must understand one thing about me. I lived by Mark Twain's quote, "Never put off till tomorrow what you can do day after tomorrow just as well."

As a result, Amrish and I ended up recording our preferences at the end of the first week – the very last day possible. We headed to our coordinator's cabin. It was tucked away in an empty part of the administrative block. I hesitantly knocked on the door and poked my head in. Thankfully, he didn't have an angry secretary! He swivelled his chair to face us. "Hey guys! Come in!" he exclaimed, gesturing for us to sit down. "Um, Sir, we came about the elective registration..." I began. But his face grew serious and my voice trailed away. "Is there a problem, Sir?" Amrish asked a little nervously. Professor

Swaminathan regarded us with a poker face that would have been more at home in a Vegas casino than a college for Computer Science. Finally, he answered, "It depends." In time, I would learn that this was his favourite phrase. But I still didn't know him well enough and so I grew concerned.

"Depends on what, Sir?" I asked openly. "On whether you like having a choice or not," he replied coolly. "Isn't that the point of an elective?" I asked, regretting the words as I said them. "It depends," came his considered response. "On what?" Amrish and I asked in unison. "On how quickly you register. It seems most of your batchmates have opted for Chemistry. So, we have too many Chemistry students and too few Biology students. As a result, you both will have to settle for Biology," came the answer. That's when I delivered my well-rehearsed speech about why I should be studying Chemistry. I even left in the joke about 'slides' (which I figured would win me some points!). However, Professor Swaminathan was unmoved. "Don't worry. I'm sure you will love the classes," he said reassuringly. Only later did I find out just how right he was.

I was extremely sceptical about what my Biology professor could do to make the subject more interesting. However, I was pleasantly surprised by how he began the class. He introduced himself as Professor Vishnu Nayar. Then, he said something that I still remember – "I don't care about whether you all memorise the textbook or not. I'll be a satisfied professor if you can look out the window and enjoy the natural surroundings." He loved Biology and wanted to make the subject interesting for us. Instead of hours spent in the lab, we would visit Lal Bagh for our practical classes and eat at one of Bangalore's most famous snack points – Vidyarthi Bhavan. On the other hand, the unfortunate Chemistry students had to identify salts and study the Hamiltonian operator (whatever that means!). They always looked overburdened with work, while we never had a single assignment all through the semester.

However, even Professor Nayar came with his own set of problems. He tended to repeat himself. This was so acute that sometimes when he was in the middle of a sentence, he would go back to the beginning and start afresh. He also had a strong Malayali accent. It was so bad that when he introduced himself, we thought he was wishing us a Happy New Year!

But the "unkindest cut of all" came in the form of an end-sem exam for which he gave us a warning of just one week! And yes – he had expected us to mug up the Biology textbook! I guess you can take the professor out of the exam set-up, but you can't take the Indian exam mentality out of the professor!

CHAPTER 8

The next couple of weeks sped past. Classes continued in full swing and work seemed to follow me home. There were a few interesting incidents that spiced up our lives. Our English teacher, Professor Kasturba, accidentally wrote on the smart board with a white board marker. That permanently ruined the board, as only a special stylus was supposed to be used to write on the smart board. In addition, we had a photo shoot with Narayana Murthy – which was pretty exciting, except for the fact that he didn't show up! Apparently, he had to cancel at the last minute. So, we had to make do with our coordinator. All was right at ICSI.

But there remained one unresolved issue in my life – who could I pick as a debating partner? Then, one day, the answer bumped into me and I mean literally. It was a rare Biology lab session in which we were actually doing some work. We were preparing transverse sections of the hibiscus stem. I had just about finished mine and was viewing my slide under the microscope when someone bumped into me and made me fumble with my slide.

"Hey, watch it!" I exclaimed angrily. I was horrible at lab work and didn't need it being screwed up by somebody else. "I'm so sorry. Let me help you with that," a voice offered. I turned in the direction of the voice and saw... nothing! "Ahem! I'm down here," the voice said again. This time I looked down and noticed a guy Amrish had earlier introduced me to. His name was Preetish. I hadn't spoken to him much, besides the usual "Hi" and "Bye".

He was small and scrawny, but liked to swagger around as if he owned the college. This probably came from the fact that he was best friends with the most macho guy in our batch, whose name was John. John was a big bruiser of a guy whom nobody messed with. He was almost as imposing as Professor Scindia. There was one misguided fool in our batch who made the mistake of calling John a "pansy" because he used a skipping rope in his training routine. The next day, that guy showed up with a black eye.

I examined Preetish again. I could tell he was a Brahmin from his sacred thread. He wasn't all that scrawny after all. It's just that he wore clothes which were too big for him. He had a slightly nasal voice, but not an annoying one. The most striking thing about him was his resemblance to a mountain goat. He had a scraggly, little beard which consisted of only 4 hairs. To compensate for the lack of a beard, he had a slight fuzz on his upper lip trying to pass itself off as a moustache. All in all, there were better things to look at in this world!

But, as I had learnt from Soorya, genius is often unattractive. So, I muttered a "Thanks" under my breath. But he seemed to be in a sociable mood. He carefully replaced the slide under the microscope and (before I could stop him) peered at it. "Your section is a little too thick," he continued, turning to face me again. "I'm guessing you followed Professor Nayar's advice and tried to extract it with one clean sweep of the razor. Use a sawing motion instead. Just do what I do..." he explained, preparing another section so that he could demonstrate the technique.

I followed his instructions and, sure enough, I got a thin translucent section rather than a thick, opaque one. "Hey, thanks! That really did the trick," I said, looking down at him (that sentence did not come out right!). "So how come you know so much of this stuff?" I asked curiously. "My elder brother's a doctor, so I used to help him whenever he was preparing slides and stuff like that. Do you have any siblings?" he asked. "Nope. I'm an only child and quite happy being one," I replied. Suddenly, I realised he had effortlessly taken control of the conversation and was chatting away.

"You can easily strike up a conversation. Have you ever debated?" I asked. "Well, I haven't really debated, but I used to participate in a lot of Model United Nations (MUN) competitions at school," he replied. I grew hopeful. "Well, the thing is there's this debate a couple of weeks from now and I really need a partner for it. You have to appear in teams of 2. It's an extempore debate – you have half an hour to prepare. Then, one person speaks 'for' the motion and the other person speaks 'against'. It's being held at Synergy College, down the road from ours. So, do you wanna go?" I asked, hoping against hope that he would agree.

"Well, it depends," replied Preetish immediately. Oh no! Not another carbon copy of our coordinator. I had almost given up hope of finding a debating partner. There were plenty of guys in my batch who were smart enough, but mumbled in front of an audience. Knowing Preetish was a public speaker, but would probably refuse, only made it worse. So, I figured I'd tell him the truth. "Well, the fact is, there's this girl I'm hoping to meet there. I, uh, have met her before. But I was uh...hoping to catch up with her again..." my voice trailed away as his face broke out into a huge smile. “Well, technically I can’t go because I’m on the college basketball team and we have a match coming up in 2 weeks...” he began.

This was news to me. I had no idea that there *was* a college basketball team, much less that Preetish was on it. I felt crushed knowing I’d probably never see Naina again. “But...” Preetish continued, “I’d much rather attend a debate organised by Synergy College girls! So, count me in.”

My heart leaped for joy. My slide was perfect, classes for the day were done and I had a debating partner, after all. Things were definitely looking up.

Preetish and I decided to hold our practice sessions in his room after class every day. At that time, John would be at the gym for an hour or so. That meant we had plenty of time to do what we wanted. As a result, I soon realised that Preetish had tremendous experience...at losing! He had somehow made it through every MUN he had attended. He tried to beat his opponents by talking too much, but he had no substance to speak of.

He tried to handle the first few sessions like the pro he was not! His first session was about how girls shouldn’t smoke. I thought he would pick one side and I would pick the other and then we would debate. I still didn’t know Preetish well enough. He spoke for half an hour (I’m not exaggerating!) on how girls who smoked were corrupting our society and how it was against *dharma*.

After a few days, even I could tell he needed to be taken in hand before he became another Nathuram

Godse! While I hadn't debated much, I had participated in the Frank Anthony Memorial debate for ICSE schools all over the country. As you can probably guess, I got knocked out in the second round. But the format was identical. So, I figured we could start with some of the topics I had practised back then.

I usually let Preetish pick first and then chose the opposing side. We started off with a few simple topics. Stuff like, 'Schools are better off without uniforms', 'Absolute power corrupts absolutely', etc. We then moved on to topics which required some general knowledge, like 'Man, not machines, should be exploring space' and 'Reservations are essential at the school level'. We spoke for a few minutes each. After both speeches were done, we would look for holes in each other's arguments and try to ask each other difficult questions. Our question-answer sessions lasted about 2 minutes. Soon, we were pretty comfortable with speaking to an audience of one!

Meanwhile, we also began to hang out together. After our sessions were over, we would go over to the college's trophy collection and boast about bringing back another. While our training sessions were going well (maybe "well" is too strong a word – more like okay-ish), we got dumped with another problem which neither of us had anticipated. We ran into someone else who wanted to compete in the Synergy debate! And for some strange reason, he had got it into his head that I wanted to be his partner, despite my vociferous objections. I guess I should go back to how we first met...

CHAPTER 9

His name was Venugopal and he was standing in front of me at the canteen. I knew him vaguely as "a bit of a weirdo" (in Amrish's words). I've already talked about Amrish's habit of judging people too quickly. So, I was willing to give the guy a chance before jumping to conclusions. But it had been a long and tiring morning filled with Real Analysis and Python programming. I wanted to grab lunch and head off to join Amrish, Ramesh, Soorya and the other guys we hung out with. But Venugopal stood in front me and kept piling curd rice onto his plate. Now, I'm allergic to milk. So, the sight of an entire tray of curd rice made me feel like vomiting.

"Excuse me!" I finally said. "You're holding up the line. Do you mind moving along?" I asked in a slightly irritated tone of voice. He turned back to face me. This was the first time I got a good look at him. He had a crew cut and wore a pair of very misshapen glasses. He was of average height, but had a slight hunch. I was expecting him to be angry or at least annoyed with me for disturbing him. But he just laughed, "Heh-heh-heh!" He then turned away from me, took some more curd rice and finally left the queue. I quickly heaped my tray with food and carried it over to Amrish's table. But I got there too late! All the seats were taken.

I cursed Venugopal and headed to the other end of the canteen. I saw a table for 2 and plonked myself down there. I was just about to lift a spoonful of 'dal' to my lips, when I was suddenly stabbed in the ribs! You're probably thinking that someone had come at me with a dagger and was watching as the blood gushed out. Well, nothing so dramatic happened. You know how you jerk when someone pokes you in the ribs? Imagine that while you're holding a spoonful of yellow 'dal'. I jumped and spilled the 'dal' all over my favourite white T-shirt.

I spun around to find the person responsible. It was (no prizes for guessing) none other than Venugopal. I was ready to whack him with the tray, while he stood there grinning and laughing his weird laugh – "Heh-heh-heh!" Finally, he spoke in a guttural voice, "Watch out for my finger electrodes!" He then plonked himself down opposite me.

I resisted the urge to smack him and sank back into my chair. I wondered if this was payback for me hurrying him up in the line. I was still annoyed, though my anger had reduced somewhat. The reason was that I realised most of what I had spilled was water. For once, I was grateful that the ICSI 'dal' was so watered down. As a result, my T-shirt was only lightly stained. A good wash with enough Surf Excel ought to do the trick.

"So, what's up?" I asked cautiously, not sure I really wanted to know the answer. He ignored me and began to shovel curd rice into his mouth. I decided that he would hopefully ignore me for the rest of lunch and wolfed down my lunch in a few bites. That's another thing I should probably mention, when I say I eat fast, I mean *really* fast. I usually pretend to eat during most of lunch break and then shovel my food down in the last 2 minutes. In fact, if I wanted, I could probably pile my plate with food and wolf it down by the time I walked over to the nearest table. But Venugopal had freaked me out. So, I quietly finished my lunch and was just about to get up and go.

He suddenly spoke up, "I heard Preetish and you are going for that Synergy College debate. Do you guys need a partner?" Yeah, as much as we needed a third wheel! And before you make the obvious joke, this wasn't an autorickshaw...it was a sleek bike! In spite of everything, however, I didn't want to hurt the guy's feelings too badly. So, I tried to soften the blow. "Well...not really. But I'm sure there's other stuff we can work on together! Besides, I'm sure there will be plenty of other debates. Are you a good public speaker?" I asked tentatively. "No. I am very bad. That's why I want you to help me. I liked that talk you gave on Oscar Wilde. I thought we could team up for the debate since you were going. Why don't I talk to you now about some personal experience and you give me some pointers on how to improve?" he asked eagerly. He sounded like an enthusiastic puppy. I just couldn't say "No" to him.

I sighed. I really didn't want to listen to this, but it looked as if I had no choice. "Okay, go ahead," I told him. He laughed again and then proceeded to tell me in excruciating detail about how he had been circumcised! By the end of lunch, I rushed off to puke. Trust me, this had nothing to do with my milk allergy and everything to do with his story. But, I had endured the worst...or so I thought!

The next day, I met up with Preetish for our practice session. There were about 10 days left for the debate.

We were excited, but also a bit nervous. We were just getting started when Venugopal knocked on the door and peeked inside the room. "Hey! I wanted to attend one of your practice sessions. Just to improve myself," he said and laughed that annoying laugh of his.

I figured things would probably go smoothly if we let him watch. Yes, yes. I was wrong as always. Anyway, I said okay. Our topic for the day was 'The mouse is mightier than the sword'. Preetish was going to speak first and was speaking 'for' the motion. But, he had barely begun, when Venugopal jumped up and said, "You can kill a mouse with a sword. How can this topic make sense?" Did the guy not understand metaphors? Why had the college let him in? And why was I studying in a college with guys like him? Was I really such a lost cause?

Preetish ignored him and carried on. For a while, Venugopal was quiet. Then, he suddenly got up and started pacing the room. He kept fidgeting during my speech too. Finally, he lashed out with his fist and hit the wall! Preetish and I just couldn't focus. We decided to cancel the day's session. We hoped he'd take the hint and disappear.

But he showed up the following day and the day after. We tried shifting our venue from Preetish's room to an empty classroom in the academic block. But nothing worked. He would just follow me all around the college after the end of lectures for the day. It got so bad that even Amrish and his gang began avoiding me. Preetish clearly told me that if I wanted him as a partner, I needed to get rid of Venugopal.

I tried to talk Venugopal out of following me. But he didn't let up. He kept saying he wanted to improve his English. I couldn't get rid of him without either physically restraining him or telling a professor. I didn't want to do either. He wasn't really a bad guy. It seemed like I was going to blow my chance with Naina. But, one day, inspiration struck!

After our class in Python programming, Professor Kumar told us that he was planning to start a maths club and everyone who was interested ought to register. I had always enjoyed maths (except for Professor Mukherjee's classes!), so I rather liked the idea of a maths club, especially if it was run by a non-IIT professor. Of course, Venugopal (my stalker) also signed up. Professor Kumar handed out some sheets to all the registered students. They contained a bunch of maths problems and were apparently from some journal called *American Mathematical Monthly (AMM)*. The problems were submitted by professors, students, researchers and enthusiasts from all over the world. Solving a problem meant your name would be published in a subsequent issue of the *AMM*. This was apparently a big deal in the maths community.

I was still studying the problems intently as I walked to lunch. I sat down at my table and began gobbling up food. I barely noticed Venugopal when he sat down opposite me. Then he interrupted my flow of thought, as usual. "Are you getting anywhere with those problems? I'm still stuck!" he exclaimed and laughed. That's when the idea hit me. "Hey, do you wanna team up to solve a problem? Forget the debating sessions. We could work on a solution. We'll set up a meeting time and brainstorm together. But first, a couple of ground rules..."

I told him not to stalk me, not to disturb our debating sessions and talk to me if and only if I was free. To my relief, he agreed to all my terms and conditions. I allowed myself a smile of satisfaction. I headed off to find Amrish, leaving Venugopal with his beloved curd rice.

CHAPTER 10

There were just 2 days left for the debate. Preetish and I were both suffering from nervousness. Thankfully, there was something going on at college to distract us, namely, the Student Council elections. The elected representative would be responsible for organising events, along with our coordinator. He/She would also have to arrange opinion polls for the class, ensure that there was no ragging or other forms of misconduct amongst the students and generally act as a go-between for students and professors.

Those interested had to register at the office a week in advance. They could try to canvas votes for a week. Finally, they had to give their speeches, after which the rest of the class would vote on a special polling platform, designed by our seniors. I wasn't quite sure why we couldn't just write down our preferences. But being part of ICSI meant making sure that IT was everywhere!

Surprisingly, some people had suggested I stand for the post. One of them was Preetish, so you can imagine how bad an idea this was! Some had even suggested Amrish stand! But Amrish and I were veterans of tons of student body elections in school. Both of us knew that the post of student representative was basically a fancy way of saying 'peon'. The unfortunate person who was elected would be constantly running errands for different professors. On top of that, professors and students always disagreed, so the Student Council members were harangued by both sides.

In any case, by the time the final day came, there were only 2 candidates left – both boys. Originally, 2 girls and another boy had also registered for the Student Council elections. But they soon realised that they didn't have a chance, so they dropped out. One of the candidates, though, was really serious about the whole thing.

His canvassing took the election to a different level. For the entire week, he had kept printing out posters of himself. He had stuck these all over the boys' hostel and had paid (yeah, actually *paid*!) one of the girls to put these up in the girls' hostel. He was so desperate, he had even put posters inside the classrooms before the professors had told him he wasn't allowed to do that. It had then taken him nearly 3 days to get them all down – that was how many posters he had put up just in the academic block!

His name was Lokesh. Every poster sported a huge picture of him and screamed out at the casual onlooker, "Vote for Lokesh!". The fact of the matter is that Amrish and I are lazy bums who like to make fun of other people's hard work. But Lokesh impressed even me with his sheer determination. I have to admit that he did look a little cheesy in the posters, but I have to give him credit for the way he advertised himself. Soon, his name was on everyone's lips. However, many people were critical of his attitude and those who knew him said he liked to suck up to the MTechs. I don't know if this was true or not, but I admired his persistence. I figured Lokesh was a sure-fire winner.

Not that I knew much about the other guy. Amrish had told me his name was Tushar. He came from Kota,

Rajasthan. Yeah, that same Kota that churns out IIT products. Actually, a fairly large proportion of our batch was from north India. There were only about 6 Bangaloreans in the batch. I counted myself as a Bangalorean because I've spent pretty much my entire life here. Though I'm actually Bengali, I visit Kolkata only once a year, usually during my summer holidays. I hate the weather, but love the food. But aside from visiting my grandparents, I still consider myself to be a good south Indian. Amrish is a hardcore Kannadiga. The little Kannada (and it really is very little!) that I know I picked up from him.

So, as we headed into the room where the candidates would speak, I figured I would vote for Lokesh. He seemed sincere and had studied in Hyderabad – which happens to be my birthplace. Amrish, I knew, also intended to vote for Lokesh. But he said that he wanted to hear both speeches first before finally making up his mind. As everyone filled the room, Tushar and Lokesh took their positions at the front of the podium. Tushar was going to speak first. I assumed it would just involve him bragging about his JEE-Mains rank. But I was pleasantly surprised.

Tushar started by introducing himself and mentioning how most of the class might not know him, since he hadn't plastered his face on every available wall. We all laughed at that. He didn't sound pushy or over-enthusiastic. He talked a little bit about himself and his family and how he thought he could help the batch. He seemed like a less in-your-face version of Lokesh. At the same time, he seemed to have a quiet air of efficiency about him. He was the type of guy who would get things done, without anyone noticing. As he finished his speech, he was greeted by warm applause. I began to wonder if I would have been better off picking him as my debating partner!

Then, it was Lokesh's turn. A hush fell over the class. Everyone had seen the posters and was eager to know the person behind the advertisements. Lokesh stepped up to the podium and began to speak, "As all of you know, I'm Lokesh and you should definitely vote for me, if you have any sense!" I think he meant it as a joke, but the batch didn't respond too well to being ordered around. When he realised his attempt at humour had been unsuccessful, Lokesh continued, "I'll be very active on our behalf. In fact, even before you all elect me, I'm in charge of the freshers' party!" He acted like we should fall at his feet and worship him. Okay, maybe I'm being a bit harsh, but Lokesh's entire attitude struck everyone as more demanding than compromising.

In any case, whether or not Lokesh should be elected became irrelevant after this. That's because Amrish chose this moment to seal Lokesh's fate. He said from his seat (loudly enough for everyone to hear), "Yeah. That's why we still haven't had a freshers' party!" Nearly everyone in the room began laughing at Lokesh. Some people even began whistling in appreciation of Amrish's remark. I felt Amrish had been unfair to Lokesh. To be honest, I felt kind of bad for him. People say humour is a nice way of making a point without drawing blood. But as Lokesh's face fell, I realised just how dangerous a weapon humour could be turned into. Despite my sympathy for Lokesh, I decided to vote for Tushar.

We voted at our desktops in the lab. The results came in after 2 minutes and surprised no one. Tushar had won by a landslide. Lokesh had got only a handful of votes from his closest friends. By that evening, we had a new Student Council member...and I was pretty sure we had made the right choice.

But Preetish and I were really excited for another reason – there was now just one day left for the debate! I spent a sleepless night thinking of the many ways in which I could embarrass myself and not get Naina's number. The next day, however, I felt a steely resolve. We were going to do this...and win!

CHAPTER 11

The puppy didn't know tonight would be its last. For a fortnight, she had cultivated its trust. She had fed it and left a bowl full of water for it every one of those nights. When she had first met it, it had been a scrawny little thing. She had rescued and looked after it. Though she was a hostelite, she had found time to meet it in the evenings and be back before the curfew. The stray lived at the end of the lane on which her college was located. Her friends thought she was out with a boy...they wouldn't understand her peculiar fetish.

At first, the stray had been wary and its white and brown face had snarled at her. But every day she had fed it till she finally won its trust. At the same time, she had left a bowl full of water for it and watched from afar before she walked away. At first, the puppy had ignored the water. But Bangalore could get very dry. Soon enough, the puppy had begun to lap up the water in the bowl. Nowadays, she would arrive in the evening, feed the puppy, leave the water and head far away. After playing with her and wolfing down the food, the puppy would lap up the water and fall asleep.

Tonight, though, there was a slight change in the menu. Instead of water, she had filled the bowl with acid. She had picked it up from a hardware shop, claiming that she wanted it for cleaning a drain. Right on time, the puppy showed up, eagerly wagging its tail. It gobbled up the food. Then it began to lap up the acid. It had been a dry day and the puppy's throat was parched. She hid herself behind a tree and watched the show. Too late, the puppy realised its insides weren't burning up from the heat. By the time it stopped lapping up the acid, the damage had been done.

It let out a horrible wail and ran up the street, towards her college. It bit a guard there, trying to find some relief from the burning sensation in its gut. It was frothing at the mouth. She watched the guards pound it to death, thinking no doubt that it was rabid. Then, smiling and satisfied, she walked away.

CHAPTER 12

Preetish and I bunked college that day. In any case, we missed only Biology, C and Real Analysis. We arrived a bit early. The Synergy campus was much bigger than ours, but not as beautiful. We wanted to explore the campus a bit – I wanted to find Naina and Preetish wanted to find her friends! Thus, with the noblest of intentions, we headed towards their imposing main gate.

Thinking back, I did notice a few odd things. There was a strong stench of rotting flesh. There were also a lot of flies swarming around the area. Finally, there was a faint smell of acid. But I didn't connect the dots until it was too late.

Anyway, there we were, trying to weasel our way in to meet some girls. I decided to walk in with a bold, decisive attitude. I told the guard that we were there for the debate. He looked at me with an expression between drunk and confused (probably a bit of both). Preetish casually stepped in front of me and spoke fluently in Kannada to him. The guard immediately got to his feet and saluted. Then, he proceeded to let Preetish in. He looked at me warily and then jerked his head towards the entrance.

We had just cleared the first hurdle and already I was being treated like a terrorist, while my pint-sized partner got the royal treatment! Oh well, it was useful having him around. I scrambled through the gate and into the college.

Though the campus wasn't as green as ours, it had a lot going for it. It had gigantic blocks for the various departments. The campus also had a large number of hostel blocks. Finally, they had a central administrative building with a banner hanging in front, inviting participants to the Synergy Debate Competition. After going around the campus and seeing the sights, Preetish and I decided to head in.

The moment we entered, we spotted a sign indicating where we had to go. We followed the sign until we reached the registration desk, where 2 girls sat looking mildly bored. However, when they saw us, they seemed to perk up a bit (if only I could say I have that effect on all women!). One of them asked, "Which college are you guys from?"

I was about to answer when Preetish smoothly stepped in and said, "We're from ICSI. Are we the first ones here?" The girl smiled at Preetish (completely ignoring me) and replied, "Yeah, you guys are actually pretty early. We're expecting around 25 colleges. So, you guys can check out the auditorium and the inside of our campus while you're waiting." Both girls were sweet, but not stunners like Naina. Nevertheless, I wasn't about to be outdone by my mountain goat of a partner! I decided the time had come to make my presence felt.

"Could you give us a call when it's time to come back for the start of the debate?" I asked, casually. "Sure! Let me just get your name and number..." she replied, whipping out her phone. Before Preetish could make any more moves, I quickly gave them my name and number.

"I never caught your name," I said as coolly as I could. "It's Meghna," the girl replied, smiling at me. "By the way, you should try our filter coffee. It's amazing!" she added. "I'd need a guide to get me there. Your campus is massive. I don't suppose you'd care to show me the way?" I asked hopefully. Meghna smiled shyly. "I wouldn't mind, but you'd have to pay!" she exclaimed laughing. "Then I guess we can share a coffee with the prize money," I said, trying to sound confident, though I was already worried that I would be a disaster on stage.

"Ahem! Do we have to fill out any forms or anything like that?" Preetish piped up from near the floor. Talk about your mood-dampener! Meghna stopped smiling and handed out some boring-looking forms for us to fill up. We spent the next 15 minutes registering and were then shooed away. With time to kill, we headed towards the main auditorium and the canteen.

The main auditorium was gigantic! Half of our college could probably fit in there! It would easily be able to accommodate 2,000 people. It was housed in a complex that also contained 5 smaller auditoriums, besides the main one. Each of these could probably seat around 200 people. We checked out the auditoriums, wondering where the preliminary debates would be held. We were both pretty nervous by now, so we figured we'd try the famous filter coffee.

Preetish offered to treat me. This was quite convenient since I had no cash on me! I guess the guy had some uses. He bought us each a filter coffee and some snacks. My only regret was that I was having a filter coffee with Preetish and not Meghna! Their canteen even served non-veg food. I wanted to pig out on that, but

Preetish considered it "impure", so I had to make do with vegetarian snacks. After we had eaten and drunk our fill, Preetish wanted to keep exploring. So, we headed over to a map of the campus, situated just outside the canteen. "Hey! They have a gym here. Why don't we check it out?" suggested Preetish. I'm guessing having John as a roommate meant fitness was always top of mind.

Having nothing better to do, I agreed and we headed over to the gym. The gym was fairly compact, compared to everything else on this XL-sized campus. But it was well-equipped with plenty of free weights, weight machines and cardio equipment. At first, I thought that Preetish would start lifting some heavy weights and try to impress me. But, as he explained to me as if he were my gym trainer, "You have to start out light." So saying, he went and picked up the one kg dumbbells and started his bicep curls. So much for being a macho guy! Even I (who barely knew the difference between a dumbbell and a barbell!) lifted 10 kg for my bicep curls. I was about to burst into laughter when I heard an audible click. I whirled towards the source of the sound. It came from the main gym doors. We reached the doors only to find them padlocked with a whistling guard walking away!

Both Preetish and I banged desperately on the glass door till the guard turned around and came back. He looked surprised to see us. When we started thumping the glass and mimed turning the key, he shouted through the glass, "Don't break door." With that he turned and walked away again. So much for his coming to our rescue. Our one shot at getting out had left us here!

By now, we were both truly desperate! So, we started banging the door again. We also started hollering through the glass for help. The guard simply strolled out of sight! It was getting late. The debate could start any minute and there we were, trapped inside the gym! I silently cursed Preetish for his stupid idea and myself for listening to him. I was just getting ready to ignore the guard and break the door when a familiar face sauntered into view. "Well, this is a surprise. You really don't have to be a macho man for little old me," said Naina with her familiar Cheshire-cat smile.

Thankfully, Naina had shown up in the nick of time. She had more luck in persuading the guard to let us out. The guard finally unlocked the door when she flashed her student ID and explained why we had come to their college. After assuming responsibility for the incident, she got the 2 of us out and back to the auditorium, grinning the whole time.

As we were walking back, my phone started ringing. It was Meghna. I didn't want Naina to see the caller ID. So, I hurriedly answered and said, "We're on our way back." I hung up before she could say anything in response. Naina cocked her head and seemed to silently ask me who it was. I felt compelled to answer, "It's from the reception desk. They want us to come to the auditorium as soon as possible." Naina just smirked like she knew exactly what was going through my mind and nodded. Preetish, of course, was oblivious to this silent exchange and asked, "Was it Meghna?" I wanted to strangle the little guy, but he was my debating partner, so I had to make do with, "I don't know her name." Naina laughed at that and said, "Oh, I doubt that very much!" She laughed heartily, much to my embarrassment. I was grateful when we finally reached the auditoriums.

We reached just as the last of the teams showed up. There were 25 teams in all, including us. It seemed like no college had dropped out. So, there were going to be 5 debates, one in each of the smaller auditoriums. The 5 winners would participate in a final debate in the main auditorium. We were led by one of the volunteers to a room, where 4 teams were already present. Just as we walked into the room, the door slammed shut behind us and I felt like I was trapped in there with the other participants. I wondered if anyone else was as nervous as I was. Preetish looked supremely confident. Then again, he always did! I thought to myself that this was a bad idea and that I should leave while I still had the chance. Just as I was about to turn around and rush out of the room, the volunteers interrupted my thoughts and guided us to our seats around a central podium. We were seated on the stage with a special seat dedicated to the Chair. As we sat down, everyone in the audience quietened down and I realised it was time to get this show on the road...

CHAPTER 13

The participants were seated in a semi-circular fashion around the podium. Each team had a desk on which were notepads, a couple of pens and water bottles. Right next to the podium was the Chair's seat. The audience – consisting of Synergy students and friends of the participants – was seated in horizontal rows in front of the podium. The 3 judges were seated right in front. All of the judges seemed to be in their late-thirties to early-forties. Two of them were women and one was a man. The Chairman looked slightly older. After all the teams were seated, he rose to begin the proceedings.

"Let me begin by thanking Synergy College for hosting this incredible debate!" he exclaimed. This was greeted by loud applause from the Synergy students. "I'll start things off by introducing myself. I'm Dr. Hegde, a proud member of the Toastmasters' chapter in Jayanagar and an alumnus of St. Stephen's College," he continued.

I sighed, though even I wasn't sure whether it was from regret or relief. I mean if I had gone to St. Stephen's, one day that might have been me over there – invited to chair debates and stuff. But, on the other hand, did I really want to end up as chairman of a debating contest, listening to guys like Preetish and me? Before I could make up my mind, Dr. Hegde carried on, "I'd like to thank Synergy for inviting me. Let me now introduce our esteemed panel of judges..." he continued in his deep baritone voice.

I must admit, I started daydreaming for a while. I didn't really want to listen to long and boring introductions of people I'd probably never meet again. The man was a journalist with *The Times of India*. One of the women was a publisher and the other was a columnist. That's about all I gathered. I started thinking about whether we had any realistic chance at all. I wondered if Naina was really interested in me, or if she was just kidding around. I thought I saw her face in the audience. Wait a second, there was someone who closely resembled Naina in the last row. Was it her?

Just then, I felt a nudge in my ribs. Preetish was trying to get me to focus. I stifled a yawn and tried to pay attention to Dr. Hegde. He was going over the rules, "I will announce the motion, after which teams will have 15 minutes to prepare. One participant from each team will speak 'for' the motion and the other will speak 'against' the motion." Preetish and I looked at each other in alarm! We had counted on having half an hour to prepare. I waited for somebody to correct Dr. Hegde, but he simply carried on. There must have been a last-minute change of plan which nobody had bothered to tell us about!

Meanwhile, Dr. Hegde went on, "Each speaker will have exactly 4 minutes to speak. A bell will be sounded after 3 minutes. After the speech is done, the speaker will then field questions from the audience and the other participants for 2 minutes." He then held up a thin envelope and extracted a slip of paper. He continued, "The motion is: 'The 21st century will find the world on the brink of disaster'. Your preparation time starts *now*!"

I looked at Preetish who seemed *really* flustered. He whispered to me, "How come they halved the preparation time? They didn't inform us, right?" I hesitated before saying, "Well, about that...the thing is I checked the rules nearly a month ago on their website. I didn't bother to go through them again later. They must have changed it closer to the actual date." Preetish looked at me furiously. I didn't want another lecture. I tried to distract him with the debate topic. "Look, forget the past. Let's just try our best and hope things work out. Sound okay?"

Preetish just grunted. I assumed that was a "Yes". I felt more confident and asked him, "So, which side of the motion do you want?" I wasn't sure why I was giving him the choice. Probably because I was too nervous to think straight and also because I didn't want him turning into a midget-sized volcanic eruption! A look of intense concentration crossed his face. Now, he looked like a midget with anger management issues. Thankfully, though, he stayed focused on the motion.

"Okay. I'd prefer going 'for' the motion. But if you come up with any facts which you think might be useful, let me know. I'll do the same for you. By the way, are we going to carry a paper to the podium or not?" he asked. I hadn't thought about that point. "I guess we can carry a sheet with us. Just remember, let's focus on a few points and cover them in detail. Don't try and cover too many points. Also, like you suggested, let's show each other the final list of points we make, so that we can figure out the other side's basic argument. One last thing – if you're speaking 'for' the motion, you'll have to go first. You okay with that?" I asked.

"Yeah, no worries. I've got it covered," Preetish replied. So saying, he went to work on his speech. After ripping a sheet out of the notepad, I picked up the sheet and wondered what points to start jotting down.

There comes a time in the life of all public speakers, when they want to run screaming from the podium and become something like a security guard, a bus conductor or a driver. Pretty much anything that does not involve addressing an audience which is looking for an opportunity to exploit their slip-ups. I was experiencing that right now as I looked at the terribly inadequate number of points I had jotted down. I glanced at Preetish. He looked supremely confident, as ever. This was in spite of the fact that he had jotted down fewer points than me!

After 10 minutes, Dr. Hegde asked for a representative from each team to come forward and pick a number. This would decide the order in which the teams would speak. I hoped Preetish might have the magic touch, so I sent him. He picked number 3. I wasn't sure whether that was a good thing or a bad thing. I was glad we didn't have to speak first. But the first and last arguments are typically all that the audience remembers. Number 3 is a position that's easy to forget, especially for the judges.

When 15 minutes were done, a bell sounded and the murmuring audience quietened down. Dr. Hegde raised his hands till there was pin-drop silence. Then he said, "I would like to invite Varun Das from R.V. College of Engineering to begin this debate. Please give him a round of applause.

I blanked out from tension while the first team spoke. I half-paid attention to the speaker from the second team, speaking 'for' the motion. He was from PESIT and kept talking about how technology had always brought us closer to the brink of disaster and how any sort of technological progress would adversely affect society in the long run. He began to get on my nerves. So, I decided to ask him a question.

I said if his statement was true, then why had the Cold War never led to a nuclear apocalypse? Also, was technology inherently evil? Didn't the way technology was used better fit the description of good or evil? Finally, I went for the kill. I posed the question that if technology had always harmed humankind, then how come we could calmly sit and debate such matters in a technologically-driven world, unlike our ancient ancestors who would throw stones at each other to settle an argument.

The poor guy looked totally lost. After a long pause, he just asked, "Could you please repeat the question?" That brought a lot of laughter from the audience. I gave him a shorter version, which he tried (and failed!) to answer convincingly. I could see from the judges' faces they were not impressed.

Finally, it was our turn. Preetish strutted up to the podium, clutching a piece of paper, but looking as confident as ever. I was worried that he was going to start off with our decaying moral standards. Thankfully, he didn't. I guess all that practice had paid off! I didn't pay attention to his entire speech because I was too nervous about my turn coming up. But I could tell from the judges' expressions that he made a good case.

I followed the basic gist of his speech. He talked about the COVID pandemic, our exploitation of natural resources, the rise of terrorism and the menace it presented, and about how our politicians now consisted of muddleheads. Finally (you guessed it!) he began to talk about our moral standards. But the bell soon rang, forcing him to wrap up – which in my mind was an excellent thing!

Next, he had to deal with the questions. A speaker from R.V. College asked him whether terrorism was another manifestation of the violence that was present in humankind. Preetish looked confused for a moment, but he quickly recovered and claimed that terrorism in its current form was very much a 21st century phenomenon. After that, a member of the audience asked him if he believed that the world had reached such a state that all attempts at governance would eventually collapse and anarchy would reign. Preetish deflected the question, claiming that the future was "in our hands". That brought some cheers and applause from the audience. He fielded a couple of more questions, but he handled them pretty easily. When he walked back towards me, he was treated to a warm round of applause. The wait was over. It was my turn to speak.

I walked, as slowly as I could, up to the podium. I gazed at the sea of faces in front of me...and I completely blanked out! I had no idea what to say. I stared down at the paper, but I couldn't read my own handwriting. I was in the grip of a terrible panic attack and I couldn't control it! There was a hush all around the room. I was actually counting the seconds. When I reached 15, I did the only thing I could.

I remembered my English professor Kasturba's advice: "When you can, bang on your facts. When your facts fail you, bang on your speaking skills. When your speaking skills fail you, bang on the podium!" Heeding her advice, I banged hard on the podium. That shook me out of my blank state and seemed to recharge the audience.

I promised myself I would take back all the nasty thoughts I had ever had about Professor Kasturba and was grateful that she had taught us English after all. It was then that I had a flash of inspiration. I didn't really need a new speech. I could just deconstruct Preetish's! I merely had to prove that he was wrong and that would do the trick for me. So, that's precisely what I set about doing.

"Ladies and gentlemen, the opposition has shown you the tip of the iceberg and tried to distort the course of history itself. The truth is that we are facing many challenges today. But we have pulled back from the edge of disaster. All hope is not lost and we don't need a bunch of 'Avengers' to rescue us," I began. The last sentence was greeted with a smattering of applause and caused quite a few laughs. I continued, "While it is true that COVID has struck the world in a manner we could never imagine, it is also true that thanks to the IT boom, we are able to continue working from home and not interrupt our work-life balance. Further, vaccines have been deployed all over the world to combat this menace. During the Cold War, we faced the possibility of nuclear war. But, together, we have reduced that likelihood in this century. People might believe that we are on the road to environmental ruin. But thanks to organisations like Greenpeace, we are now moving forward in the right direction. India's own Supreme Court quashed the allocation of coal blocks. This has been heralded as a victory by environmentalists and humanitarians alike. We now possess roomy, self-driven electric cars which provide sufficient mileage to compete with their fossil-fuel equivalents."

I was warming up now and went on, "The opposition might talk about how race, gender and religion have become far more divisive today than in the past. Some might cite the Nirbhaya rape case as proof of our moral decay (I guess I owe Preetish for that one!). But the truth is that the subsequent outcry and legislation have tried to restrain the cruel and vicious sociopaths who live among us. Eve-teasing in many public places is no longer tolerated with the excuse, 'boys will be boys'. The legislation of gay rights in India is another major step in the right direction."

Finally, the bell rang, interrupting my flow of thought. I had to wrap this up quickly. "When it comes to religion, divisions have always existed from the time of Christ to the Crusades till today. However, more and more people are now aware of the value of tolerance. And just as it is wrong to judge all Romans for the crucifixion of Christ, it is equally wrong to label all Muslims or Hindus or Christians as terrorists. With the election of Barack Obama as President of the United States, a new era of racial relations has been ushered in. Thus, ladies and gentlemen, I believe we have come to a time when the human race is better equipped to take on the challenges of today. Therefore, I disagree with the motion, 'The 21st century will find the world on the brink of disaster.' Thank you!" I concluded.

I was greeted by thunderous applause as I finished my speech. I'm guessing it was because they were glad it was finally over. Of course (and yes, I'm a big fan of my work!) I like to think it was because they found it a powerful speech. The opposition seemed so taken aback at the audience reaction that no one dared to ask a question for a long time. Or, maybe, they were just bored to death. In any case, I was about to step away from the podium when one brave soul from Jain College raised his hand.

His question was as annoying as his voice: "What about individual freedoms? I mean my grandparents had more time to play, while my mom would scold me if I didn't finish my school homework first. So, haven't we lost a lot of freedoms in this century?" Suddenly, I found myself blanking out again. I tried to think of a witty comeback, but I could barely form a sentence in my head. "Well, when you talk about freedoms..." my voice trailed away, as I wondered what to say next. Then, suddenly, as if I were on autopilot, the words popped into my head, "Would you rather be fed to the lions for your religious beliefs like the Christians in ancient Rome than be scolded by your mother? I...think not!" This time the crowd laughed and clapped at the same time. As I stepped away from the podium, I felt triumphant!

My feeling of triumph lasted until I heard the next speaker. He sounded convincing, forceful and compelling. He proceeded to dissect my speech one point at a time. My only consolation was that he kept quoting me and referring to me as his "learned opponent". I felt good that he had based his entire speech on mine and had gone to the trouble of remembering exactly what I had said. At least one person had stayed awake!

I kept worrying that the applause he received was louder than mine. I tried to go over his and my speeches and felt like there were gaping holes in mine. I was in such a state of anxiety that I couldn't even manage a question! Finally, when he returned to his seat, I felt nervous and relieved at the same time.

The remaining speeches left me feeling even more nervous and on edge. I was close to a full-blown panic attack by the time it was over. I tried to remember what each speaker had said, but the words all jumbled together in my head. The one thing I felt certain of was that we were going to lose and I was going to have a heart attack if my heart kept up this pace. I glanced at Preetish who looked cool as a cucumber. I wondered how he did it.

Dr. Hegde went to the podium after the last speaker had finished. He gestured for silence, giving a very good imitation of a fat bird trying to fly! Once the audience had quietened down, he began speaking, "The judges will now confer and the qualifying team will be announced shortly. I request all the participants and audience members to return here after 10 minutes to hear the results. Thank you all. I wish you a great day!" There was a round of applause, after which everyone started leaving the room. Preetish and I joined the crowd. We had just stepped outside when I heard her voice.

"Congratulations on your speech. I really liked it," she whispered in a husky tone. I turned to face her and was struck by her resemblance to Naina. Her hair was a little browner and she was a little shorter. But she too had captivating charm. She wasn't as thin as Naina, but she was equally enchanting. She had extended a hand to shake. But I was so startled that an attractive girl was complimenting my speech, that my brain froze. Thankfully, Preetish saved me from further embarrassment by doing something even more idiotic.

He took her hand and shook it firmly. She looked a little taken aback, which was exactly how I felt! Seemingly oblivious to the fact that this girl had aimed the compliment at me, Preetish continued shamelessly, "I wasn't sure everyone here connected with it, but I'm confident the judges will appreciate it. I'm Preetish, by the way." Preetish was still firmly holding her hand. She flashed him a half-smile, probably wondering how she had got into this mess! She desperately tried to extract herself from Preetish's clutches.

Finally, she rolled her eyes and asked, "What are you both – dumb and dumber? One can't speak and the other only speaks stupidly?! Just my luck!" By this time, she had pulled her hand free from Preetish's. She looked like she was about to storm off in a huff. That's when my brain activated itself. I stepped into her path to block her. She stopped suddenly and gazed at me warily. She looked at Preetish and asked, "Are you his mouthpiece?"

Trying to act casual, I forced a laugh. She looked at me like I was crazy. "No, I'm his!" I exclaimed stupidly, making no sense to anyone. What on earth was I doing? Why was I babbling?! "No, wait. That's not true. We're not each other's. I mean we are. We are definitely partners... intimate partners," I began and stopped when her eyes widened in shock. "No! Not that. I mean we're debating partners. But we aren't gay now. Or ever, for that matter. Not that there's anything wrong with it. We just aren't. At least I'm not!" I laughed weakly as I babbled away. I bumbled through the blank space that was my mind, trying to find the right words to say. Finally, I covered my face with my hands and muttered, "Can we just rewind this conversation back to where you complimented me? Please?"

I uncovered my face, fully expecting her to be long gone and was pleasantly surprised to find her still there. Her expression simultaneously bordered on amused and curious. "You're not much of a first-impressions kind of guy, are you?" she asked, a smile tugging at her lips. We both laughed, a little more comfortably. By this time, Preetish was standing behind her and gesturing at his watch. I desperately waved him away with both hands while laughing. I obviously looked like an idiot. She asked, "Are you spastic?" Forcing my hands as deep into my pockets as they would go, I replied, "No! I was...I mean I...It's like this...I was...chasing a wasp. There was a huge one! Right over your head."

"So, I guess you only speak well in public. Conversation doesn't seem to be one of your strong suits. Anyway, it was nice running into you...Pranav. I'm Nisha," she laughingly said. She held out her hand again and I shook it firmly. "See you in 10 minutes for the results?" I asked hopefully. "Yup. See you then," she replied, before vanishing into the crowd outside.

I should probably have mentioned this earlier, but the debate was a very formal affair. That meant formal shoes, clothes complete with tie and college blazer. Personally, I've never been too fond of formal clothing and today was no exception. While the air-conditioning had been great inside the room, I was still sweaty from anxiety. So, as soon as Nisha left, I went to the bathroom to freshen up a bit. Thankfully, this also gave me a brief break from Preetish. I took off my blazer, loosened my tie and undid my collar button. Slinging my blazer over my shoulder, I walked out of the washroom, feeling refreshed.

I tried to find Naina in the bustling crowd, but couldn't see her anywhere. Instead, I was spotted by

Preetish, who immediately came hurrying over. "Are all the girls here attractive, or what?" he asked excitedly. I murmured in agreement. "Let's quickly head over to the canteen and get some more filter coffee!" he exclaimed. I looked at him like the idiot he was and said, "Coffee?! Really? You're surrounded by good-looking girls and all you can think about is coffee? What's wrong with you, man?"

"Don't worry. They will be even more impressed when they hear we've won!" he replied with his usual confidence. "Won?! We were lucky they didn't have anything at hand to throw at us! Are you crazy or something?" I retorted. "Chill, bro. Save your passion for the next round," Preetish said complacently. So saying, he pushed his way through the crowd and headed towards the canteen. Sighing, I followed him. I hadn't spotted Naina and I probably wouldn't in this mad rush of people. Plus, he had the money and yeah – I'm a total loser.

We finished our coffee and then headed back to the auditorium. We sat down at our desk and waited as people slowly shuffled in. Finally, Dr. Hegde and the judges strolled in. Once all the teams had arrived and the audience seemed to have settled down, Dr. Hegde began speaking, "I have been informed by the judges of their decision. However, before I reveal the winner, the judges would like to give their feedback to the teams."

The next few minutes were absolute agony for me. The judges pointed out a few loopholes in Preetish's and my arguments, but their only major criticism was that we hadn't asked enough questions. I heaved a sigh of relief. I was still sure we had lost. But I was glad we weren't going to be publicly ripped to shreds.

Suddenly, Preetish piped up, "Don't you think it's a little chilly in here?" I didn't think so and told him as much. "Maybe you'd be more comfortable if you buttoned your shirt and put on your blazer," he carried on. I was getting sick of getting fashion tips from Preetish. So, I just said, "I'm fine, bro. Let's wait for the last team to be dissected and then head out." The judges were almost done with the last team. As they finished, Dr. Hegde stood up and walked over to the podium. Suddenly, Preetish snapped at me, "Fix your tie and wear your blazer!" He sounded like an angry puppy. I'd never seen him so forceful! So, I quickly complied.

Just as I shrugged my blazer back on, I heard Dr. Hegde announce, "And the winning team is none other than...ICSI!" I was so stunned by the announcement that I forgot to stand. Preetish literally pulled me to my feet and started dragging me towards Dr. Hegde. I plastered a smile on my face, while my heart still hammered away from all the adrenaline. "Subtlety just doesn't work on you, huh? Now do you get why I wanted you to put on your blazer?" Preetish whispered beside me. I was so happy with our victory that for once I didn't even want to whack him!

CHAPTER 14

The final round involved a face-off between the 5 winners from each of the preliminary debates. We headed to our labelled desks on the stage. I glanced around the main auditorium and was surprised to see it more than half full. Obviously, this debate was more popular than I had expected. I scanned the audience for any sign of Naina. However, there was no trace of her. I did spot Nisha, though. We made eye-contact for a moment and she flashed me a thumbs-up. I offered a weak smile in return. Then, she disappeared in the crowd. Next, 3 people (who I took to be the judges) came and sat right at the foot of the stage. The last to arrive was the chairman – Dr. Krishna.

Just before he arrived, volunteers went to the 5 desks, handing out water bottles, pens and notepads to the participants. Unfortunately, Naina was not amongst them. The volunteers also checked that the podium mic was working. Finally, one of them came up to our table. He vaguely resembled an uglier version of Soorya. He mumbled something in Kannada. I looked completely blank (which was happening today more often than I liked!), but Preetish replied fluently and then pointed at me. At this point, I felt like a human sacrifice being offered up. So, I interrupted the dialogue and asked Preetish just what was going on.

"They want a participant to light the lamp, along with the chairman and one of the judges. So, I said you'd go," replied Preetish casually. "Maybe you can ask me next time before volunteering my services?!" I snapped at him angrily. Preetish looked like he was dealing with an annoying child. "You want me to turn him down?" he finally asked. I sighed and said, "No, it's fine. I'll do it." The volunteer was looking from Preetish to me and seemed to be wondering what was going on. Preetish must have reassured him because he went away looking pleased and thanking me a lot.

You're probably wondering why I was so reluctant to light the lamp. Well, the truth is that I'm not so smooth with my hands. No, wait. That came out wrong. You know how people sometimes say that if you're good with your hands, you're popular with the girls? Well, I definitely didn't mean that I was bad with girls. Okay, I actually was, but I didn't mean to admit it a few sentences ago! What I meant was I just wasn't cut out for manual labour. That's probably the understatement of the century. When I was in kindergarten, my teachers thought I might be retarded because I couldn't cut paper with a pair of scissors. When I was in Grade 4, we had stitching. I got my grandma to do my assignments, while I tried to figure out which side of the needle was the eye. In Grade 12, I couldn't get the circuit for Ohm's Law to work, so I forged some values and got away with my Physics practical. For those of you who have forgotten (or never knew) Ohm's Law, consider yourselves lucky! It's a simple concept in theory, which never works in practice! But the most obvious example of my clumsiness was when I tried to build a taser from scratch and ended up electrocuting myself!

As a result, I was understandably concerned about lighting the lamp. I kept dreading it all through Krishna Sir's introductory speech and his ramblings about the format of the debate. He introduced the judges – 2 gentlemen and a lady. Finally, he called on one of the men and me to light the lamp along with him.

A volunteer handed me a candle as I stepped up to the lamp. He then pointed at the wick I was supposed to light. Dr. Krishna and the judge had already started on their wicks. I figured it couldn't be that hard and began trying.

I *assumed* the wick would catch fire if I held the candle to it. But nothing of the sort seemed to be happening. The wick refused to catch fire! I tried changing the orientation of the candle, then I ducked the wick in oil before trying to light it. No luck. By now, the audience was getting restless and the volunteers were getting desperate. Frustrated, I jabbed the wick with the lit candle...and ended up dropping the candle into the oil! Instead of three lit wicks, the lamp now blazed away like a bonfire. All that was missing were marshmallows. There was only one thing left to do.

I walked over to the podium, ignoring the shocked faces of the volunteers and the gaping mouths of the judges and Dr. Krishna. I adjusted the mic and said, "Ladies and gentlemen, I'm here representing ICSI and I like to think I follow the guidelines of my college in everything I do. We never settle for medium and always push for well-done – whether we are eating steaks or pursuing our passion!" I stepped away from the mic and was greeted with loud laughter and applause from the audience. I had goofed up, but managed to cover my disaster. I just hoped Preetish and I weren't going to be the main course!

Dr. Krishna waited for the audience to stop hooting and quieten down. He invited a member from each team to come forward and pick a slip. This time, Preetish insisted I go. After checking what number I had picked, I discovered that we would be speaking fourth. Well, it could be better and it could be worse. Speaking fourth meant that we'd have more time to reflect on our opponents' points. But the audience and the judges might grow bored by the time our turn came. Finally, it was time to announce the motion. Dr. Krishna began, "Participants, please pay attention. Your motion is...". Here, he made a great show of coughing and clearing his throat. I began to wonder if he was going to start gargling with his own phlegm. Finally, he spit it out – the motion, not the phlegm! "Your motion is... 'Scepticism is crucial to debates about climate change'. Your time starts now!" With that, a bell sounded and our preparation time began.

I was feeling fairly confident. I again offered Preetish first choice. As I had expected, he wanted to argue 'against' the motion. I tried to play it cool, but I couldn't resist a slight grin. Catching my grin, he asked, "What's so funny?" I told him not to worry and to focus on his speech.

I couldn't believe how easy this was going to be! Sure, at first glance, arguing 'for' the motion might have seemed difficult. I mean you have to be pretty thick-headed to completely ignore global warming. But one had only to consider the wording of the motion to find the loophole. The motion didn't state that scepticism was crucial to proven scientific facts. It merely claimed that before something was accepted as a fact, one had to be sceptical about the opposition's arguments. Actually, that was true for any branch of science. After all, evolving an optimal climate policy requires an ongoing and engaging debate. If you looked at the words right, the debate actually favoured those speaking 'for' the motion.

Plus, I had thoroughly researched the topic in preparation for one of our practice sessions. We had been debating 'Climate change is a catalyst for human evolution'. I had spent a considerable amount of time studying how much money environmental engineers earned and had discovered that it was on par with engineers from more traditional disciplines (especially overseas). To paraphrase Stan Lee, "With great wealth, comes great responsibility." Then, the starting bell rang and snapped me out of my reverie. It was on!

This time, I felt way less nervous than I had in the previous round. I also posed many more questions to the teams before us. Some of the speakers came up with clever retorts, but I managed to poke some major holes in our opponents' arguments. Once the first 2 teams had spoken, I was more confident than ever. All that changed when the third team's (the team from NLSIU) first speaker began his speech.

His speech was nearly identical to the one I planned to make. He covered the same basic outline, and argued how scepticism was crucial to all debates and how we couldn't be expected to swallow everything that was thrown at us without testing it out. Then, he went on to quote the salaries of engineers of different disciplines and point out how environmental engineering was lucrative as a profession. By the time he sat down, I was virtually in tears.

He'd covered my entire speech! If I spouted the same lines, the judges would assume that I was simply copying him. There was nothing for it – if his speech had logic and sense, mine would have to depend on wordplay and rhetoric.

After a while, I felt a sharp poke in my side. I looked sideways and noticed Preetish gesturing towards the podium with his head. The previous speaker was heading back to his seat. I supposed it was my turn. I pulled myself out of my chair and dragged myself over to the podium. I adjusted the mic slightly. The moment the bell rang, I began.

"Ladies and gentlemen, the opposition has tried to frighten you with ghastly, apocalyptic visions of the future. They claim that if immediate action is not taken, climate change could wipe us all out. And the point, ladies and gentlemen...is that they are right!" I had barely finished my first sentence when confused murmurs broke out throughout the auditorium. I waited for the murmurs to subside before continuing.

"Yes, I realise my statements might seem contrary to the motion. But the point is that climate change is a reality that is not going away because we choose to ignore it. However, having accepted certain phenomena, like global warming, what actions need to be taken to stop them from harming humanity as a whole? Many from the opposition have decided that we must forego development to achieve planetary equilibrium. But is that necessary? If science can tell us what harm is being done to the environment, perhaps it can also provide us with the solutions. After all, Newton discovered gravity, but that didn't stop humans from reaching the moon!"

My last sentence was met with a burst of applause. I was grateful for the delay as this gave me time to collect my thoughts. I carried on, "This is where room for debate comes in. As environmentalists and policy-makers consider different options, only through debates and discussions can we come close to an optimal policy for dealing with climate change. While Greenpeace's attempt to prevent unfair coal block allocation is laudable, NGOs alone don't have all the answers. For instance, Greenpeace's decision to shelve nuclear energy based on Fukushima might not be the best policy. World leaders need combined advice from scientists across various disciplines."

I paused for a moment because I blanked out. Then I decided to gun for the guy who had got me into this fix. "As my friend from NLSIU pointed out, environmental engineers are earning relatively high salaries. He believes this should cause us to suspect the authenticity of their results. However, I say this – pump in more money into this line of work. This will allow a better peer review ecosystem to evolve."

Now, came the problem. I wasn't sure how to wrap up. I could virtually feel time slipping through my fingers. Then suddenly, it hit me. Once again, it was as if someone had taken over my body and I was speaking on autopilot. "In conclusion, this is the age of social media and unscientific trends – from what one should eat to how one should live. People shouldn't believe advertising and PR. Science always demands a healthy dose of scepticism towards everything we encounter. In an article by Jug Suraiya, I read about how people are moving from a firm grounding in reality to a virtual social media image of themselves. In fact, it's gotten to a point when even your body needs to be perfectly sculpted. In other words, we are being led from reality to the 'abs-tract'! Thank you, ladies and gentlemen!"

The bell sounded just as I finished. I felt sort of hazy and confused. I fielded the few questions directed towards me and wearily made my way back to my seat. The audience was laughing and clapping. I wasn't sure if they were laughing with me or at me. Frankly, I didn't care. I was just glad that it was over!

CHAPTER 15

The audience was laughing and clapping as he made his way from the podium back to his seat. She waited for the final team to speak before heading for the exit. She knew the judges would be conferring now. But she didn't really care. She had scented her prey and had decided what to hunt. She no longer had any need for the final judgement to be pronounced. She knew from the judges' faces who was going to win. Not that she'd had much doubt. There was something different about this one. He was...unusual. And she enjoyed that.

She headed back towards her hostel room. Being a volunteer, she should probably be more involved in cleaning up after the debate, but she didn't really care. After all, she had something far more exciting back in her room.

She climbed the 2 stories that led to her room. She knew her roommate wouldn't mind if she dropped in now. All the first-year girls in her department had to share their rooms, with 2 girls allotted to each room. Her roommate would be busy – in the thick of things – back at the debate. Besides, her roommate didn't need to see what would happen next. She frowned in concentration as she tried to unlock the door. Her hands were trembling... from anticipation!

The 2 beds were placed side by side. She cast her eyes over the room once. Her roommate (sloppy as usual) had left her bed unmade. The very sight disgusted her. When she had first been assigned to the same room as this girl, she had been thrilled. Now, though, she was just bored. All she wanted to do was cultivate her fetish.

She made her way over to her bed, which was right next to the window. She got down on all fours and retrieved the prey from under her bed. The sleeping pills in the ball of dough had been enough to knock her prey unconscious. She watched it now, as she held it up to the light by its tail. It was a rat – a giant one! There had been an infestation of them a few days ago. The college had immediately had the girls shifted to a guesthouse and sent for exterminators. But, after returning, she had spotted a rat 2 nights ago. It had scurried down the corridor and vanished from sight.

She had picked up the dough and the sleeping pills the next day, crushed the pills into a powder and mixed the powder thoroughly with the dough. Then, she had left the door open that night. She had patiently waited all night. She hadn't been able to sleep. She had been so excited!

She had heard the snuffling of the rat as it had entered the room. She had willed it to go under her bed and had been ecstatic when the snuffling and nibbling sounds began. After a while, silence had reigned. She hadn't moved a muscle, though she had been itching to. She had been uncertain about how many pills needed to be powdered to knock the rat out without killing it. She had also needed the rat to stay asleep for a long time. She had been waiting such a long time for an opportunity like this. She hadn't wanted to mess this up now. But she had had to work on her instinct.

She had waited till morning arrived. She had waited for her roommate to finish her bath and leave the room. Finally, she had made her move. She had stooped down and checked that the rat was asleep. Then, she had dropped it in a perforated metal box bought the previous day for just this purpose. Then she had left.

Now, she had returned. The very sight of the rat filled her with loathing. Yet, somehow, she was filled with the desire to touch it – even caress it. Just as these thoughts flashed through her mind, the rat twitched. It was now or never. She was ready. She carried it with steady hands into the bathroom. Holding it by its tail with one hand, she switched on the exhaust with the other. The exhaust was situated right above the commode. It spun so fast that a few years ago, a girl had lost her finger here, according to college gossip. However, the girl had miraculously survived, despite the blood loss. Today, there would be no survivors.

She lifted the rat up ever so slowly. Then, without a second's hesitation, she flung it into the exhaust. There was a spray of blood all around the room. She screamed, which was only natural for a girl who had been traumatised. She kept on screaming till fists pounded on the door. She kept on screaming as she moved to open the door. She twisted her face into a mask of horror, as she flung it open. She continued to play the role of victim as her friends hugged her and consoled her. She kept the mask of horror on her face. But for a moment, she smiled...

CHPATER 16

"I think our speeches were the worst. I have no idea why I thought we could, or should, do this! This is probably the most embarrassing day of my life. We were pathetic," I droned on and on, after the speeches and questions were done and the judges were conferring. I kept thinking about how much the audience had clapped for the other teams' speeches. At least no one else had set the lamp on fire! Not only had I publicly humiliated myself, I had made a laughing stock of my college too!

"Will you relax? I think your speech was pretty good. Of course, mine was better. Despite that, I think we stand a good chance of winning," said Preetish, trying to comfort me. "Besides us, only the NLSIU team has a good chance. But don't worry so much. We'll know soon enough whether you'll get your girlfriend's number! Till then, relax!" continued Preetish.

I was sorely tempted to throw Preetish into the bonfire that had been the lamp till a few minutes ago. But at that very moment, the judges signalled to Dr. Krishna. Dr. Krishna took a sealed envelope from the judges and walked over to the podium. The miniature forest fire which had once been the lamp had finally extinguished itself. Dr. Krishna began, "Without further ado, I will now reveal the judges' decision. As you all know, the winning team and the runner-up will receive trophies. A special cash prize of Rs. 10,000 will be awarded to the

Best Speaker." So saying, he extracted a piece of paper from the envelope.

"Let me begin with the award for the runner-up. The team selected as runner-up for this debate competition is...NLSIU!" There was an enthusiastic burst of applause from around the auditorium, followed by some loud cheering from the NLSIU contingent. Once the audience had quietened down, Dr. Krishna resumed, "And now, the moment you've been waiting for! The best team for this debate competition is...ICSI!" The entire auditorium seemed to erupt with shouts and hooting. I was so dazed at the time that I thought they might be booing us! Preetish and I (looking like a distorted version of Laurel and Hardy) walked up to the podium and were presented with a giant trophy by Dr. Krishna. Finally, we resumed our seats and the spell broke. I felt a rush of adrenaline course through my system. Preetish and I stared at each other in shock. Neither of us dared to believe it. But we had done it! I slumped back in my seat.

But the surprises weren't over yet! Dr. Krishna was announcing the Best Speaker, "And the award for Best Speaker goes to...Preetish S.!" Normally so cocky, Preetish continued sitting, while Dr. Krishna smiled expectantly in our direction. Finally, I kicked Preetish under the table and he rose to receive the award. He was greeted by a standing ovation. Just kidding! I made up the standing ovation bit to see if you're still paying attention. I had been worried about Preetish, but he had proven the old proverb – "Dynamite comes in small packages!" After receiving the envelope containing the money, he returned to his seat. There was one final round of applause for Synergy College and then everyone began to disperse.

I felt light-headed from the victory. But as the other teams mingled with the audience and each other, I searched for Naina in the vast crowd. I didn't see her anywhere. I didn't see Nisha either, though she had been in the audience at the beginning of the debate. I shook outstretched hands and quickly thanked all my well-wishers and others who were congratulating me. Suddenly, a voice called my name. I turned to look at a girl right behind me. It was none other than Meghna – the volunteer who had first greeted us!

"Hey! Preetish finally won the money for that coffee you were talking about. I figure I can borrow a little from him. You free for a quick cup?" I asked, unable to think up something more sparkling to say. She laughed and said, "Well...you did promise. Maybe I'll take you up on the offer some other day. Today, I'm busy cleaning up after this debate. No rest for the volunteers. Actually, I'm here on behalf of Naina. She wanted to be here in person, but something awful happened to her. Anyway, she told me to give this to you and said you'd know what to do," said Meghna. She pushed a piece of paper into my hand, turned and walked away. I was about to ask what was wrong with Naina. However, before I got the chance, Meghna was gone. I looked at the piece of paper crumpled in my hand and whooped for joy. It was Naina's number! I was so happy with this discovery that I didn't try and find Meghna and get her to tell me more about what had happened to Naina. But I suppose that's the great thing about life. No matter what you imagine, the truth is always more complex than your imagination.

CHAPTER 17

Preetish and I returned to college the next day, feeling triumphant. We intended to present the trophy to our Registrar together before classes began. That was when Preetish decided to drop the bomb.

"Hey, you do know we have a test in C today, right?" he asked casually as we stood outside the Registrar's office. There went my perfect morning! "What are you talking about? Why on earth didn't you tell me earlier?! You had my cell number!" I shouted at him. He just shrugged as if it were no big deal. "Hey, it's just a programming test. How hard can it be?" he offered as an explanation. I was about to punch him when the door swung open.

The Registrar was a tall, lean man with a pair of glasses which were always perched halfway down his nose. He gave us both a stern look. Finally, he spoke, "Don't you know shouting in the hallways is against the institute's rules?" I was about to gently explain that we were just excited about our victory at Synergy and attribute our enthusiasm to that. But, as usual, Preetish leapt in front.

"Sir, we won this at Synergy College's debate yesterday!" he exclaimed, proudly presenting the trophy. The Registrar cast a glance at the trophy and then continued his lecture (ignoring Preetish). "Is that why both of you were missing in all the classes yesterday?" he demanded. I looked at the floor and Preetish looked at me. Finally, I answered, "Yes, Sir." The Registrar looked furious and said, "Don't you know that classes at ICSI are sacred?! We never miss classes for anything! Anything!"

I thought he was going to lecture us for so long that we might just end up missing class. But then his anger seemed to vanish and he smiled. He said, "You boys have done the institute proud. I'll speak to the Principal. He'll want to show this off among our other trophies." Thankfully, Preetish didn't say anything and I just said, "Thank you, Sir," and bobbed my head up and down like Dhanush. That seemed to do the trick. The Registrar dismissed us with a wave of his hand. However, just as we turned to go, he called out to us again.

I turned around, not sure what to expect. But he was still smiling. He said, "I have a feeling you 2 might be up to mischief like this again. So, I'm informing you – if you want to attend a fest, tell me a couple of days in advance." I finally relaxed. Our Registrar looked like the Laughing Buddha on a starvation diet.

Then, his frown returned. "Now, go to class quickly. I don't want you missing your classes again!" he exclaimed and shut the door in our faces. Preetish and I bounded up the stairs. I tried to keep a cool head. Like Preetish had said, it was just a programming test. How hard could it be, right?

I stood outside Professor Scindia's office. I silently cursed myself and Preetish! How hard could it be? Really hard! I had just been slaughtered in the most merciless manner. Professor Scindia had asked us to write a program in C to perform some abstract calculations from graph theory.

If you think graph theory has anything to do with bar graphs and pie charts, think again! It's to do with abstract notions of points joined by edges and is filled with complicated theorems by Euler, Djikstra and a whole host of other unfriendly mathematicians.

It was a 90-minute test. I had kept a level head and got my code to run after 80 minutes. I felt very pleased with myself and submitted my code early. Unfortunately, Professor Scindia hadn't told us that we couldn't use certain predefined functions in C (at least, I never heard him say so). Plus, he wasn't manually checking the code. Instead, he had written a program to automatically test our code. This was really cool and I would have been impressed if the program hadn't given me a big, fat zero for using those predefined functions!

Thankfully, I wasn't the only one who hadn't heard Professor Scindia. A lot of people had got zeroes for the same reason. However, most of them were too terrified to object. Only one other person joined me in asking Professor Scindia to forget the results of this test and conduct a re-test. His name was Romik.

I didn't really know him. I mean, he hung out with Amrish and gang, so we had chatted briefly. But I'd never had a private conversation with him. Since he was a Bengali, I decided to converse in Bengali to break the ice. If there's one thing all Bengalis love, it's fish curry and rice. So, while conversing with him on this topic, I took the time to take a closer look at the guy.

He was only a little taller than Preetish with long hair which reached his shoulders. He was reed-thin and wore a T-shirt proclaiming, "Relax...I'm just a ninja!" Obviously, I had a hard time taking him seriously. He never walked. He seemed to swagger and waddle at the same time. The good thing was that he was here with me to fight for some marks.

"So, how do you think we should ask Sir?" I asked Romik, hoping he had some valuable insight to offer. He pushed his hands into his pockets and closed his eyes. "Hmmm..." he intoned. I wasn't sure whether he was meditating or sleeping or had passed out. I was just about to call for medical attention when he opened his eyes.

"...mmm. I don't really know. I was thinking of saying that we didn't hear him properly. At least, I didn't," answered Romik lamely. "I'm not sure he's going to change everyone's marks if 2 kids out of 50 say they didn't hear him. I was thinking of something along the lines of asking him to give us an extra test and counting the best 5 out of 6 for each student. What do you think?" I asked Romik. However, I never heard Romik's reply because at that moment the door opened and we entered Professor Scindia's office.

"Hi, guys! Come in," said Professor Scindia, as he welcomed us into his cabin. The room was lit by the sunlight which filtered in through the blinds. The cabin was pretty big with enough room for a desktop and several laptops, all of which were running different programs. But when compared to someone as big as Professor Scindia, the room felt cramped! There were two chairs around a circular table and one swivel chair in which Professor Scindia sat. He gestured for us to sit down.

"Right, right. So, how can I help you both?" he asked and grinned at us. I wasn't entirely sure whether he would be willing to help us. His grin made me wonder if he was considering our potential as dumbbells. I decided I had to say something since Romik was staring silently into space. I honestly wondered if he was high on some drug or the other.

"Well, Sir. It's like this. We were wondering about the test. I'm not sure whether a lot of us heard you right or not," I began, but Professor Scindia held up a hand and cut me off. "Tell me your roll numbers. I need to check something," he said, swivelling around to face his desktop. "I'm IMT2012036," I replied anxiously. If he saw our marks, he would just brush us away. Romik chimed in, "I'm IMT2012037, Sir." Professor Scindia got a serious look on his face. Then suddenly, his frown disappeared and his face brightened. He turned back to face us.

In my head, I could see how this conversation might play out. He would ask us how we got zeroes. We would tell him we hadn't heard him correctly. It sounded like a lame excuse, even in my head. He would then ask how some people had heard him. I could hardly tell the guy he wasn't audible. He had a lapel mic attached and spoke into a podium mic as well. Besides, why this sudden urge to look out for our batchmates? We had no business sticking our noses into this. We were basically begging for our own sakes. I figured I might as well tell him the truth rather than pretend to represent the batch.

I opened my mouth to speak but, once again, he held up a hand to stop me. Then he said, "I see you guys have got zeroes along with a lot of other students. But I'm proud of y'all. I ran my plagiarism checker and you're both clean. That's more than I can say for a lot of students who scored 100. So, I'm going to hold a re-test for the class, since I don't want to have to punish so many people for plagiarism. Now, what did y'all want to ask?"

I opened my mouth and closed it dumbly. This felt like speaking to Nisha all over again. My brain was trying to process the fact that he had agreed to a re-test without our having to say anything. While I opened and closed my mouth like a goldfish, Romik spoke up, "Sir, can you please hold an extra test besides the re-test and count the best 5 out of 6 for the final grade?"

Professor Scindia seemed to hesitate for a long time. Finally, he spoke, "Okay. I'll think about it. But if any one students (sic) objects, I won't hold an extra test. In any case, don't worry. Each test counts for only 5% of your total grade. So, even if you get zero in one, it doesn't matter much." Romik looked reassured and got up from his seat. Now that he knew the test counted for only 5% of the grade, he seemed happy.

Professor Scindia looked questioningly at me, as I sat there with my mouth half-open. "Anything else?" he enquired. "Student," I replied without thinking. He looked surprised. "I know you are. But what did you want to tell me?" he asked again. But the only thing I could think of was his slip of the tongue. It was a common enough mistake – he had said, "if any one *students* objects", when he should have said, "if any one *student* objects". I had made more than my share of such mistakes both in public and in private. So, it wasn't really a big deal. But for some reason, my mind kept coming back to it. Obviously, I wasn't about to tell him the truth. He would probably gulp me down along with his protein shake! Finally, I blurted out, "I'm really enjoying the classes, Sir. This is my 'favourite' course!" He smiled at me, probably wondering if I was a special needs case. He replied, "Thanks for the feedback and next time, I want both of you to score 100!"

CHAPTER 18

A week after the Synergy debate, Romik, Sachin and I ditched lunch at the college canteen in favour of a momo joint (recommended, of course, by Ramesh). Sachin was a friend of Ramesh and Amrish. He was short, wore big spectacles and had a Hitler-like moustache with no beard. My grandmother always said, "Men with moustaches and no beards are those whom puberty forgot about half-way!" Sachin bore a striking resemblance to a rabbit. But he was a cool guy and didn't mind the jokes.

The momo place was about a kilometre away from our college. We were all non-vegetarians, so the thought of chicken momos for lunch was more than enough to tempt us away from the same old college food.

We had just reached the place when Romik got a call. He swaggered off as Sachin and I ordered 2 plates of momos each (yes, we were that hungry!). Suddenly, Romik came rushing back. "Guys, I got a call from Prayuj. He said that the Principal is meeting everyone in our batch on a one-on-one basis and it's almost our turn!" I knew Prayuj. He hung out with Romik a lot. I knew Romik and him well enough to tell that this was no practical joke. The Principal wanted to meet us. I could hardly be excused so that I could eat momos. Talk about a case of bad timing!

"Okay. Let's take an auto and head back to college. We'll just forget the momos this time," I suggested, hoping Sachin and Romik would agree with me. But Sachin surprised me by saying, "It's okay. My roll number comes a little later. You guys give me the cash and I'll pack the momos for y'all. I'll meet you back at college."

Romik was literally tugging on my T-shirt's sleeve by now. "Come on, hurry up! We're going to be late. I don't want the Principal to be angry with me from the first semester itself!" Romik exclaimed, panicking. Okay, I admit it. I panicked too. I didn't know why the Principal wanted to see us...but I sure wasn't going to keep him waiting! I handed over 80 bucks to Sachin and headed to the auto stand on the other side of the road with Romik following me like a lost puppy.

Romik kept glancing at his watch and tapping his foot impatiently. He reminded me of a (much) uglier version of Naina, when I first saw her. Neither Romik nor I spoke Kannada. We finally managed to find one guy who spoke in broken Hindi. At first, he didn't seem to understand where I wanted to go. "ICSI? Opposite Infosys campus main gate?" I asked hopefully. He looked blankly at me and tilted his head to one side. "*Woh* Infosys *ke* opposite *wala* parking lot (That parking lot opposite Infosys)?" he finally asked. I should probably have been more agitated about my college being designated a parking lot, but I was in too much of a rush to care.

Before I tell you anything more about what happened then, I should probably back up a little and tell you how my mom brought me up. Don't worry. This isn't some kind of psychoanalysis, where I attribute all the problems in my life to my parents. According to my mom, the ultimate sin in life is to allow auto drivers to cheat you. She always says, "Don't ever fight anyone in anger. Always ignore an insult to your ego. Don't hold grudges or seek revenge. But...fight for what's right. For example, you *must* fight with an auto driver who is trying to rip you off." In all the years I've known her, my mom has never given another example.

So, I was willing to pay the auto driver the 30 bucks that he was due and not a paise more. I asked him the fare. He asked for 60 bucks. I laughed at him. I dismissed this and reminded him that in Bangalore, he could charge at most 30 bucks for 2 kilometres. He claimed that Electronic City didn't fall strictly within the city limits. I didn't have enough money to pay the guy even if I'd wanted to, since I'd left my momo money with Sachin! I hesitated, not sure what exactly I should do next.

But Romik took off running, like Usain Bolt! I figured he'd run off to find a cheaper auto. I kept calling him, but he ignored me and kept running. I was forced to race after him like a madman. I finally caught up with him. "What are you – crazy? Where are you suddenly haring off to anyway? The auto stand is in the opposite direction!" I exclaimed while puffing and panting. Romik replied (without even breaking a sweat), "It's only a kilometre to college. Should make for a good warm-up. Real men burn calories, not fuel!" I wondered if he was secretly the brand ambassador for a gym! Seriously, who says stuff like that except gym trainers?! "Come on, you can do it too. Just keep pace with me," he said casually, as if he was out for a leisurely evening stroll.

I realise there are a lot of fitness freaks out there who would laugh at the thought of running *just* a kilometre!

But I also know a lot of people (like me!) who feel like they've climbed Mt. Everest if they can go the distance. Just as I felt my lungs were about to explode, I saw the ICSI gate. I don't think I've ever been happier to see college.

We raced inside and (finally!) stopped. We walked to the academic block and the Principal's office. Oddly, there wasn't a queue in the waiting area. That seemed weird. I wondered if we were too late and began imagining getting expelled from college. Just then, the Principal's secretary came into the waiting room with a cup of coffee in her hand.

"What are you boys doing here?" she asked curiously. I was out of breath, so I let Romik describe his conversation with Prayuj and explain why we had come running here. She replied, "Oh...sorry. I thought the rest of your batch would have told you. Sir had an important meeting to attend, so he promised to continue the interactions some other time." I felt exhausted and frustrated at the same time. As Romik and I headed towards the canteen, Romik saw that Prayuj had called him several times after the initial call. However, we had been too busy dodging traffic to hear the phone.

Suddenly, we spotted Sachin cheerfully entering the hostel. I ran to catch up with him and asked him for my momos. "Oh...about that..." he muttered grinning widely. "I-uh kind of ate them all," he mumbled. "What?!" I couldn't believe what he had just said. How did a skinny guy like that eat 24 momos?

Sachin tried to explain, "See, Prayuj called me too and said not to worry because the whole meeting thing had been called off until further notice. I figured y'all had reached college as it takes just a minute in an auto. I thought you guys would eat at the canteen and I could treat you later."

I'm not sure who I was more irritated with then – the conman or the confused one! Oh well, I guess you have to learn some lessons the hard way!

CHAPTER 19

She woke up suddenly. It was pitch dark. But she could sense something. Her heart hammered wildly in her chest. Was this some kind of nightmare? She moved her hand towards where her bedside table should be. Her fingers grazed the bottom of her phone. That's when she knew this was no dream. Suddenly, a flash of lightning lit up the sky, giving her a chance to get a good look at them.

There were 2 men. Both wore masks and were dressed in filthy T-shirts and pants. They had black hair and piercing black eyes. They were bending over her. One was holding a needle and the other a handkerchief. They were here to kidnap her! She was sure of it.

Just then, the man with the syringe grabbed her arm, pinning it to the bed. The other man covered her mouth with the handkerchief. "Nooo...mmm!" she shouted through the gag. Her roommate stirred on the other side of the room. "Hey, you okay?" came her roommate's sleepy voice. She tried to reply, but the handkerchief was in her mouth now. She could even taste the horrible sweaty fingers of the man. She bit down as hard as she could. The man cried out and fell back. His companion stuck the syringe into her and pushed the plunger.

She didn't know what she had been injected with, but she knew she might soon lose consciousness. She had to act fast. She used her free hand to pick up the glass from her bedside table. She smashed it into the face of the attacker with the syringe and then dropped it, so that it fell onto the floor and shattered into a million fragments. Her roommate was now fully awake and sitting upright in her bed.

"Listen, we're going to be okay. I promise. Just try and calm down," her roommate said reassuringly. But she could already see that the two men were recovering from her attack. She felt her blood turn to ice as one of them headed towards her again. No! She refused to be a helpless victim. She had to get out of this room.

She grabbed her phone and dazzled her assailants with its flashlight. She scooped up one of the glass fragments and held it in the other hand. Then, she ran towards the door. She was surprised to see that it was still locked from the inside. How had her kidnappers entered?

But before she could figure that out, her roommate tackled her to the floor. She lashed out and gave her roommate a nasty cut, using the glass shard. Her roommate screamed and took a step back. That was the opening she needed. She leapt to her feet, unlocked the door and bolted from the room.

She fled the hostel, screaming as she fled. Doors were unlocked and girls began appearing to see what the fuss was all about. She ran down the stairs, taking them 2 at a time. She could hear footsteps behind her, but she didn't dare look back. And then, suddenly, she was out in the pouring rain.

She called her brother from her mobile. She willed him to pick up the phone, but it was no use. Water clogged the screen as she ran through the rain. She didn't know which way she was going, or where she should head. She just kept running madly in the pounding rain. Suddenly, she felt as if she was losing control of her body. It was weird and disorienting. It was like an out-of-body experience. It must be because of the drug they had injected her with. With sudden clarity, she knew she had to get it out of her bloodstream before it killed her. She slashed her arm with the glass shard, still clenched in one hand.

The pain was intense. She could barely move. Then, blood mixed with rainwater and formed a pool beneath her. She tried to run, but was too dizzy. She could see the main gate now. There were security guards running towards her. She stumbled and fell. The last thing she heard was her name being called. Had she got away in time? She blacked out before she could be sure...

CHAPTER 20

It was 2 weeks after the Synergy debate. I cradled the phone in my hands, wishing Naina would answer. But, as usual, the phone kept ringing with no response. It hummed in my hands till I heard the same prerecorded message. I turned off speakerphone and wondered why all those prerecorded messages had to sound so very cheerful!

You're probably wondering why I hadn't tried Naina sooner. As a matter of fact, I had messaged her on WhatsApp every day since the debate. But there had been no response. I knew she had seen the messages. But she didn't bother replying. I finally decided that enough was enough. I wouldn't message or call for a while. In fact, I resolved not to pester her till she responded to my old messages. The ball was in her court now.

My steely resolve lasted for a royal total of a day. The very next day, I texted her on WhatsApp and later tried calling her. But it was no use. She ignored my calls and messages completely. I wondered if she liked to dangle herself flirtatiously and then disappear without a trace. I might be a total loser when it comes to a pretty face, but I still wasn't about to lose what little dignity I had left by marching up to the Synergy gate and demanding to see her. Thankfully, though, I still had an ace up my sleeve.

Yeah, you guessed it – her brother. I had noticed him from afar when I first met Naina. He had a distinctive face. He was around my height, wore rectangular glasses and had quite a stubble. I knew his name was Vijay from one of his batchmates, who was our Teaching Assistant for C programming. I had seen Vijay again at the freshers' party. Yes, we did finally have a freshers' party! But I had never spoken to Vijay in person. After waiting for Naina's call for 2 weeks, I steeled myself to go up to him without any introduction.

I saw my chance one day at the canteen. He was sitting alone at a table, looking glum. I walked up to him, trying to decide what to say. I was sure the guy wouldn't recognise me. Plus, he seemed a bit of a loner (even in his own batch). So, my prospects seemed pretty bleak. I could hardly walk up to him and say, "I'm your sister's stalker/ wanna-be-boyfriend!" The guy looked like he could pound me into the dirt. I was rehearsing equally awful lines in my head, when he looked up and noticed me.

"Need something?" he asked in a deep voice. I have to say, I was tempted to squeak, "No!" and get as far away from him as I could. But I just grinned and motioned to his table, "Mind if I join you?" I asked. "Go ahead," he mumbled before resuming his meal. I sat down and toyed with my food for a while. Suddenly, both of us began talking. "Don't I know you..." he began, while I said, "I'm Pranav Dasgupta..." We both stopped midway and began chuckling. Then he spoke again, "Right, you're the debate guy. My sis told me about you." I came back with an amazingly brilliant remark, "Yeah. The debate guy. That's me." He had a faint smile on his face. "So...how can I help you?" he finally asked. It was now or never. I had to trust him.

"Is anything wrong with your sister? I've been trying to connect with her for 2 weeks and she seems to be avoiding me," I said. He narrowed his eyes at me suspiciously. I quickly carried on before he told me not to stalk his sister, "The thing is...she left me her number after the debate and suggested we connect. I don't want to sound like a stalker or anything, but I just want to know if she's okay." For a minute, Vijay tensed his body as if he was getting ready to punch me. Then he exhaled and slumped back in his chair. He answered, "If *she* gave you her number, then I guess it's okay for you to know. My sister's been sick for a while. That's probably why she hasn't replied. Hopefully, she should be discharged from hospital soon."

I hastily nodded and got up from the table. I felt like a jerk for thinking Naina was the type of girl who didn't really care about anyone, except herself. She was fighting some disease and here I was wondering if she liked me! If only I had known. If only...

CHAPTER 21

The time had come at last. The time I had been dreading since I joined ICSI. Exam time. Everyone had been desperately trying to prepare for the various subjects. The last week had flown by too quickly for anyone's liking. You have to remember we were all still in competitive exam mode. The engineering entrance exam preparation was still the way we worked.

Anyone who's been through college in India knows that after a few exams, you sort of get less caught up in trying to stay on top every time. But your first and last set of college exams have you studying late into the night, filling your brain with stuff you'll forget by morning.

Most of us had our own private rituals. Amrish was busy oiling his hair. Ramesh ate a record number of momos. Soorya finally shaved his stubble and Venugopal had his martial arts exercise routine. What about me? Well, I tried reading the textbooks. But I just wasn't dedicated enough to mug them up. So, I basically ended up reading my notes (which were mostly squiggles) and discussing possible exam questions with everyone from Dhanush to Lokesh. After I was suitably tense, I binge watched Netflix and tried to forget the fact that I was probably going to fail every paper.

Finally, exam week arrived! Our first paper was English. One of the key topics we had been focusing on during the course was how to make a good presentation. You're probably thinking that it would make sense for us to have to make an actual presentation, right? Wrong! Our English teacher had us write a pen-paper exam. One of the questions asked us to list the "seven C's of good presentations". I didn't remember a single one, of course. So, I came up with things which sounded promising, such as clarity, conciseness, etc. Thankfully, no one had paid much attention in class. And since the marking was relative, everything seemed right with the world.

The next day was Real Analysis. The only one who looked happy to be entering the exam hall was Soorya. But, then again, he was the only one who understood anything in the class. Professor Mukherjee hadn't spared us. He seemed to want to remind us why we weren't IIT material. All of us felt like we had hit rock bottom after 3 hours of torture. The paper had wiped the smile from everyone's face – even Soorya's. Like a true IIT professor, Professor Mukherjee was strict in his correction. I managed to score in the low sixties. That actually meant I was among the top 5 in class!

Other people (probably brighter than me) scored in their thirties and even twenties. Amrish landed up with a 27! And this after a full bottle of oil! Soorya obviously topped the class. But even he only managed a 75. Most of the class actually failed the exam! Originally, Professor Mukherjee had intended to give 50% weightage to the mid-sem exam and 50% weightage to the end-sem. But after seeing our performance, he decided to give the mid-sem 20% weightage, the end-sem 50% and added 3 class tests with total 30% weightage. But after the paper, we didn't have time to sit and mourn. It was time for our Python programming exam!

The next day found us sitting at our desktops, fully expecting to fail. Professor Kumar arrived with his customary laugh. He had claimed that it would be an open-book exam. In fact, he had even said that we could search the internet and use Google if we thought it would help. When a professor offers so much help, there's always a catch. As a result, we were all freaked out about the exam and Professor Kumar's lack of concern only added to our worry. A lot of us thought Professor Kumar was going to give us some kind of open problem (that's Computer Science lingo for a problem which is yet to be solved) and see if anyone could solve it.

Professor Kumar tapped some commands into his laptop and our screens lit up with the question paper. It had only 2 questions. But after reading them, I knew 3 years wouldn't be enough for me to solve them, forget 3 hours! The first was some horrible maths technique for approximation called the Newton-Raphson method (don't ask me what that means, since I have no clue till date!). The second was about vectors embedded in 4-dimensional spaces. I was in no shape to solve either. I was desperately trying to Google solutions, like everyone else. That was when I first noticed it.

My right hand started trembling a little. At first, I thought it was just nerves. After all, anyone about to score a big fat zero would be nervous. When I clenched my hand into a fist, the shaking stopped. So, I just ignored it and kept hammering away furiously at my keyboard, trying not to panic and desperately attempting to make my code look nice – even if it didn't run. Professor Kumar had promised partial marks for the source code itself and not just for the final result. Hey, if Dhanush could pull it off, I figured I should give it a shot!

Then, my left hand began trembling too. I brought them both up to my face and realised that the intensity of the trembling had increased a lot. Still, I tried to will it away which worked for a while. It was only then that I figured that something was seriously wrong with me. The air conditioner had me shivering, but I was still dripping with sweat, like I was John after a workout session!

While I was trembling and trying to wipe away the sweat, I had a sudden flash of inspiration! I thought I knew how to solve the first problem. But I had a bigger problem on my hands – hypoglycaemia (hypo).

That's basically just a fancy way of saying that the amount of glucose in my blood was below normal. That meant that I immediately needed to eat something sweet. Sounds fun, right? Trust me, it isn't. The early signs can be shakiness, anxiety, sweating, fatigue. As the hypo worsens, the symptoms can include loss of consciousness and even death. Diabetics get hypos when they miscalculate and inject themselves with too much insulin (which helps the body break down glucose). So, basically every time you miscalculate your insulin dose, your life is on the line.

I actually had a bottle of Coke in my bag for just such an emergency. But I figured I'd finish coding the first answer before explaining why I needed to glug down a bottle of Coke in the middle of an exam. I finished the last line of code. My fingers were trembling so much that I could barely type. I had just begun to run it, when... my computer crashed! It kept saying memory error. Apparently, not only did my program not run, but it was also deadly enough to crash any computer which ran it!

"Sir, I seem to be experiencing some technical difficulties," I joked. Yeah, even though my brain was shutting down, I still retained my sense of humour. That was my last thought before I blacked out.

CHAPTER 22

She awoke to harsh neon light. She squinted and tried to figure out where she was. The last thing she remembered was being pursued...oh no! She sat up in a bed. Had her kidnappers decided to keep her here? She felt a burning pain along her left forearm. Glancing at it, she noticed a deep and jagged scar. Her other arm was covered with needles. No doubt sedatives to make her easier to handle.

She was on the verge of yanking the needles out and throwing them aside when the door creaked open. She froze, paralysed by indecision. Should she hurl herself on whoever was coming through and make a break for freedom? Or should she pretend to be asleep from the sedatives? She lost the few seconds needed to make the snap decision. So, she was entirely unprepared for what followed.

Her brother stepped into the room, accompanied by someone who looked like a nurse. Suddenly, all the tension of the last few minutes vanished. She knew that she ought to be able to take care of herself, but it felt good – knowing her big brother was looking out for her. Tears of joy came to her eyes.

The nurse came over and examined her in a brisk and business-like fashion. She peered at the scar, which was still red and then turned her attention to the various medicines which were being administered to her. Meanwhile, her brother stood in the corner, chewing his lower lip – like he always did when he was concerned. Finally, the nurse asked her how she felt. She thought for a while and then replied honestly, "Tired." The nurse smiled at her and said, "Don't worry. You'll feel better soon. Now, let me get you some food."

The nurse then bustled over to her brother and had a whispered conversation with him, before leaving the 2 of them alone. After the final bang of the door, they smiled at each other. "Hey, I'm so sorry..." he began, but she cut him off. "It doesn't matter. All that matters is that you're here now. Promise me you'll always be there for me, no matter how crazy life gets. The 2 of us against the world, right?" she asked pleadingly. Was it her imagination or did a flicker of uncertainty cross his face? Then he squeezed her hand reassuringly. "I promise," he said.

"What do you remember of the night you got that?" he asked, pointing at her scar. She paused, uncertain how much to reveal. "I was being chased by 2 men. They were trying to kidnap me! They injected me with something. I had to get it out of me. That's why I did this!" she exclaimed in a frenzy, pointing to her scar and hoping that he'd understand.

He pushed her gently back onto the bed. His eyes looked troubled. He spoke soothingly, "Last night, you called me from your cell phone. When I couldn't hear anything, I came running from ICSI. But the guards and some of your friends from the hostel had already brought you here. They said you were tightly gripping the phone in one hand and a chunk of bloodied glass in the other."

Her brother carried on, "I insisted they give you a separate room. The doctors wanted to keep you under observation. You woke up once this morning before I got here. Apparently, you had some juice. But this is the first time you've spoken properly. Is it coming back to you?" he asked her pleadingly.

But she just shook her head. "I don't remember any of that. What about the 2 men? Has there been any sign of them?" she asked, already knowing the answer. "I'll ask around. But nobody else mentioned 2 guys in the hostel," he replied. "Still, I'll check it out," he promised. He carried on, "I better run. Visiting hours are over and I have another patient to look in on." She was curious. "Who?" she asked. "The other victim of your little adventure..." his voice trailed off suggestively.

She felt sleep approaching. The sedatives must be working, she thought. She caught one final glimpse of her brother and managed to say, "Tell her I'm sorry. I'm sorry..." Then, sleep engulfed her.

***

Since then, 2 weeks had passed. She had been in the hospital for all that time. She missed the warmth of the sun on her face and the cooling rain on her brow. Her parents had driven down from Chennai for the first few days. Once both they and the doctors had been satisfied that she was no longer delusional, they left.

She had spent most of the time watching Netflix on her phone. Her college had been supportive and she was allowed to continue her courses via correspondence. The only thing she couldn't do from hospital was take the exams. But her college had assured her that she could do so during the holidays.

Her friends had dropped by for occasional visits. But most of the time, she had been too tired to make much conversation. Her brother had been the only constant. He had taken to sleeping right outside her room. Finally, even the guards had given up trying to chase him off and had allowed him to stay with her late into the night. She had been grateful for the company, though there were times when she would wake up and scream despite his presence.

During the 2 weeks, a number of strangers had come into her room. Thankfully, the kidnappers hadn't returned. But every day, new faces would show up. Some of them were caring and gentle, others were insane and evil. In one part of her mind, she knew they couldn't be real. But what was real? Was her brother real? What about the doctors and nurses? Maybe, this was all some kind of twisted nightmare. She knew she was being given antipsychotics. But wasn't that a fancy way of admitting that she was crazy? How could she be crazy?

She hadn't wanted to do it. But she soon realised there was no other way. If she ever wanted to get out of this place, she needed to convince the doctors and nurses that she was fine. So she had ignored reality and gone along with the pretence of being alone in the room, except for her brother. She had taken all their pills and told them what they wanted to hear.

Today, she would finally be released from this dreadful place. She couldn't wait to get out of here. But there was one final exam to pass before they let her go. She looked excitedly towards the door as it swung open.

Her doctor (Dr. Ravi) walked in with a nurse behind him. "Hope you're feeling well today, my dear?" he asked, dangling the carrot of freedom in front of her. She just nodded and smiled.

"Just a few standard checks before we release you today. I'll just check your temperature, blood pressure and mouth. I'm sure you haven't vomited out the medicines we gave you. You've been a good girl, haven't you?" asked Dr. Ravi. "Yes, doctor," she replied automatically. Dr. Ravi completed his checks. Satisfied, he put away his instruments and smiled at her. She smiled back, wondering what he would do next. "I have one final question, my dear. How many people are in this room, excluding you?"

He studied her intently, like a predator studying its prey before it strikes! However, after so long, she could lie to him with a straight face. She donned her poker face and said, "Only 2." He sat back, relieved and satisfied. "Well done, my dear. Just keep taking the medication and you will be fine. Why don't you step out and meet your brother, while we complete the formalities?" he said, winking at her.

She cautiously slid off the bed. She waved the nurse away and walked with her back to the doctor. She approached the door slowly, all too aware of the gun barrel trained on her back. The 2 men from that night had returned!

CHAPTER 23

I awoke in the comfort of my bedroom to see the sun setting. For a minute, I wondered if this was the afterlife. Then, my bedroom door creaked open and my mother stepped in. Suddenly, my heart pounded. As I saw her, I remembered the Python exam – how I had been getting a hypo, how I had ignored the symptoms and how I had blacked out. That still didn't explain how I had ended up back home though.

"Ma, what happened?" I croaked. My limbs felt really stiff. In fact, my entire body hurt all over. Just getting those words out was an effort. "Don't you remember?" she began. "You were in the middle of your exam when you suddenly lost consciousness. Thankfully, Amrish was there. He'd seen you get hypos before. He told Professor Kumar that they had to get you home as soon as possible," she continued.

"Did you come and pick me up from college?" I asked. My brain still felt fuzzy. "No. Amrish and some other boys from your batch picked you up and carried you to Professor Kumar's car. Professor Kumar was kind enough, to drive you home. Thankfully, he drove fast enough so that he arrived in time for me to revive you with glucose," she concluded.

My mom looked like she was on the verge of tears. I tried to comfort her. "Don't worry, Ma. I'm good now.

That's all that matters," I reassured her. I slowly lifted myself from the bed and awkwardly embraced her. "I'm sorry that I scared you. I should have had the Coke earlier. I guess I'll have to repeat the semester now," I said thoughtfully.

"What?!" her head snapped back and the old, familiar fire ignited in her eyes. You see, it's just a question of pushing the right buttons. For any good Bengali, the three M's of life – 'maach' (fish), Marxism and marks – are very important. Most Bengalis have fish every day. They will also debate and discuss Communism with anyone willing to listen. And finally, there is the question of marks – especially children's marks. All parents want the best for their children. But Bengali parents equate 'best' with 'best marks'. That's why I knew I would touch a nerve with all this talk of repeating a semester. No good Bengali could let a sentence like that go unquestioned.

"No child of mine is repeating a semester!" she declared forcefully. "I've already spoken to Professor Kumar and he's promised to give you a make-up exam before the end of the semester. And anyway, you're already prepared for tomorrow's paper, so go ahead and rest for the day." Great! Not only did I now have a make-up test to worry about, but I also had to sit for tomorrow's exam in C!

I know how my mom sometimes gets when she's very passionate about something – like about me sitting for all my papers come what may. If she hadn't been stopped by my school, she would probably have sent me off to write my exams when I had chicken pox! But, for the first time, I had seen a chink in her armour. So, I decided to push my luck.

"Ma...about tomorrow's exam...do you think it's okay if I don't go? I'm feeling pretty sick..." my voice trailed off as she gave me the 'disappointed mom' look. What is this look? You know the look that your parents give you when you ask them if you can do something they really don't approve of? That's the look. For example, I know a lot of people who want to eat meat, even though their parents are vegetarians. Well, whenever they ask their parents if they can eat a chicken finger or something, their parents give them this really pained look. It says something like this – "Well...you'd be letting us and generations of your ancestors down...but, if you really want to do it, you can..." Now, you know what I'm talking about. And that's why I knew I would end up sitting for the next exam!

The next day, I landed up in college late and wasn't able to have last-minute discussions with anyone. However, as I scanned the uploaded paper, I started feeling better. You're probably wondering why I would be happy about a paper I had barely prepared for. But that's just it...the questions came from exactly the material I had used for preparation. Yesterday, the only thing I had the energy to do was go through my old assignments and hope Professor Scindia would give similar questions in the exam.

Not only similar, the questions in the exam were *identical* to the ones from our assignments! Of course, there was less time to finish them. But after staring at the code all evening, I had practically memorised it. There were 5 questions in all with a total of 3 hours to solve them.

This time, when I glanced up from my desk to look around the class, I saw way more smiling faces than during the Python exam. If there was a prize for 'favourite' professor, Professor Scindia would be pretty highly ranked after today.

As the bell rang, signalling the end of typing time, the class broke up into clusters of students discussing the paper with each other. Most everyone seemed to be in an upbeat mood. And me? Frankly, I just felt tired. I wanted to go home and forget about the exam and all college-related things for a while. I was just getting ready to leave, when they stopped by my table.

They were standing between my desk and the door, waiting for me to look at them. I got up and saw Amrish. He was facing me along with Preetish, Dhanush, Venugopal and Romik. "Hey, guys!" I said, getting up gradually. "What's up?" I asked casually. They waited till everyone else had left. Then Amrish spoke, "*Macha*, you really scared us yesterday. Thankfully, I knew what to do from school. Otherwise..." he left the word hanging. "Okay...well, thanks guys. I really appreciate it. But I'd best be going..." I stopped mid-sentence as a thought struck me.

"Hang on a second! Did the 5 of you carry me to the car yesterday?" I asked as realisation struck. They all smiled (probably because of how slowly my brain was functioning) and nodded. I have to admit, I choked up for a moment. I'm not normally an emotional type of guy. But the thought that I had such caring people in my life was a nice one.

"So, we were wondering, could you tell us what to do in case this happens again?" asked Amrish. I spent some time talking to them about the symptoms I might experience in case my sugar dropped and I got a hypo. I explained how they ought to give me Coke, juice, glucose or anything sweet before I started convulsing. In case of convulsions, they ought to rush me to the nearest hospital. Finally, they volunteered to tell all the other students and professors about my condition.

After thanking each of them, I promised myself that I would always try to return the favour whenever I could (no matter how annoying they became!). It was the least I could do. As we continued chatting, the topic turned towards the C exam.

Only Dhanush seemed to have got all the test cases to run (besides me, of course). Amrish and Preetish had failed one test case each, while Romik and Venugopal had failed 3 each. Dhanush's head bobbed up and down like a jack-in-the-box with a superior smirk plastered all over his face. He had gone from heroic to annoying in a couple of seconds. I wanted to burst his bubble. But I remembered my promise to myself. So, when he asked how I had done, I simply said, "Not as well as you." With that, I spun on my heel and walked away.

CHAPTER 24

She ran as fast as her legs would carry her! She raced unthinkingly into the traffic, dodging this way and that – desperately trying to shake off her pursuers. She threw herself aside at the last instant just as a truck rumbled past.

She had complied with every request the doctors had made. But she couldn't ignore the goings-on at her college forever. She had pretended for so long that those men weren't watching her constantly from behind. But she knew that they were there – every minute of every hour of every day. She had tried to focus in class, but the pills prescribed by the doctors had made her sleepy. As a result, she was falling behind in every course and she hated it.

But her so-called 'friends' had hurt her the most. They had been the most vicious in making her suffer. They had smeared ketchup all over her bed and claimed it was blood just to frighten her. Someone, no doubt as a sick joke, had put posters all over the campus, advising people to "buy pot from the crackpot". This had led to a serious college investigation as to whether she was involved with drugs or not. Nothing came of it. But the thought of people going through her things and looking at her suspiciously had made her feel hollow inside.

She had felt like she had lost all reason to live. Even when she had run to the bathroom to lighten her burden by crying tears of frustration, she had found those wretched posters all over the walls. Suddenly she had felt a violent urge cutting through her depression. She had torn down every poster from the bathroom walls.

She had then proceeded to make her way to her hostel. Just as she had entered the hostel block, she had spotted 2 girls laughing about something. She had looked at them and the words had burst out of her – "SHUT UP!" Before she had been fully aware of what she was doing, she had launched herself at the 2 girls. She had tackled them to the cement floor. She had scratched at the first girl's eyes and had bit the second's fingers.

Suddenly, she had heard footsteps approaching as more girls from the hostel had gathered and tried to pull the 3 of them apart. She had felt several pairs of hands grip her firmly and drag her away from the other 2 girls, who had looked terrified. All of a sudden, her murderous rage had subsided. She had gone limp as she had felt the barrel of the gun poke her side.

Then, the reassuring face of her roommate had appeared. She could have wept for joy. She had let herself be escorted to her room. Her roommate had said something to the other 2 girls. It didn't matter anymore. Soon after, the men had arrived and she knew they would stay. She might as well accept her role as a victim. It was the only way to survive.

The next day, she had been called to the Principal's office. The 2 girls she had attacked had reported her actions to the college authorities. Just as she was about to knock on the Principal's door, it had opened a fraction. "Come in," a deep voice had commanded.

The Principal had a huge office with a long, rectangular table right in the middle. The Principal himself had been seated at the head of the table. The 2 girls she had attacked yesterday had been seated to his right. They had stared at her as if she was some kind of monster. The Principal had motioned for her to sit down. Her feet had obeyed, though she had still felt like an external observer.

Once she was seated, the Principal had begun in his deep voice, "I understand there was...a 'fight' of some kind between the 3 of you yesterday?" She had sensed the question mark at the end of the sentence and had nodded mutely as his gaze fell on her. "She attacked us!" exclaimed one of the 2 girls she had assaulted yesterday. "Yes, Sir," the other one had agreed. "We were sitting together and laughing when she attacked us and started scratching and biting us like some kind of animal." The Principal had nodded seriously. He had then gazed at her again.

"I have numerous eye-witness accounts which confirm this story. Now, I realise your 'condition' makes you volatile. But I'm afraid we can't tolerate such behaviour on our campus. Unless you are able to interact normally with your peers and professors, you leave me with no choice but to ask you to leave. Is that understood?" the Principal had asked seriously.

She had just nodded mutely. The Principal had seemed satisfied. "Then I suggest all of you carry on to your classes." As she had turned to leave, he had stopped her. "Just a minute. Let the others leave. I'd like to ask you something," he had said. She had waited obediently, while the other girls had left the room. Then he had addressed her, "I want you to think about what I'm about to say carefully. Do you want to repeat a semester?"

She had heard herself say, "No, Sir." "Is there anything else you'd like to tell me?" he had asked gently. She had found herself saying, "No, Sir," in the same mechanical tone of voice. She had cried deep inside – feeling helpless – as she had left the office.

That brought her back to the present moment. She was running away from college towards ICSI. She could hear the heavy footsteps of her pursuers. They were out in force. All of them. And this time, they had one mission – shoot to kill. She had been lucky so far. But sooner or later, one of the bullets would find its mark. Then suddenly, she was blinded by the lights of a bus headed towards her. She froze – like a deer in the headlights – and was jerked out of the bus' path by a strong pair of hands. She lashed out violently. But the hands had a firm hold on her. She could hear a familiar voice calling her name. But each sound was so loud that she couldn't piece the syllables together.

Then she heard the voice ask, "Do you want to be expelled from college?" She shook her head. "Good...then come back with me," the voice coaxed. Gradually, she let herself be led onto the pavement, where she collapsed. The day's exhaustion hit her like a physical blow.

She had heard one of her pursuers remark, "Finish her the moment she leaves the campus. No witnesses. And this time...shoot to kill." Her first thought had been to run to her brother in ICSI. She had known that she had to reach him and tell him everything. She had decided to risk the possibility of being shot dead and run crazily into the traffic in the hope of losing her pursuers. She had wanted to create a scene and draw as much attention to herself as possible, since she had wanted to make sure there were plenty of witnesses wherever she went. Her roommate had followed her and rescued her from certain death. But what kind of life was this – one where she was always on the run, always being hunted?

"Come on," the voice coaxed, "let's head back. They won't even let you into the ICSI campus if you show up like this. You better have this first." A pill was handed to her. She swallowed it automatically. In just a few moments, her sense of panic subsided. She got to her feet shakily. She put her hand into her pocket and pulled out her phone. She quickly messaged her brother, saying she would meet him tomorrow. Having done so, she put herself in the capable hands of her roommate, who steered her towards college.

CHAPTER 25

Thankfully, the Biology students didn't have a mid-sem exam. That meant we spent Friday chilling and making fun of the Chemistry students – who had a gruelling paper complete with Schrodinger's equations and other types of nasty stuff. Finally, after the week was over, we all breathed a sigh of relief. The mid-sems were over and we had a week's break to celebrate.

Around a week after college had re-opened, our coordinator strolled into our Python class just before lunch. He was smartly dressed (as always) and seemed to be bursting with excitement. Professor Kumar stopped mid-sentence and stepped away from the smart board. No doubt, he was as eager to get to lunch as the rest of us.

Professor Swaminathan began, "You all must be wondering why I'm here. Don't worry, I won't take up too much of your lunch break. We professors get hungry too, you know!" Once again, his poor joke was met with silence. Not to be daunted, he continued, "There is going to be an international programming contest held day after tomorrow. It's called IEEE-Xtreme. It's a contest for college students from all over the world. It starts at 9 a.m. and lasts for 24 hours. So, bring your snacks and sleeping bags!"

The mention of snacks made me remember the lunch I was missing out on. But there was a buzz of excitement around the class as everyone understood the nature of the competition. It was a long haul, but winning a competition like this might be well worth it. Professor Swaminathan held up his hands for silence. He continued, "Each team can consist of at most 3 members. You will have to code your answers in a programming language of your choice and upload them from the registered account. I hope you don't have any further questions?"

Everyone was still digesting the format of the competition, when he seemed to decide that he had spent enough time with us. "Good. In that case, register with your team names and members at my office by noon tomorrow at the latest." He was about to step away from the podium when he seemed to suddenly remember something. He returned and finished his (really long!) speech, "In case of any plagiarism, not only will you be disqualified from the contest, the institute will also take strict disciplinary action. Good luck!"

So saying, he strode out of the classroom. Professor Kumar was right on his tail. By now, I was ravenous. Frankly, I was more concerned about lunch than winning international programming contests. I had just stepped out of the door...when I realised that I had walked into an ambush! Ramesh and Soorya were standing a little to one side. The minute they saw me, they hurried towards me. I pretended not to have a clue what this was all about.

"Hey, guys! What's up?" I asked lamely. Ramesh spoke in his usual direct manner. "We want you to join our team. You in or out?" Soorya seemed to sense my discomfort (but obviously not my hunger!). He added, "We saw that Pacman game which you and Amrish had programmed. We were impressed and would really like you to be on our team."

I inwardly cursed. As part of our CBSE Grade 12 Computer Science project, Amrish and I (okay, mainly Amrish) had developed a variant of the popular Pacman game in C++. Amrish had been showing it off lately to impress our batchmates. The thing was that he had coded most of it. I had just tagged along for the ride. Now, I was about to join a team consisting of a genius and a mafia don. But the more I thought about it, the more sense it seemed to make. I could leave the hard work to the 2 of them and pretend to help out. "Okay. Let's do it!" I exclaimed. It couldn't be all that bad, could it?

The day of the contest, I landed up at college at 9 a.m. sharp. Ramesh had already registered our team the previous day. Our team name was 'Semicolon Expected'. Naming the team was my greatest and only contribution to the contest. We had named ourselves after the famous programming error which every programmer has seen at some stage or the other.

Soorya and Ramesh were waiting for me in the lab. Apparently, they had spent the last 2 days going through programming challenges online. I listened to them talk about matrices, searching, sorting and all kinds of horrible mathematical things I had never even heard of. So, I refrained from commenting and tried to look wise and knowledgeable. However, I have a bad feeling that I ended up looking pained and sleepy!

We had 3 desktops to ourselves. The idea was that we could divide the work amongst the 3 of us. Finally, Soorya would take care of the actual uploading. I still wasn't sure how I could best hide my ignorance. Then, before I knew it, Soorya and Ramesh were opening the IEEE-Xtreme webpage to check out the questions. I could see the questions, but I could also see there was no way that I could solve any of them!

The first question was a horrible one, involving permuting the letters of a word to obey certain specific rules. The second one was about performing multiplication on sparse matrices (matrices where most of the elements are zero). As if these 2 weren't enough, we also had a third question. This involved doing something called an LU-decomposition of a matrix (don't ask me what that is...I still don't know!) and then doing some other mathematical tricks to get the final answer.

Of course, Soorya and Ramesh wanted to get started on all of them at once. And (of course!) they knew all the maths involved. Ramesh started on the first question and Soorya on the second. So, as usual, I ended up in last place with the hardest question! I tried to argue with them, but they tried appealing to my ego! As Ramesh put it, "You've programmed more than any of us, so you do the hardest one." I fell victim to their flattery and started slogging.

Finally, after 3 hours of slogging...I had nothing! You're probably imagining me hooked to my desktop, an unstoppable force, bent on cracking the problem I was working on. You couldn't be further from the truth. In my defence, I had started out with the best of intentions. Firstly, I got Soorya to explain what the LU-decomposition of a matrix meant. He dropped some heavy-duty maths jargon which left me more confused than I had been in the beginning. Secondly, I had Soorya explain what the jargon meant. I now understood what the LU-decomposition would yield, but no idea how to perform it. As a result, I couldn't code it. So thirdly (I guess you know how this is going!), I had Soorya illustrate it with a simple example. For those of you who thought of the movies when I said "matrix", all I can say is...you have your priorities right! In any case, Soorya finally dumbed it down to my level and explained it to me. I felt like I had just unlocked the mysteries of the universe. But now I had to code it.

By then, I could tell that Soorya was getting flustered and wanted to start work on his own question. I figured I'd give us both a break and return to our respective questions. The only one who didn't seem in the least bit bothered was Ramesh. He continued to code on his own, like he was in a trance. The 3 of us spent the next 4 hours in complete silence, coding hard. Well, Soorya and Ramesh coded. I tried my best for a while. But though the process was simple enough, programming it was a nightmare!

I kept supplying different (slightly modified) versions of the same slow code to Soorya. Every version of my code took too long to run on one or more of the test cases. So, I kept getting time errors. Soorya and Ramesh weren't doing that much better than me. We all ended up with time errors. After a while, I tried playing Counter-Strike online, while avoiding the vigilant gazes of Soorya and Ramesh. I was pretty sure they would kill me if they saw me playing. But after 2 hours, I had 20 kills. Not bad for someone who hadn't played in a long time!

After a while, my gaming came to an end when Soorya realised I was just giving him slightly modified versions of the code to upload! So I pretended to work, while stalking Naina on Facebook. Yes, I admit it – I'm a total loser when it comes to girls. Most of her posts dated back to the time of the debate. After that, she had only put up a few sad poems about suicide. I began to wonder what exactly she was suffering from. Then the lunch bell rang and I cried, "I'll just grab some lunch and be back!" Before Soorya or Ramesh could object, I reached the door and raced for the canteen. College food had never smelled so good!

I was one of the few IMTech students in the canteen. There were a few others, but they were mostly sitting in their respective groups and discussing code. But since I had come early, I got a nice table to myself. That afternoon, lunch consisted of gobi manchurian and fried rice. I wasn't sure what the occasion was, but I sure was glad that no one else was busy piling their plates high with positively *good* food (for a change)! I chewed each grain of rice to extinction before swallowing it. I wanted to make this lunch last as long as possible. I had no desire to return to programming.

I was so focused on my plate that I didn't register the fact that Professor Swaminathan was walking towards me. One minute he was nowhere in sight, the next he was trying to loom over me (which was kind of hard for someone so short!). Perhaps I should have laughed at more of his jokes! I certainly hoped he wasn't going to try them on me now.

“Not busy coding with your team?” he finally asked with a smile. “Waiting for inspiration to strike, Sir,” I replied, grinning nervously. “So how many questions are you done with?” he asked, still smiling. “Um...well, we’re sort of done with, uh...actually none,” I stammered. “Then how can you think of having lunch?” he demanded. “A programmer’s place is beside his computer.” I nodded my head like Dhanush. He then asked, “So do you feel confident or overconfident now?” I was about to assure him that I would get back to work immediately. But the opportunity for a perfect comeback popped into my head. Without thinking it over, I said, “It depends.” He seemed surprised that someone had used his favourite phrase against him. “On what?” he finally asked. “On whether or not we win,” I replied and coolly walked away.

Yeah, yeah, you’re right. I was just acting cocky with that last line. I might not be smart, but I do know how to be a smart alec! But when the adrenaline had ebbed, I was left feeling useless again.

But all wasn’t lost yet. I had the outlines of a plan. Arriving back at the lab, I noticed not everyone was working with the same intensity as before. There were a lot of frustrated and bored faces. But not a single happy one. I started to feel more positive about my plan. Now I just had to convince Soorya and Ramesh to accept it. Otherwise, I had no idea how to spend the next 19 hours!

“Hey, guys!” I exclaimed, greeting them. “Any luck so far?” Soorya just shook his head, while continuing to code. Ramesh looked at me like I was a monkey who had turned on a computer (which was admittedly not too far from the truth!). He briefly mumbled a “No,” and went back to work. So much for my motivational speech!

“Okay guys, listen up. By the looks of the other teams, I am assuming that they haven’t cracked a single question either. So, instead of trying to multitask, how about we all focus on one question at a time?” Soorya and Ramesh actually stopped work to look up at me. I took that as a positive sign and carried on. “Think about it. We’ve got 3 hours before I have to leave for home. Let’s spend one hour on each question. After I get home, I’ll keep coding till the deadline and I’ll mail you guys the code. How does that sound?” I asked, coming to the end of my well-rehearsed speech.

Soorya and Ramesh exchanged the briefest of glances. Then Ramesh said, “Let’s do it. But first...I need filter coffee!” For most of the next 3 hours, I spent my time listening to Soorya and Ramesh talk about various approaches to the problems they had been working on.

Finally, we came to the moment of truth. My code was about to be examined. Soorya and Ramesh would obviously want me to explain what I had been doing till lunch. Then they would go over the code themselves, after which we would discuss how to improve it. I knew for a fact that if Soorya or Ramesh saw how little I’d done, they’d throw me off the team. So, instead of focusing on functionality, I had transformed my code into a work of art! And by art, I mean those vague and abstract things which nobody understands, but people still pay millions for! Even I wasn’t completely sure which part of the code did what and what the end program returned.

So, when asked to explain how the program worked, I repeated what Soorya had said in his morning explanation to me. Needless to say, Soorya was not at all impressed. "Show code!" Ramesh ordered like a boss. I opened the code for them to see. The 2 of them stared at it for a long time. Finally, Soorya pointed to a block of code and asked me, "What does this do?" Thankfully, I knew the answer to that one. "That's for getting the input from a file," I replied, trying to sound more confident than I felt. "But you're supposed to get it from a user, not read the input from a file!" exclaimed Soorya, staring at me as if he was just beginning to understand how stupid I really was. "Oh, yeah! Of course...I knew that! What I meant to say was, um, I read the input from the file and then pass it to the program like a user. It's a standard trick for making programs run faster. Every programmer knows that!" I was pretty sure the opposite was true, but I was just trying to make myself seem smarter. Also, Soorya took programming tricks and good coding practices very seriously and I acted like I had a lot of experience in that regard. If I sounded like a veteran coder, Soorya would be more willing to accept my rubbish! The good thing was that the code was so complicated, even Soorya couldn't prove I was wrong.

"So, what does this next chunk do?" he asked after reading a block of code 4-5 times. "Well, that's an excellent question! You see...actually, it's like this...the thing is it does the *thing*." Soorya continued to stare at me. I realised he expected me to say something more. So, of course, I said the first thing that came to my mind, "It does *the* thing. The LU-part and the next block of code decomposes!" I finally exclaimed.

Soorya began to scowl slightly. "Hahaha! No...I'm just kidding, guys. Well, you see this entire block here," I said, gesturing vaguely at the screen, "Well, it supervises the decomposition which is done by subprograms all of which are controlled by this segment."

Soorya looked at the screen again. "Why have the subprograms? Don't they take more time to run?" He was absolutely right (as usual!), but I couldn't admit it. "No, I've used several tricks to make them run in parallel and reduce the time taken. It's a standard technique!" I said, forcing what I hoped was a winning smile onto my face. Soorya finally sighed and looked at me. "Can you try to give us a version which is easier to understand? I don't get this code."

I felt like leaping for joy. That made 2 of us! Finally, Ramesh said, "Let's start this from the beginning." I quickly agreed and glanced at my watch. It was already 4:30 p.m. "Listen, guys. I'll tell you what. You both try and work on the other 2 problems. I'll head home and send you another version of this in a few hours. I won't finish it here in time to beat the rush-hour traffic. Sounds good? Awesome! See you later!" I jumped up from my seat, grabbed my bag and ran out of the lab before they could protest.

I reached home smelling of coffee, stale air and stinky feet (all of which our lab was filled with!). So, I had a long bath with nice hot water. It was around 7 p.m. by the time I sat down at our desktop. I was hoping to finish the code and grab dinner by 9 p.m. Then came my favourite part of the day – binge-watching Netflix! You're probably wondering how I intended to code in 2 hours what I hadn't been able to in 4. But I had an ace up my sleeve.

Before sitting down at my desktop, I took a book that had belonged to my grandfather. It was called *Numerical*

Recipes in C++. I found the code for LU-decomposition of a matrix and (as usual) had no clue how it worked! But that didn't stop me from mailing the copied code to Soorya and Ramesh. It was around 8 p.m. by the time I finished. In a few minutes, Soorya mailed me again, asking me to explain the code. I was about to cook up some more rubbish when my phone pinged. I glanced at it...and forgot everything else. On the screen were two simple words – "Hi. Wassup?" The user ID was Naina.

CHAPTER 26

"Hey yourself. I'm doing great. What about you?" I messaged Naina back, pushing aside all thoughts of the competition. Soorya's and Ramesh's emails and messages remained unanswered. I quickly made up some excuse, saying I was feeling sick and might have to rush to hospital. I shut down the desktop, grabbed a bite to eat and retired to bed, focused on messaging Naina without being disturbed.

"Are you done already?" my mom asked as I switched off the computer. "I thought the contest was supposed to go on all night," she remarked. "Um...yeah! But that book really helped. I think we've answered the questions correctly," I managed as an explanation. "Wow! You must have some smart members on your team!" she exclaimed. "Thanks, Ma! I'm touched by your faith in me and my abilities as a programmer!" I replied sarcastically.

"No, sweetie, it's not that. It's just that I thought you were working on one problem. What about the other 2?" she asked, honestly curious. "Uh...oh, right...the other 2! Well, um...we divided the work and I'm pretty sure I gave them the basic idea needed. I have full confidence that they can code the rest," I stammered in reply. "But don't you want to be sure?" she asked, adding, "Why don't you check the code they send back to you?" That was obviously the sensible thing to do. But I could hardly tell my mom that I had lost all interest in the contest and now wanted to spend my time running after a girl I barely knew!

"That book was *really* helpful! I think they'll know what to do. Anyway, I might stay up messaging them. So, don't worry, Ma!" I hugged her to muffle any further protests and ran off to my room.

That brings me back to the moment I replied to Naina's message. She messaged back almost immediately, "I'm so depressed and sad! I feel like I need to talk to somebody desperately..." This seemed too good to be true! There weren't going to be any awkward ice-breaking moments here. All I had to do was be a sympathetic listener. I saw that she was typing, but beat her to the punch. I sent a message saying, "Hey, it's okay. Don't worry. I'm here for you whenever you need me. Tell me all about it." She sent her message a few seconds after mine. It read, "I was being sarcastic, dude! Are all you IT guys this gullible?" Okay, that was a cheap shot. I felt like a total lame-brain, falling for the bait she had dangled in front of me.

I was about to chuck the phone away in disgust when it pinged again. It was Naina. "Don't worry! Even if you're not funny, you're still cute!" it read. Wow! She had actually called me "cute". Maybe I hadn't blown my chance after all. "So, what are your hobbies, besides debating and stalking girls you barely know?" she messaged teasingly. I decided to lie shamelessly. "I'm into hiking and trekking and stuff like that. I'm an outdoors kind of guy," I messaged back. The truth was the only outdoors I'd ever been to were my neighbourhood parks. But I figured she'd prefer the outdoor stud guy.

"So, which was the last place you went trekking?" she responded. That left me stumped. The last 'hill' I had climbed had been a small mound of grass at Lalbagh. But I had to sound like a veteran hiker. So, I threw out a name I had heard Romik use sometimes – "Skandagiri". She seemed impressed. "Wow! You went all the way to the Himalayas?!" was her quick response.

Maybe it was the excess enthusiasm in her response, but I sensed a trap. And after my last disaster, I decided to check up on Skandagiri. I Googled it and found that it was near Nandi Hills...nowhere near the Himalayas. As soon as I knew the truth, I messaged back, "Nice try. But since I've actually been there, I know it's near Nandi Hills, not the Himalayas!" I felt very proud of myself. If I was going to be boyfriend material, I'd need to stay on my toes with her! She replied with a smiling emoji and said, "Either you've actually been there or you just Googled it. So, what's the truth?" I couldn't resist a cheesy comeback, "Get to know me better and find out!" She seemed immensely pleased with my response – "Oooh! A man of mystery! I like that."

I felt like I had crossed the first hurdle. I was now in the 'friend zone'. But (as every wannabe boyfriend knows) it's moving on to the next level that's the real challenge. The second thing I felt was disappointment. I was "cute", but apparently failed to make "hot"! So close and yet so far!

"You go to a college full of hot girls. Introduce me to some of them," I messaged her. "You're texting one," was her reply. Wow! Things were definitely heating up. She was flirting now, right? I was about to reply, but she messaged me first, "Okay. They've come for me now. Ttyl." I was left staring at the phone and wondering what the cryptic message could possibly mean. If I'd only known...

At the time though, I wasn't thinking so much about the line itself as about the last phrase – "Ttyl". Yes, I hate to admit it, but I'd never come across the acronym before and had no idea what it meant! Even now, I'm not familiar with a lot of slang used by my generation. For this reason, I generally prefer face-to-face interaction. However, attractive girls leave me lost and tongue-tied in person or via messages. I generally stick to safe slang acronyms like 'Lol' or 'Omg'.

However, at one point in time, I wasn't sure whether to interpret 'Lol' as 'Laugh Out Loud' or 'Lots Of Love'. For that reason, when a girl I was dating messaged me that her grandma had died, I replied with an 'Lol' for 'Lots Of Love'. As you can imagine, she dumped me the next day!

Now the smart thing to do in a situation like this is to Google the acronym. So, of course, that was the one thing I didn't do. I decided to spend all my time trying to guess what the letters could stand for. As you can imagine, it didn't end well. After sending Naina a whole bunch of messages and getting no response, I decided that she had tried to type 'Totally' in short, but had mixed up the spelling. Now I just had to figure out why she would say that.

I lost track of time while my deductive juices were flowing. There was a knock on my door and my mom entered. I didn't have the presence of mind to switch from my WhatsApp chat with Naina. "Still working?" my mom asked, stifling a yawn and looking at my phone. She was close enough to my bed that she caught sight of the name. "Who's Naina?" she asked, instantly alert. "No one. Just someone I met at the debate," I answered. "I see. And you're messaging this girl, rather than helping your teammates?" she asked frostily. "Don't make such a big deal out of it, Ma. We're almost done with the code," I replied reassuringly. "You're an adult and you're free to make your own choices. But that doesn't mean I have to support them. If you want to be a slacker, then so be it! But remember, if I don't like your behaviour, you have to get out of this house!" she announced in a deadly calm voice. If my mom got into one of her moods, there was no stopping her. I knew I had to patch things up immediately. "I'm sorry, Ma. You're right. I should be helping Soorya and Ramesh. I'll stop messaging this girl for good. Okay?" She smiled and nodded. "I knew you'd see sense. Good night," she said. Then, she seemed to remember something and asked, "I thought you said you were done with the code?"

I cursed myself and my big mouth. I'd completely forgotten what I'd told my mom when I had shut off the computer. "Well, yeah. We had solved them, I mean, we *have* solved them. We're just trying to make our code more efficient," I said, struggling to come up with a reasonable explanation and failing! "So...let me get this straight. Your 2 teammates are staying up the entire night to improve the code you're submitting, while you're going to sleep?!" asked my mom, smelling something fishy in my story. "Besides, you can help them out better if you're also at the computer," my mom continued relentlessly.

"Don't worry, we're almost done with the code. They'll send it in soon. But for now, I better get my beauty sleep. Tomorrow's another busy day!" I exclaimed, hoping that she would go away and leave me in peace. "But tomorrow's a Sunday," she protested mildly. "Haha! Yeah...just joking," I replied feebly.

Sighing, probably in equal parts acceptance and exasperation, she left the room with a "Good night." My phone pinged with a WhatsApp message from Naina. It read, "Ttyl=Talk To You Later. Good night dummy!" I spent the rest of the night trying to memorise every slang phrase out there!

CHAPTER 27

I was really anxious about going to college on Monday. Naina hadn't messaged me after Saturday night. Plus, I still had no idea how Soorya and Ramesh had done in the competition. I could almost imagine Ramesh assembling a hit squad to take care of me – permanently! As I headed to class, I suddenly realised that I was being followed. I spun around to confront my pursuer(s)...only to find (surprise, surprise!) Professor Kumar! Like a fool, I had let myself be trapped.

I tried to dodge towards my left, towards the bathroom. But he just came after me. I knew I was never going to shake him. So I turned, determined to confront my fate head-on. "Good morning, Sir. Did you want to see me about something?" I asked as innocently as I could. I knew he was going to raise the question of the make-up exam. If only I had been alert enough to avoid him...Oh well! I might as well get this ordeal over with.

He came to a stop with a serious expression on his face. "Hello, Pranav. Yes, there actually is something I wanted to discuss with you," he began. Then his face broke into a smile and he thrust his right hand towards me. "I just wanted to say congratulations. I knew you had it in you!" I put my hand in his. He crushed mine in a grip like a vise. I was interested in why he was congratulating me. Was he being sarcastic or was he plain delusional?

"Hahaha! Um...yes, Sir. But, uh, what exactly are you talking about?" This seemed to strike him as even funnier than anything I had said before. He laughed so much that his face turned red. "That's a good one. But you can drop the modesty with me," he said, once he had stopped laughing. "Right...well, it's good to know that I've impressed you so much. I'd still better get going." So saying, I hurried off to class. I had a bad feeling about what had happened and was reluctant to meet Soorya or Ramesh right now.

Of course, that's why I ran into them standing in front of the classroom door. There was no way to avoid them. With a hollow feeling in the pit of my stomach, I approached the 2 of them. If I was right, they were going to be *really* angry with me. But I was determined to finish our little showdown. As soon as they noticed me, they turned in my direction.

I stopped right in front of them and nodded. I was not prepared for what came next. "Why do you look constipated?" asked Ramesh. So much for my resolved look. I put on a neutral look and asked, "What's up guys? Why so serious?" I was prepared for screaming and shouting. I was worried Soorya would vow never to help me with maths again. I was worried that Ramesh would sit on me!

But both of them started smiling. Ramesh just said, "Thanks and congratulations!" Soorya elaborated by adding, "We came first in ICSI. The only problem that we managed to solve successfully was the one with the LU-decomposition. And it was all thanks to your code!"

I wasn't sure I had heard right. The 3 of us had come first from ICSI? With that scrappy code I had put together? I puffed up my chest with pride. I knew I didn't deserve the credit, but who was I to say no to praise? It wasn't like anyone was going to question me any further on the matter, right? Wrong! Ramesh chose that moment to drop his bombshell. "Come fast. The Principal wants to see us. You can explain the code to him!"

We reached the administrative block, where our coordinator Professor Swaminathan was waiting for us. "Where have you boys been? On second thought, it doesn't matter. Come along, quickly. The Board meeting is about to commence and I've begged the Principal for a few minutes of his time. He's arranged for a photoshoot with all of you and this could very well be carried in some newspapers! So, I'm glad you've all dressed smartly. Now, follow me!" said Professor Swaminathan, hustling us along.

I was kind of hoping we wouldn't have to waste too much time on our code and how it worked. I was more than happy to smile for the camera. But I was not prepared for what happened next. We entered the Principal's waiting room. The Principal's secretary looked up as we entered. "We have an appointment with Sir. We're expected. Actually, the 3 of them are 'Semicolon Expected'!" exclaimed Professor Swaminathan, laughing at his own joke. As usual, nobody else laughed.

"Let me check if Sir is free," said the secretary. She picked up the intercom, spoke rapidly into it in Kannada and nodded her head a few times. Then she hung up. "Sir will see you now," she announced and opened the door to his office, which we entered hesitantly. The Principal, Professor Gowda, was seated behind a vast, teak table. The office was enormous. It could easily accommodate

20 or more people. Just like the Dean of Admissions, Professor Gowda too was very energetic and jumped up to shake our hands. He then gestured for us to take our seats.

Professor Swaminathan began to speak. He went on about how grateful we all were for Professor Gowda's precious time. I tried to look grateful, but Ramesh later told me I ended up looking like a chimpanzee. Professor Swaminathan then told Professor Gowda, "I'll let them tell you about the contest, Sir." We were all unsure of what to do next.

Being the boss he was, Ramesh took charge of the situation. He continued, "Actually Sir, we only passed all the test cases on one problem. That was the problem that involved LU-decomposition of a matrix. Pranav gave us the basic code for that problem and Soorya finished the job." Having made his announcement, he sank back into his seat, looking highly pleased with himself. I dreaded what was going to come next.

Professor Gowda turned to me and asked, "So, how did you deal with the problem?" I hoped for a flash of inspiration, but came up with...absolutely nothing! "Well, the thing is Sir, the problem didn't directly ask for the LU-decomposition of a matrix. In fact, it was Soorya who figured that bit out. Maybe he should explain?" I asked, hoping Soorya would rescue me. But it just wasn't my lucky day! "Don't be modest, son. I'm sure you must have paved the way for your team's success. So, tell me what you did," he encouraged me.

Not knowing what to do, I blurted out the truth. "I copied it from a book...No, not *that*. What I meant was I-uh copied it to a book, no...not book, file. But I was keeping a book as well." What had I just said? Everyone was staring at me in shocked silence. Finally, Professor Gowda broke the silence. "Son, what are you saying? You were bookkeeping? As in gambling?" I was desperate for a miracle – and then got one in the form of Professor Swaminathan! He obviously couldn't pass up the opportunity to crack a bad joke, "Sir, maybe he was gambling on the program to work for his teammates?" Professor Swaminathan and I chortled with laughter. Everyone else maintained a stoic silence. The guy had just saved me. I promised to laugh at every joke of his in future.

Just then, Professor Gowda looked at his watch and said, "Oops! I'm running late for my Board meeting. I'll listen to this story some other time. Let's finish the photoshoot." We quickly arranged ourselves around the 2 professors and smiled for the camera. In the end, no newspaper published the photo or mentioned ICSI. Newspapers have more important things to feature – like ads! But that was all right with me. I would have posed for a thousand photographs, as long as no one asked me to explain the code again!

CHAPTER 28

She had almost finished her dinner. She was always one of the last ones to eat. She hated the looks that people shot each other behind her back. She hated hanging out with the girls and the boys just avoided her. That's why she was surprised when one came over and sat opposite her.

"Hey," he said in a surprisingly rich voice. "You look familiar. Have we met?" he continued. "In your dreams..." she murmured. The last thing she needed was a boy falling for her. She just wanted to be left alone.

But he persisted. "No way! I never have dreams that good! Sorry, I should have introduced myself. I'm Ram. Oh, hey – wait, I know where I've seen you. You were the one on those stupid posters..." his voice trailed off as he realised how rude he must have sounded. Despite herself, she smiled. "So, do you flirt with girls by calling them crackpots?" she asked teasingly. "Just the pretty ones!" he replied, smiling wolfishly. She realised in that moment how much she hungered for body warmth. He seemed to sense her need and leaned towards her. She grasped his face in her hands and kissed him. It was a long, passionate kiss. Finally, he broke away.

"I'm sorry. I should be going," she said, quickly getting up from the table. "No, I'm sorry. I didn't mean to pull away like that. I was just surprised...that's all," he replied, looking at her with eyes filled with lust. She looked closely at him. Had she really kissed him? She felt so mixed up. Suddenly, her heart began to pound. Had she taken her medicines? Probably not. She had to run away from here! She wanted to head away, but he tried to draw her close.

"Hey, don't worry, okay? Just relax. I'll keep you safe. I'll protect you," he murmured soothingly. "There's nothing to be afraid of. We can go for a walk together if you want. I just want to get to know you better. And trust me, I don't give a damn about the fact that there's something wrong with you. To me, you are truly wonderful!" he said admiringly. But she could barely hear his voice anymore. The people in purple were speaking in muted tones, but she couldn't ignore their voices. The more she tried to ignore them, the louder they got. She had to get away.

Suddenly, she lashed out at Ram, using her nails to scratch his face and claw at his eyes. "Let me go, let me go, let me go!" she screamed, gradually losing all control. She needed the pills. But who would give her the pills? Why couldn't she remember? Everything was so fuzzy. She just knew that she had to escape from this place!

She let out a shrill, high-pitched cry, like a siren. She kept screaming, as her knees buckled under her and the world faded out of focus. Suddenly, there was a power failure and all the lights went out. She and Ram were alone in the darkness. By then, he had released her, but she still kept screaming. She screamed till people arrived with flashlights. She told the guards that Ram had attacked her.

Finally, some professors came and assured her that appropriate disciplinary action would be taken against

Ram. By then, she had calmed down somewhat. She let herself be led to her room. But as she lay, tossing and turning, she knew there was no going back. She had tasted blood...and she wanted more!

CHAPTER 29

Almost 2 weeks had passed since Naina had messaged me. It was a pretty busy time. We were picking our partners for the C programming project. For those of you with short memories, this basically involved programming one or more robots to perform a task of our choice. This was the day when Professor Scindia first showed us the robots. They looked like little *idlis* on wheels. You've probably seen them being sold as Roombas for vacuuming houses. They are also known as iRobots. Professor Scindia gave us some code which allowed us to control the robots' motion from a computer.

I must admit it seemed kind of cool that we would be handling these robots! I mean every wanna-be mad scientist dreams of something like this, right? Unfortunately, there were some hitches. I originally thought of partnering with Amrish, Soorya and Ramesh. However, Soorya and Ramesh seemed to have learned from their past mistakes, and had formed a group with Amrish and two girls I didn't know.

We had to form teams of 5. So, I got the 4 worst possible partners – Preetish, Romik, Venugopal and Sachin! None of them knew how to code properly...and (more importantly) neither did I! But that wasn't the main problem.

Aside from the fact that none of us could code, we also had no idea what our task should be! We were supposed to submit our project proposals in 2 days. Only if that was approved, would we be allowed to start coding. Amrish and gang had already decided what they would do – a *rangoli* robot. I have to say, it sounded cool.

In comparison, pretty much all I could come up with was a sad excuse for an interactive game. The game involved 2 iRobots. We would allow the user to control one iRobot and try to make it bump another. The other iRobot would be controlled by software written by us and would try to avoid colliding with the user-controlled robot. The user got more points the more times he/she got his/her robot to bump the computer-controlled robot. Our game was supposed to be like a game of tag. But the problem was that each robot couldn't detect the other's approach unless it was actually bumped by the other robot. That was the tricky part we had to overcome.

Late that night, Naina messaged me again. I must admit I was hoping for something like that! "Still awake? Give me a minute to take my pills and then we'll chat," she typed. I responded, "Yeah, like all good nerds! Busy preparing for the finals. But tell me, why do you still need to keep having pills? I thought you were cured." There was a long pause after this and I wondered if she had fallen asleep. Then my phone pinged. "I was sort of in an accident and these pills are like my pain-killers. Anyway, I prefer not to talk about it. So, let it be, okay?" I was just trying to be friendly. But I had obviously overstepped my bounds. So, I struggled to do some damage control.

"I'm sorry. Didn't mean to pry. Just wanted to let you know that I'm here if you need me," I messaged her. She replied with a curt, "Thanks." I was silent for a while, not sure whether she'd appreciate any more questions from me. All was quiet.

Then, out of the blue, came the question, "So, any lucky girls in your life?" I responded with the cheesy line, "Yeah, but she doesn't know how lucky she is to be messaging a hunk like me!" She replied immediately, "Ha-ha! Lame. I was hoping you'd have a long list of girlfriends, so that I could boast about hooking you and reeling you in!" I cracked a smile at that. "By the way, yesterday I kissed some random guy who was trying to make a move," she messaged casually.

"What?!" I messaged back – totally shocked. "Why? Are you jealous?" she taunted me. I have to admit, I was a little annoyed. Was she just trying to get a rise out of me? Or did she honestly not care how I felt? She continued, "All you guys are the same. You just want to get into a girl's pants and then take off without any kind of commitment." But I was no longer in the mood for games.

"If you know so much about me, why bother to message?" I knew I was probably overreacting, but I had honestly thought we had something special. "Time pass!" she messaged back. I was really annoyed now. "And I guess all you girls care about is how many hearts you break! I guess your beauty is only skin-deep!" She replied, "There's plenty of depth to me. You're just too stupid to figure it out. I guess I was wrong about you. You're nothing special." I answered angrily, "And neither are you!" I tossed the phone away and fell into a fitful sleep.

CHAPTER 30

The next day, I woke up late. I felt bad and very sorry for myself. I also felt intensely angry. It's not as though Naina had done anything wrong. It wasn't as if we were in a committed relationship. Still the thought of her going around kissing strangers, made me mad. I think I was angrier with myself than anyone else. Plus, nothing seemed to go right that day.

I got stuck in Bangalore's terrible rush-hour traffic. As a result, I ended up missing half of the first class, which was Real Analysis. Definitely not my strongest subject. Plus, with end-sems coming up, I would have to catch Soorya and get him to explain more of these mysterious concepts to me. After that, we had English in which Professor Kasturba read out poetry, which almost put me to sleep. Then, it was time for lunch.

That was when they cornered me and decided to ask me about the iRobot project. All of my teammates were present – Preetish, Romik, Sachin and Venugopal. Of course, they all looked happy and content. Romik said, "Mmmm...we were just wondering when we should book a slot for practising on the iRobots. Professor Scindia announced in the morning that there were only 7 iRobots to go around. So we thought we'd ask you what time is good."

We had C programming immediately after lunch. I decided our team would approach Professor Scindia before class began and ask him if we could work with the iRobots as soon as classes were over for the day. He said, "Right, right." My spirits lifted. But then he continued, "But I don't think there's a slot free today till 8 p.m. You can use them and then return them before 9 p.m. Each team has been allotted 45 minutes, but since you guys are last, you can take an extra 15 minutes." I heaved a sigh of resignation.

After classes of both C and Python programming, I went over to study some code which Venugopal had written for controlling the iRobots. It seemed to make sense. But it kept giving us errors. We wanted to run only error-free code on the iRobots. So, we roped in Sachin and managed to fix all the errors. The biggest problem was that we still couldn't get the iRobots to sense the other's approach. All of a sudden, Preetish came running into the room.

"Hey, guys! I think I've solved the problem. Let's test my code on the iRobots tonight!" he declared. I suggested that we take a look at his code. But he tried to act cool. "Don't worry, man. I've got it all sorted," he replied calmly. I suddenly felt ashamed of neglecting Preetish's hidden talents.

We watched movies, listened to music, grabbed some pizza and waited for 8 p.m. to arrive. Finally, it was time. We took the iRobots from Amrish and his group (whose *rangoli* robot looked even more impressive) and set to work. I used Professor Scindia's code to run one of the iRobots and let Preetish run his code on the computer-controlled one.

The computer-controlled robot moved slightly away from my robot. Then it came and rammed my robot! "Preetish!" I muttered through clenched teeth. "What the hell does your code actually do?!" He coughed in a slightly embarrassed fashion and said, "Well, it just moves the robot in a random direction, rather than making it dodge your robot..." As he was speaking, the robot went here and there and then came to a halt. It refused to budge.

Finally, Romik (who would have guessed!) figured out that the robot was out of charge. We needed to plug it in to recharge it. "I can fix my code by tomorrow, once we recharge the robot!" Preetish piped up. I tried to remember my promise not to lose my cool, but I had had enough of a bad day. "Will you just SHUT UP!" I yelled at poor Preetish, venting all my frustration on him. "You guys are totally useless! We haven't managed to make any progress today. Anyway, book an early slot with Professor Scindia tomorrow. I'm going home." I turned and walked away.

I felt miserable as I headed home and went straight to my room. I plonked myself down on my bed, holding my head in my hands. I couldn't get the damn program to work. More importantly, I had pushed Naina away. I didn't even bother to change. I just pulled my blanket over me and browsed the net on my phone. I wasn't hungry. I had had way too much pizza.

Suddenly, my phone pinged with a WhatsApp message. I hoped it was from one of my partners telling me that they had finally fixed the problem with the robots. I opened WhatsApp and was surprised to find the message was from Naina! It was short, but sweet – "Sorry. I was just kidding. Truce?" After reading it, everything in my life seemed better. I messaged back, "No way! You broke my heart! You're gonna have to fix it." To that, she replied, "Looking forward to it!"

CHAPTER 31

She was in that vague, dream-like state the drugs always left her in. It was a weird feeling. She felt like she was trapped in her body, while her spirit yearned for freedom. But at the same time, she didn't want to be just a floating spirit with no anchor to the real world.

Tonight, she had taken her pills, so she could see her 2 captors, but no one else. They were standing near the door, just like every night. But the door was open. That was odd. She could have sworn it was shut when she went to bed. Of course, her roommate always slept later. So, she could have forgotten to shut it. That seemed like the most logical explanation. But her roommate was the most efficient and organised person she knew. It just didn't seem like her to leave the door to the room wide open. So, what was going on here? That was when she noticed it from the corner of her eye.

There was a figure in black, standing just beyond the moonlight streaming in through the window. She willed herself to move her head and look at the figure. But it was no use. She could sense everything around her, but she couldn't act on her impulses. She was a prisoner in her own body.

She couldn't even make out if it was a boy or a girl. That struck her as odd. How had she known it was a youngish person and not a slightly older man or woman?

She seemed to recognise the figure from somewhere, but she couldn't be sure. The figure in black picked up a pillow at the foot of her bed and moved towards her head. She was going to be smothered to death! Somehow, she just knew it. Then the figure stepped into the moonlight and she saw...herself! Before she could process the thought, the pillow was on her and she was being killed!

She fought through the sleep induced by the drugs and woke up...to darkness. She could feel something pressing down on her face. But now, she was in complete control of her body. She clenched her fists and threw her hands and feet about, trying to throw her attacker off-balance. At first, she thought she had succeeded because the pressure on her face lessened. But soon it was back, twice as hard as before! She struggled to make a noise, but she just couldn't. It was the weirdest sensation in the world. It wasn't just that her mouth was muffled and so she couldn't make any meaningful sounds. She was actually incapable of making any sound whatsoever. She wondered if this was how the gang had planned to kill her. She could hear the beat of her heart and feel the pressure building in her chest.

Then, all of a sudden, the pressure was gone. She stared into the concerned face of her roommate. "What happened?" her roommate asked. "Somebody was smothering me. A-a figure in black. But why was the door open?" she asked weakly. "Huh? The door was shut. Are you okay?" her roommate asked anxiously. She nodded. But she knew someone was out to get her. And somehow, she knew that it was someone from her college!

CHAPTER 32

I woke up feeling cheerful. What a contrast this was to yesterday! The sun was peeping out from behind the clouds. The birds were singing. The flowers were blooming. It looked like it was going to be a perfect day. The fact that Naina had resumed contact with me meant that I had forgotten all about my other problems. I felt Naina and I were destined to be together and that we could solve all the problems in the world.

Unfortunately, my mom was feeling unwell that day, so I had to make do without any breakfast. I have heard some people claim that they can survive on a liquid diet for several days. I try to avoid such fitness freaks as much as possible. My stomach grumbled in protest at being forced to endure the journey to college without any food. I decided (since I reached a little early) to treat myself to a *samosa*. My spirits revived a little at the thought. I could almost hear Romik telling me to avoid such an unhealthy snack. I told the imaginary Romik to shut up and enjoyed my first meal of the day. In no time, I was happy again. I knew I'd have another boring day of classes. But somehow, Naina's message kept me going.

As I was heading for class, I bumped into my team for the iRobot project. Obviously, they had been waiting for me. I can't really say that I was surprised to see them. I had been hoping for such an opportunity, so that we could work together as a proper team and not just come up with random bits of code by ourselves.

"Hey, guys! Great to see you all. Did we get a better time slot?" I asked casually. All of them looked seriously at me, except Venugopal, who just laughed his usual laugh. Finally, Preetish spoke up, "If you think we can't do anything without you, then why don't you just take charge of the project? We're trying our best too, you know!" He practically shouted the last sentence.

That was when I realised I shouldn't have yelled like that last night. I tried to apologise, "Listen, guys. I'm sorry, but..." when Preetish interrupted me. "Save it. The 3 of us will try it our way and you try it yours," he said, indicating that Romik and Sachin were with him. Romik jiggled his head from side to side. I assumed he was agreeing with what Preetish had said. Though, for all I knew, he might have had a crick in his neck. The 3 of them then entered the classroom. Just before the door shut behind them, Preetish said, "Oh, by the way, we got you a slot after class like you wanted. We'll be there too, so you have to let us try our code as well." With that, they were gone.

All this time, Venugopal had been standing to one side. Finally, he approached me and said, "Don't worry, you've got me. Plus, I had some thoughts about the *AMM* problem. We can discuss it at lunch." It looked like my perfect day was turning into a nightmare!

All day, I kept dreaming about Naina. Even walking to the canteen, I was so caught up in my daydreams that I didn't hear the voice for a while. All of a sudden, I heard a voice shouting my name – "Pranav!". It was so loud that people all over the canteen turned to look. When I turned around, I was surprised to find Vijay.

"Hey, wassup?" I asked as casually as I could. I wondered whether Naina had decided to end things after all and was using her brother to tell me to lay off. However, if Naina wanted me out of her life, I wanted her to tell me directly, not through her brother. Vijay gestured for me to follow him and headed out of the canteen. I wondered if I should just ignore him and pretend I was busy. I could always message Naina tonight and find out what it was he had meant to say.

But I was curious. I hurried after him. Suddenly, he came to a stop and turned around. "My sister wanted me to give you this. She said you'd understand. I didn't get the joke," he said and handed me a crumpled piece of paper. I opened it to see a photo of Naina. She was kissing an ass! And, I mean literally! It was obviously a neatly done job in Photoshop and it reassured me that she wasn't serious about the guy she had kissed. I started to chuckle.

"Oh, by the way, she also asked me to apologise to you," Vijay continued uncertainly. He obviously thought both Naina and I were crazy. "I have to say...I think you 2 are made for each other!" he exclaimed. "Why's that?" I asked defensively. "Because both of you are nuts!" Both he and I laughed. "I hope Naina and you don't intend to keep using me as your peon!" he said. "No, I think we're good now," I reassured him.

Then, I suddenly remembered the only cloud on my horizon. "Hey, I don't suppose you have any tips for programming robots?" I asked, expecting him to say, "No." But (to my surprise) he said, "I sometimes work in the Robotics lab. Why, what's the problem?" I explained our project to him and the problem in getting the iRobots to sense each other's presence. He thought for a while and said, "I don't know how to do that either. But..." He smiled at me and winked, "How much do you and your professor know about something called reinforcement learning?"

Before class resumed after lunch, I hunted down Preetish. He had just finished lunch and was accompanied by Venugopal. I would have preferred speaking to him in private, but I guessed I wouldn't get a better chance. Preetish tried to rush off the moment he saw me. But I quickly blocked his way.

"Hey, I had some new ideas that I thought we could try together..." Venugopal started. But I had eyes only for Preetish. "Preetish, bro, do you have your old code? The one that makes the iRobot move in a random fashion?" I asked, standing directly in front of him. He was too small to avoid me. He said, "Get lost!" Sheesh! He'd probably have shot me, given a chance.

I decided to discard all my pride and massage his ego. "Listen, man...I'm really sorry about yelling at you yesterday. I was just feeling frustrated and I lashed out at you. There was a lot of difficult stuff going on in my personal life. That's why I acted like that."

Immediately, Preetish's expression softened and he started talking. "Oh my gosh! I didn't realise, bro. Of course, we can work together now. Like a proper team. I'm sure you can solve this problem. We all have faith in you!" he exclaimed.

Finally, I had gotten through to Preetish. Now, came the tricky part. Could I convince him that Vijay's plan was the right one? I continued to heap praise on him, hoping he would be easier to convince that way. "No, Preetish. I can't solve this problem," I replied. "Don't worry, I should be able to solve it," remarked Venugopal cheerfully. "Shut up!" both Preetish and I said to him simultaneously. Then we grinned at each other. "Don't be so negative, man. You can drop the modesty around me. I'm sure you'll figure it out," continued Preetish. "NO–" the force of my reply seemed to startle Preetish. "Um...maybe you should just chill for a while?" he suggested, looking a little scared.

"No, you don't understand what I meant. Your code really is the answer to our problems. Only *you* can help save the day. So, ready to be a hero?" I asked, willing him to say, "Yes." His face took on a serious expression. I think he was trying to look heroic. He ended up looking constipated. Finally, he spoke, "Okay. Let's do this. What's your plan?"

Once I had finished explaining everything to him, he seemed to be lost in thought. But he finally agreed. "There's just one problem," he pointed out. "And that is..." I probed. He said, "This morning, one of the teams noticed that the batteries for the collision detection mechanism for the iRobots are out of charge. To run the code, we need those batteries to be replaced. We need a pair of AA batteries for the bump to be detected by the computer. But the thing is, we don't have the money to pick them up. So, could you buy a pair?" "Sure, no problem," I answered casually. I winked at Venugopal and said, "In the meantime, Venugopal...introduce Preetish to your finger electrodes!" As I turned to go, I had the satisfaction of hearing Preetish squeal!

CHAPTER 33

She had decided that things had gone far enough. She had downloaded the recorder app and kept playing it every night after her roommate fell asleep. She hoped that she would be able to catch her attackers off-guard and record their conversation.

Of course, she had felt compelled to tell her college about the night she was smothered by a pillow, even though her brother had warned her against it. "They're looking for excuses to throw you out. Don't give them any," was all he had had to say. She didn't want to hurt anyone...at least, not intentionally. But if some of the other girls were behind this, she would expose them. All she needed was solid evidence. Hence, the recording app.

Then, one night, it happened. She was gently drifting off to sleep, after several exhausting, sleepless nights. She suddenly heard the creak of the door. Instantly, she was awake again. Her roommate kept snoring, fast asleep. Then she saw 2 girls in purple T-shirts in the pale moonlight with their faces in shadow.

That was when they began to speak. One of them said, "Might as well get this over with. The boss wants results by tonight." The other one just grunted and said, "What do we do with the body?" The first replied, "Just leave it here. I'm not going around with a corpse!" The second said, "Okay. Looks like she's fast asleep. I'll hold her down. You smother her with one of the pillows. Just make sure you do it right this time." The first retorted, "Hey, you're the one who didn't want to get your hands dirty last time!"

They advanced slowly towards her bed. She wanted to see their faces. The voices had sounded metallic, as if they were fake. She figured they had probably distorted their real voices somehow. Just as they were about to step into the light, her roommate grunted and turned in her bed. The 2 girls quickly backed away into the shadows. "What now? We can't kill them both!" the first girl exclaimed. "We'll finish this some other time," the other girl muttered. The girls spun around and left the room.

It was only when they were out of the room that she realised just how terrified she had been. Her heart hammered in her chest. But she smiled a triumphant smile. She turned off the recorder and listened to the saved audio file. She had recorded their conversation. All of it. Now, it was just a question of notifying the authorities. She kept her phone on one side and slept peacefully after a long time.

CHAPTER 34

I spent the next couple of days running my (okay, Preetish's!) code on the iRobots. Once we were satisfied with the results, we all went back to preparing for our end-sem exams. In the meantime, Naina and I were back in touch, messaging each other on WhatsApp.

I should probably clear this up now. You must be wondering why we were only messaging rather than meeting face to face when our colleges were so close. The thing is, every time I raised the topic, Naina deflected it, saying she wasn't ready to meet just yet. I had to content myself with messages and hope that she would eventually agree to meet me in person.

I heard from her the day after I met Vijay. "So, did my bro give you my apology note?" she messaged that night. "What did you think of it?" she messaged before I could reply. "Hmmm...your Photoshop skills need work!" I messaged back. "So mean! And after all the effort I put into it!" she responded.

The following night, she messaged me first with a cheery, "Hey, lame-brain! How's life?" I immediately replied, "Booorrrringggg. How're things at your end?" Her next message came out of nowhere: "I think something's wrong in my hostel...and I'm really scared." She continued typing, "I'm not kidding. I feel I'm being stalked." I wanted to pipe up and write, "Yeah...I'm your number-one stalker!" But I understood that she was actually scared. It wasn't a game or a joke. Before I could reply, she messaged me again, "Do you know of an app which will help me record voices secretly? I want to keep it running, so that I'll know if anyone enters my room and talks."

I was curious. "Does this have anything to do with the guy you kissed?" I asked, puzzled. "Possibly. He might be stalking me," she replied. "Why? What did that guy do, besides kissing you?" I asked. She replied almost immediately, "He got violent and held on to my hand. He bruised my arm pretty badly."

There were no emoticons or emojis. There was not a hint of the casual flirting usually present in our conversations. Something was seriously wrong here. I replied at once, "Please tell me the next time a guy tries this with you. I've got a mind to go over there and thrash him for you!" Her teasing tone returned, "Trust me, he'd be the one thrashing you!" But I wasn't daunted. "Okay, then I have a mind to go over there and get thrashed by him for you!" I replied. Her usual fun-loving mood had returned. "Hahaha! Thanks. That's sweet of you. Idiotic... but, sweet." I decided to lighten the mood some more.

"Tell me, what's your favourite song?" I asked. Yeah, it was a totally random question, but I wanted to talk about something else to distract her. She seemed a little surprised. "Huh? My favourtie song? Why?" I replied, "For the app you wanted. I thought I'd send you an audio file of me croaking your song. If you like the quality, we can go with that app." Hey, I was making this up as I went along. So, don't judge me too harshly. "It's from the movie *Race*. It's called *Pehli Nazar Mein*," she replied.

"Awesome! I'll send you a couple of audio files from different apps by tomorrow. Ttyl!" I replied.

The next day, I was feeling pretty pleased with myself when I got home. I had got the old Pacman code from Amrish. Yes, this was the same Pacman version he had designed (and I had taken credit for!) in Grade 12. I said a quick "Hi!" to my parents, freshened up and then sat down at my desktop. I pulled the old code up onto my screen. I'd love to say that it looked familiar, but the lie would choke me. I finally found the instructions we had printed on the screen.

We had explained that the aim of the game was to maximise your score by moving the yellow Pacman figure over the white dots, while avoiding touching the randomly moving 'ghosts'. I added the following lines to the instructions: "Also, avoid kissing asses if you don't want the -100 point penalty! Flirting with the game's creator is permissible by the rules, but flirting with anyone else is not. Have fun and remember...don't let the stalkers bite!" I surveyed my handiwork and was pretty pleased with the result. It was a custom-made video game. I was going to give it to her brother to pass on to her whenever he was free. I'd give it to him on a pen drive tomorrow, but I'd tell her about it tonight. I wanted to make her wonder what I had got for her.

As I put the finishing touches to the code, I hoped the neighbours had their noise-cancelling headphones on. Yup, you guessed it – I was now going to sing. I first printed out the lyrics. After an early dinner, I retired to my room. I had already installed 5 potential apps. I decided to keep the phone in one corner of the room and stand in the diagonally opposite corner. I would sing at a normal volume. The only problem was...I had never heard the song before. So, before setting everything up, I listened to the song at least 10 times.

It was a slow, boring song which kept droning on and on in my head. There were times when I wanted to scream in frustration. The Hindi music I listened to consisted entirely of Bollywood item numbers – definitely not slow, boring songs about falling in love at first sight.

In any case, I sent her the 5 audio files and then asked her, "So...what do you think?" She sent back the message, "Honestly? I'm just feeling sorry for your parents and neighbours!" I shot back, "I was keeping it tailored for the weird senses of a girl who goes around kissing donkeys!" She retorted, "So mean! Not only do I have to listen to your singing, I have to put up with your lame jokes too?!" I replied, saying, "For you...I'm as good as it gets!" She bounced back with the line, "Whatever it is I've done to deserve you, lame-brain, I'm truly sorry!" We kept on chatting like this for a while. Then, she popped the question.

Not the "Will you marry me?" question. She asked me, "Do you think I'm crazy?" I avoided the question. "Does this have anything to do with the stalker thing?" I asked. "Yes...and no. There's just a lot of stuff going on in my life right now. I'm worried that I don't have anyone to back me up. Wow! I sound crazy even to myself!" she replied. I decided to play it safe. I messaged, "I think you're understandably paranoid after that guy hurt you. But better safe than sorry!" There was a longish gap. Then she messaged, "Awww...thanks. So sweet!"

I was glad she had cheered up a bit. I continued, "By the way, I've got a gift for you. Something to show off how cool I really am. Not that I need to prove it. It just oozes off me naturally. But anyway, I think you'll like it." Her mood lightened immediately. "Tell me what it is. I hate surprises!" I couldn't resist the cheesy comeback, "All I'll say is it's a game. Of course, I'm a player, so that shouldn't come as a surprise!" She replied, "In your dreams, lame-brain. Anyway, I've chosen the third app. So, speaking of dreams, good night!"

CHAPTER 35

She awoke the next day, feeling fully refreshed. It was a beautiful morning. "Hey, wake up, sleepyhead!" she yelled into her roommate's ear. "Sheesh! Haven't you had your pills? I thought you were the one who overslept!" her roommate exclaimed. "What time is it anyway?" her roommate grumbled, glancing at her phone.

"It's only 5," she replied, "but I just thought we should enjoy the lovely morning together!" Her roommate still looked groggy and annoyed. "You're not cracking up completely, are you?" She laughed freely, enjoying the sensation. "Hahaha! Just the opposite! I'm finally free and safe and sound again." Her roommate crawled back under the covers. "Well, good for you!"

She playfully hit her roommate on the head with a pillow. "Hey, don't fall asleep yet!" she shouted. "At last, I think I've got the solution to all my problems." A grumpy head emerged from beneath the covers. "So, what is your plan? I thought you were okay...don't tell me you're seeing and hearing stuff again?" her roommate continued, growing more and more anxious.

She decided to narrate only the relevant part of the story. "Well, actually, I felt someone trying to smother me the night you found me with the pillow." Her roommate rolled her eyes. "Look, the door was locked and you said that you hadn't seen anyone else. You've just got to treat it like a nightmare and move on!"

She grabbed her phone from the table beside her. "You don't believe me, right? But yesterday, I recorded 2 girls' voices. They were talking about killing me!" she said as calmly as she could. She turned the phone on and then let it slide from her hands and fall to the floor with a clatter. She was aware of reassuring hands on her shoulders, but she just kept muttering the same sentence over and over again – "This isn't my phone, whose is it?"

***

After she calmed down a bit, she noticed that a SIM card was lying next to the phone. On inserting it into her roommate's phone, she discovered it was her SIM card. Who would steal a phone, but leave a SIM card behind? After discussing it with her roommate, she decided to discard the unknown phone. During lunch break, she intended to drop it in one of the Lost and Found bins. If it belonged to anyone from college, he/she would have a week to collect it from the Lost and Found pile before it was discarded.

She tried to pay attention during the morning lectures. But, as usual, she was distracted. Finally, it was lunchtime. Everybody drifted towards the canteen. She headed in the opposite direction. She carefully looked around to make sure no one was watching. Then she gingerly took out the phone (gripping it with her handkerchief) and was about to drop it in the bin when a voice screamed, "Stop! Give me my phone, thief!" She spun in the direction of the voice, looking as guilty as she felt.

It was a girl she knew from her hostel. Her name was Meghna. Meghna walked up to her and grabbed the phone. She switched it on and exclaimed, "I can't believe you'd stoop to this! How dare you take my phone?!" But she wasn't going down without a fight. "Enough of your stupid joke! You got your phone. Give me mine!" Meghna looked completely lost. "Huh? Why would I have your phone? Just get lost!" Meghna angrily stormed away. Her heart sank as Meghna walked away.

CHAPTER 36

The day had come around at last. It was time to demonstrate our iRobots in action for Professor Scindia. If I was going to pull off one of the biggest cons in history, I had to keep my nerves steady. I checked that I had brought 4 AA batteries with me, along with their bill. The batteries would help the computer-controlled iRobot to detect a bump and, correspondingly, change direction. Everything was in place and I was fairly confident that we could do this.

I figured I might as well hope for the best. By the time I reached college, I was in a better mood. That mood lasted until I ran into Venugopal. "Hey, man! I wanted to talk to you. Preetish said there's a problem with his code. Apparently, as long as he *runs* it, there's no issue. But it's not terminating properly," replied Venugopal.

I don't think I had ever felt so utterly terrified. I grabbed Venugopal by the shoulders. "Where is he?" I demanded. "Everyone is in Preetish's room. They're waiting for you to arrive. That's why they sent me out," said Venugopal. I could think of plenty more reasons why they had sent him out, though I didn't bother cracking that joke. Right then, my top priority was finding Preetish and fixing the code.

By the time I reached Preetish's room, I was prepared for the worst. I nodded at Sachin and Romik and stood beside Preetish. He looked up from his laptop screen and smiled at me blissfully – like I was gonna make all his problems disappear. Then he explained, "Hey man, glad you're here. I was trying to improve our code, but I'm kind of in a mess right now."

I took a look at the code. There was no doubt about it. It would take me a full day to sort out all the variables and functions. What they were hoping I would do was impossible. I ran the code again...and again. It worked as long as it was executing, but the moment I tried to halt it, the program terminated with a 'Segmentation Fault' error. Like I've said before, this is the most annoying error in C. It gives away absolutely nothing about what is really wrong with the code.

That's when Romik spoke up, "Hey guys, maybe we can call our team 'Segmentation Fault' and claim we're displaying our credits at the end of the program execution. Hahaha!" He laughed stupidly at his own joke, while everyone else ignored him. For me, it was the last straw. I had had enough of Romik and his lame jokes. I began to shout. "This is the single stupidest idea I have ever heard. It's so stupid...that...it might just *work*!" I yelled as enlightenment hit me. This was a scam of a project, right? Why not turn the whole thing into a scam? Romik had just come up with the best idea of his life. And I intended to make full use of that. Professor Scindia had no idea what we had in store for him!

Our group was the first one up. Everyone in the team was expected to understand the basic ideas behind the code. Plus, each of us had to talk about the section of the code he/she had worked on. While Preetish ran the code from 2 desktops, I had to convince Professor Scindia that this wasn't a con job. Thankfully, Vijay had written my lines.

"You guys had one of the most ambitious projects. I sure want to know how you made it work. Explain the basic idea to everyone...and then let's see the iRobots in action!" Professor Scindia said. That was my cue. Now or never. It was showtime.

"The basic idea we used is a principle from artificial intelligence called 'reinforcement learning'. It's kind of like how humans learn through trial-and-error. One iRobot is not under our control. This computer-controlled one initially moves in a random direction. We make the iRobot under our control bump into it a couple of times. The first robot understands that the bumps are negative signals. This iRobot still incorporates some randomness, but as it is bumped more times, it begins to learn the basic path of the robot under our control. Some amount of randomness is needed to prevent the chased iRobot from fleeing the other one in a straight line. We incorporated a very basic reinforcement learning framework and used it in our implementation, which we will now demonstrate," I finished.

"Right, right," said Professor Scindia. "But before that, it's your 'favourite' question time. I'm going to ask the first – what algorithm did you use to update the weights for the randomness and the last known bump location?" Now, don't ask me what this question meant. As a matter of fact, don't ask me what any of what I had just spouted meant!

"Um...well, about that...it updates based on past history. I'm not sure that there's anything new in our approach. It basically works by, um...updating by reinforcements!" Yeah. I know. Lame! But I didn't even know what weights were, besides the numbers that tell you that you're too fat (at least, in my case)! Then I had a brilliant idea. "I think Preetish is the best person to ask about the exact algorithm used, since he was the one who programmed that part of the code," I finally finished with a diversionary tactic.

Preetish and I had already decided that he would claim to have coded the learning part of the algorithm. I agreed, since I figured he was a smooth talker and could talk himself out of a tricky situation. I was counting on the fact that Professor Scindia didn't know much about reinforcement learning. I wasn't counting on the fact that he wanted to learn more about it from us!

Preetish's response began well. He started, "We've used Q-learning in our approach, rather than a simple Markov chain. This iterative algorithm trains the iRobot and is proven to converge to the best possible path." Of course, he knew nothing of what he was talking about. I had got the lines from Vijay and made Preetish learn them. I hoped this would make Professor Scindia back off. No such luck!

"So, what exactly is a Markov chain? And what is the iteration construct you have used in *your* code? This Q-learning sounds very exciting. Please teach me more about it," he said, looking very interested. Oh great! Now what? Preetish tried to come up with something. "Well, a Markov chain is...um, a chain that satisfies the Markov property!" I could guess the next question. "And what *is* the Markov property?" asked Professor Scindia. "Well Sir, I didn't focus on the theoretical results so much. You should probably ask Venugopal about that.

He focused on the entire iterative construct. I just coded the corresponding results," responded Preetish, using the same trick as me.

Don't let anyone tell you there isn't such a thing as 'pure luck'. None of us had any idea how lucky we were to have Venugopal on our team. Little did I know that he was a maths whizz as bright as Soorya. Okay, so maybe he was a little weird. Aren't we all? But when he started talking, he was cool, confident and (most importantly!) correct! Or, at least, I guessed as much, judging from Professor Scindia's expression.

Venugopal began answering, "Sir, the Markov property means that the probability of an event occurring is dependent only on the last event in the chain and not on the distant past..." he carried on like this. He explained everything in such a way that soon everyone was nodding, as if they understood everything. If you can't beat them, join them, right? Soon, I was bobbing my head, just like Dhanush. After Venugopal finished, I started clapping. Professor Scindia and the rest of the batch soon followed.

Professor Scindia then turned to Romik and Sachin. "So, what part did you guys code?" he asked. Sachin, being a quicker thinker than Romik, hurriedly replied, "Sir, I worked on the bump detection task. I helped update the weights after a collision. So, I managed the hardware side a bit more." Professor Scindia smiled and nodded. He was clearly more of a hardware guy himself. But he still knew enough about code to know that ours was a hack job.

"So Romik, I suppose you handled the random number generation? I hope you used a better source of randomness than the built-in functions!" he said laughing. Romik had done absolutely nothing except naming our team. He stood there, looking terrified. Then, I had a flash of inspiration! "Sir, can I be excused please?" I asked. "What's the matter?" he asked in a worried tone of voice. "Um, I really need to visit the bathroom, Sir," I replied, hopping from one leg to the other impatiently. He must have thought I was trying to hold it in. "All right. Go ahead, but be quick about it," he said with a jerk of his head. "Thanks, Sir. You won't be sorry!" I exclaimed and ran out.

Why on earth had I said that? The more I thought about it, the more disgusting it sounded. But as soon as I left the room, I jammed the door open with my foot. Professor Scindia and the rest of the batch had their backs to me. Only Romik could see me.

I waved frantically at Romik to get his attention. Romik waved back! "Who are you waving at?" asked Professor Scindia confusedly. I quickly hid behind the door. "Just chasing flies, Sir," Romik replied. "Are you done?" asked Professor Scindia as I stood up again. Romik's eyes flicked from Professor Scindia to me. "Um... could you repeat the question, Sir?" he finally managed. "I was just asking if you were done chasing flies, so that you can explain how your team implemented randomness," replied Professor Scindia. I nodded my head as much as Dhanush and flashed him a double thumbs-up. Romik noted my reaction and then looked confidently back at Professor Scindia. "Yes, Sir! Absolutely! You're totally right!" he said as though he had just clarified a doubt.

I opened my mouth and mimed talking. Then I motioned for him to get started. He coughed and began to speak hesitantly. "Well Sir, the randomness we use comes from...um..." he fumbled, obviously at a loss for words. I mouthed the letters "R-S-A" through the gap. "From the same principles as RSA cryptography," he concluded. I hoped Professor Scindia would leave it at that. "So, how did you use those cryptographic primitives?" he asked. Romik looked desperately at the window for my inspired advice. I looked to the ceiling for some inspiration of my own! Suddenly, Romik had an idea, "Well Sir, I programmed that part. But you can ask Pranav for the details about the theory. That was what he focused on. He's just coming back in."

All eyes turned towards the door. I had no choice. I quickly entered the class again. "Good to have you back with us, Pranav," said Professor Scindia. "Romik was just telling us that you were the right person to ask if we wanted to understand how y'all incorporated randomness into your code," he continued. I grinned nervously and then began to write down a proof of something called 'Fermat's Little Theorem'. Don't ask the obvious questions. I don't know who Fermat is, I don't know what is 'little' about it and I don't really understand what the theorem says. But for this demonstration, I had harassed Soorya till he had explained the proof to me. So, I plodded on and succeeded in putting everyone to sleep. Luckily, Professor Scindia seemed satisfied.

"Now comes the fun part, guys!" he exclaimed enthusiastically, after my boring maths lecture. "Any questions anyone?" he asked, facing the rest of the teams. For a change, even Dhanush shook his head. "All right, then. It's time to see the result of all your hard work, guys. Start the demonstration!"

I have to admit, I was pretty scared we would screw things up. Preetish was running the code for one of the iRobots from a desktop. This was to make the computer-controlled iRobot move randomly. Preetish's code was brilliant. It essentially made the iRobot move in one direction for a while and then switch to another random direction.

I watched as Sachin took control of the second iRobot. The code running this iRobot was identical to the code Professor Scindia had supplied us with. I just hoped Sachin was up to the task.

I nodded at Preetish and he let the code run. Meanwhile, Sachin was running the other çode. For a while, neither robot moved. Then, Preetish's iRobot sprang to life and began moving away from Sachin's iRobot. Sachin quickly sent his iRobot in a wide circle to intercept Preetish's iRobot. Suddenly, Preetish's iRobot changed direction and Sachin took the opportunity to bump it. Sachin continued to move his iRobot in the general direction of a circle, going around Preetish's iRobot and looking for a chance to bump into it. Before Sachin's robot could bump Preetish's, Preetish's iRobot bumped Sachin's. Sachin carried on moving his iRobot in a circle, avoiding Preetish's which moved around randomly. Sachin had to make it seem like he was chasing Preetish's robot, but in reality, he was trying to dodge it as time passed.

Sounds too simple? Well yes, you're right. I knew perfectly well that if we kept up this charade for more than a few bumps, we'd run into trouble. But we had a plan. At a signal from me, Preetish made his iRobot keep moving till it hit a wall and got stuck. It stayed there, trying to push past the obstacle. “What’s wrong, guys?” asked Professor Scindia. “Sir, I think it might be a loose connection,” I replied as innocently as I could. “I’ll check it out,” I continued before he could get in another word.

I walked over to the iRobots. You’ll remember that I had brought 4 batteries with me. However, 2 of them were dead. I quickly slipped these dead batteries in and took out the live batteries from the iRobots. I slipped the live batteries into my pocket and headed back to my team. “Try running it again,” I suggested. Once again, the computer-controlled robot stayed stuck near the wall. Professor Scindia then got the other teams to try running their code on the iRobots. But the obstacle detector failed for all the teams which made use of collision detection. A few teams which used solely user-controlled iRobots managed to demonstrate their work, but it was a major inconvenience for most of the teams.

“It seems like the batteries are out of charge. Does anyone want to volunteer to go and get some?” My hand shot up immediately. “I’ll go, Sir!” I declared, perhaps a little too enthusiastically. Professor Scindia nodded his head sadly and waved me off. I left the campus and headed to Domino’s. After a suitable length of time had elapsed, I returned to college. I produced the bill that I had with me. Of course, this was for 4 batteries. I handed Professor Scindia all 4 batteries and he paid me back in full.

Then I asked as innocently as I could, “Sir, would you like us to continue with our demo?” Professor Scindia thought for a while and then said, “No...no need. It was very impressive. I’m glad that you guys are so thorough on such an important subject. Well done! Now, let the other teams have a turn before the charge runs out again." I silently cheered. We had done it! With a little help from Preetish and a lot of help from Venugopal and Vijay, we had pulled off the most successful con job of all time!

I watched as the other teams presented their projects. I have to admit, they were *actually* pretty cool! The *rangoli* robot was probably the most impressive of the lot. Amrish's team used the iRobot to draw a *rangoli* (pattern) using a trail of powdered pigments. But none of the projects came close to ours in terms of sheer (or should I say, apparent) awesomeness! After all the demonstrations were done, I walked out of the room with my team. We waited till all the other teams had left before congratulating each other. As we left, I said, "I love a project like this – it's easy, it's impressive and, most importantly, it's over!"

CHAPTER 37

The end-sems were finally over! I think I had done reasonably well (enough to satisfy my parents, at least!). The results hadn't been announced yet, but I had convinced myself that I would (probably!) pass most of the exams.

A few days ago, I had given Vijay the pen drive with my old Pacman game on it. He had given it to Naina, who had messaged me, highly amused by the customised video game. These days, she seemed genuinely happy with none of the morbid thoughts which had been plaguing her of late. I was glad, so glad that I had asked Vijay for another favour.

I had spent most of the weekend binge watching *Castle*. Now, it was Sunday night. As usual, I was messaging Naina, "Hey, wassup nerd? Done with exam stress?" She replied, "You're calling me a nerd?! Yeah, finally done. Can't wait to get back home to Chennai!" She continued, "What are you up to now?" I replied, "Nothing much. Killing time, waiting for dinner. How about you?" She piped up after a longish pause, "I'm heading over to a restaurant to meet my bro and another ICSI guy. My brother won't even tell me who he is. So annoying!" Before I could reply, she messaged, "Okay, I've reached. I'll let you know all the dirty details later. Cya!"

So much for our usual late-night conversations. I sighed and put the phone away. I looked around the softly-lit room as I waited for dinner. I just hoped that Vijay would come through on his promise. I wouldn't have asked him, but I was desperate. Then I heard the sound of heels clacking on the wooden floor. Heads turned towards the source of the noise. I just kept staring at the menu. I suddenly realised the clacking had stopped at my table. I looked over the menu into Naina's beautiful eyes and said, "Surprise!"

I was hoping for a reaction of pure joy. Unfortunately, she rolled her eyes and exclaimed, "I can't believe I fell for this!" After that, she looked like she was about to walk away. "Hey, sit down! I even stretched my 50-buck limit to treat you here!" I said, smiling desperately. She looked dubious, but slid into the chair opposite mine. She flashed her cute little smile and said, "I guess my brother isn't really going to show?" I shook my head. "So, lame-brain, now that you have me in your clutches, what exactly do you propose to do with me?" she asked flirtatiously. I gulped, not sure what to say.

I muttered, "You should check out the bread-basket here. It's tasty and, more importantly, it's free!" Naina looked at me like I was totally insane, which is what I sounded like even to myself! Why was I talking to her about bread? Then she laughed and the tension evaporated. "You're trying *way* too hard. Just relax. I won't bite. I promise," she reassured me. I smiled at her and she smiled back, lighting up my heart. "So, is this where you bring all your unsuspecting victims?" she asked, reaching for a piece of bread. That was when I saw her arm.

"Oh my gosh! What happened to your arm? Is this something to do with why you were in the hospital?" I blurted out unthinkingly. She stopped smiling at once. She drew her arm back and held it close to her body. "Yeah, something like that," she mumbled. "I'd prefer not to discuss my scar," she continued. "Naina, I'm really sorry. I was rude and insensitive and if you want to leave, I'll understand," I apologised. She laughed. "No way. Watching you is way too much fun," she kidded me. I tried my best imitation of an American accent (which was pretty bad!) and said, "You ain't seen nothing yet!" We laughed together.

"Hey, fun as this is, shouldn't we order now?" she finally asked. "Oh, yeah! I totally forgot about that part! Here I was thinking I could romance you with the humble bread-basket!" We both chuckled. I motioned a waiter over. Naina quickly scanned the menu and said, "One vegetable lasagna, please." I couldn't believe it! That was exactly what I had intended to order, after perusing the menu for half an hour before she showed up! I said, "Make that 2."

Naina looked at me curiously. "You know you can order something else, right?" I tried to come up with a likely explanation for my choice. "I know. Don't worry. I love vegetables and lasagna is one of my favourite dishes," I replied. But Naina wasn't ready to let it go at that. "Don't you prefer meat? That's what you once told me," she persisted. "Yeah, but you're vegetarian...and I remember you once saying that any boyfriend of yours would give up meat if he loved you enough. So, there you go..." my voice trailed away, as her eyes widened in shock. She and I sat in a tense silence, broken finally by the waiter.

"So, that's 2 vegetable lasagnas?" he asked, spoiling the moment. I said, "Yeah...and quickly, okay?" He hurried off. I turned back to Naina, who was (I couldn't believe it!) blushing a little. I guess even attractive girls get embarrassed sometimes. "So, tell me more about yourself..." she said, as we waited for the food to arrive.

I don't think I've ever opened up to anyone the way I did with her that evening. I told her about my parents. I talked about how I had lived most of my life in Bangalore. I ended up describing the first sem of college to her – how angry my mom had been when she had seen Naina's message, how Preetish had rescued our iRobot project, how her brother (Vijay) had helped and, finally, how Amrish was the real inventor of the Pacman game I had given her.

Then, once the food arrived, it was her turn. She talked about how she was good at dancing and had always enjoyed design. That was why she loved architecture so much. But Synergy, apparently, put them under a lot of pressure. Finally, she talked about how much she missed Chennai. Though, being sensible, she liked the Bangalore weather more. It was an enchanting evening.

Then, it was time for dessert. She told me she had quite a sweet tooth. I explained that I was a diabetic, so I wasn't allowed sweets. She immediately apologised and tried to cancel her order. But I wouldn't stand for it. While we were waiting, I excused myself, saying that I needed to use the washroom. In reality, I had a surprise to plan. I told one of the waiters to take a pair of earrings I had bought for her and serve it on a plate along with dessert. I also informed the manager of this plan, so I didn't end up getting robbed! Finally, I asked them to play *Pehli Nazar Mein* when they brought her the earrings.

Naina loved the dessert more than the lasagna. I couldn't really blame her. I would have preferred meaty lasagna. Just then, the song began to play. Naina looked suspiciously at me. "Your doing, lame-brain?" she asked. I was saved from answering when the waiter arrived with the earrings. She loved the earrings and the song. After I paid the (ridiculously high!) bill, we went down the stairs. I was practising different goodbyes, when she said, "I have a gift for you too, lame-brain. Hope you like it." So saying, she kissed me on the lips and I held her close beneath the (cliched) starry sky.

CHAPTER 38

The winter holidays passed relatively peacefully. I spent most of the time messaging Naina on WhatsApp. Of course, my mom grew suspicious. So, I pretended that I was messaging Venugopal about the *AMM* problems Professor Kumar had given us. I felt guilty about lying all the time. So, I did message Venugopal occasionally. He, of course, needed no encouragement from me. He wasn't content with just one. He wanted to solve all the problems. I constantly had to hold him back and tell him that it would be awesome if we had a concrete approach to any one problem. I also had to keep asking him to dumb down what he was saying, so that I could understand it. It was like talking to Soorya. Sometimes, however, Venugopal would start saying utter rubbish. So, I had to keep checking whether what he said made sense or not. The first few times might have been accidental. But after a while, he admitted to doing that just to keep me on my toes.

One night, he kept calling me. I repeatedly cut the call, since I wanted to message Naina. But he was undaunted. Finally, I answered and snapped, "Hey! Now's not really a good time. Can we talk later?" He laughed that weird laugh of his and said, "Check your email. I think I've figured out the proof to one of the problems. Let me know what you think." So saying, he hung up. I opened my mail and glanced through the proof. It looked like a lot of complicated and messy maths. So, I quickly messaged him saying, "Perfect! Let's send it to Professor Kumar."

I'm sure you can guess what happened next. Yes, you're right. He began to call me again! I ignored his call a coupe of times, then I figured if I flattered him enough, he'd stop calling. So, I picked up the phone and said, "Hey, great job, man! You solved it after all!" He started making a weird sort of choking sound. I asked him if he was okay. Then I realised he was laughing. "Heh-heh! Everything in that proof was wrong! Just wanted to see if you were paying attention." I felt like screaming, but managed a polite, "Hahaha! You got me! Let's talk tomorrow. Good night." But he wasn't done. "Seriously, though, I think I might be able to solve one of the problems, but I'm stuck somewhere. Call me tomorrow. We can discuss," he said and hung up.

The next night, as soon as I picked up my phone, I saw that he had given me 3 missed calls. A little voice in the back of my mind told me I ought to call him back. I ignored the little voice and began to draft my next message to Naina. Of course, Venugopal chose just that time to call. I knew from past experience that he'd keep on trying till I answered. So, sighing to myself, I answered the phone.

"Hey," I said, trying not to sound as bored as I felt. "Hi!" he exclaimed enthusiastically. He sounded like he'd just won the Nobel prize, rather than getting ready to discuss a lot of boring maths. "Hope you're not busy," he began. It was a statement, not a question. Nevertheless, I felt compelled to reply, "No, not at all. So, what did you want to discuss?" I hoped to finish this as quickly and painlessly as possible. He began talking, "I was thinking about that number-theory problem which used modular arithmetic..." at which point my mind went blank.

I let his words wash over me, till something he said sounded off to me. What was it? "Hang on a second!" I exclaimed. "If you're trying to find the remainder when dividing 25 by 3, you can use the direct method and get 1..." my voice trailed away, as I tried to recall a formula from long ago. "Heh-heh, so?" asked Venugopal. "But if you take the remainder of 5 divided by 3 and multiply it with the remainder of 5 divided by 3, you get 2 times 2, which is 4. So, you have to divide by 3 once again to get the remainder 1," I said, completing my train of thought.

At first, I wasn't sure if I had said something really stupid and obvious. But after a long pause, Venugopal finally shouted (right in my ear!), "I can't believe I was so stupid! This is what I was missing all along. This completes the proof. I'll mail it to you tonight. You're a genius!" True to his word, he mailed me the proof. I, in turn, mailed it to Soorya to verify. Soorya confirmed that the proof was correct and congratulated me on solving the problem. So, I happily added my name alongside Venugopal's and submitted the proof to Professor Kumar.

It was the last day of the year. Since it was a Sunday, my mom and I had gone to see a movie together, as was our usual practice. However, unknown to my mom, I was meeting Naina for lunch and dinner. I had just told my mom that I would be catching up with some friends, so she had made some plans of her own.

As the credits rolled, my mom and I got up and started walking towards the exit of the cinema hall. I felt relieved. I had persuaded my mom to go for a morning show, reminding her that tickets would be cheaper. The movie hadn't been exceptional, but I hadn't thought it would be. It was a typical Bollywood *masala* movie – lots of *masti* (fun), *gaana* (songs) and romance with a dash of action thrown in for good measure. I had told Naina that I would meet her for lunch, somewhere in the same mall where the movie hall was. I was feeling pretty pleased with myself. After the movie, my mom had plans to catch up with some friends on the other side of town. Everything seemed to be working out perfectly.

"So, who was your favourite actor in this one?" my mom asked, snapping me out of my daydreams of Naina. This was a game we had played since I was a child. The 2 of us would analyse every movie we watched in detail.

"Hmmm...I'm not really sure. What about you?" I asked, playing for time. My mom came to a halt and pondered the question for a long time. "Well, it's tough. But I think it would have to be..." I completed the sentence for her, "Shah Rukh Khan!" She smiled at me and said, "Now you're making fun of me!" I laughed, "Hahaha! No way, Ma. I'm too scared of you to do that!" By this time, most everyone had left the hall. As we moved with the flow, I turned back and suddenly caught sight of them. At first, I thought I was imagining things. But unfortunately, it was true. Naina and Vijay were here. They were among the last few stragglers in the movie hall. What's more, they had caught sight of us and were hurrying to catch up!

I don't know how you would react if all your well-laid plans started to unravel. But I went into panic mode. My brain shut down and I started saying rubbish. "Ma, let's go find the bathroom together!" I exclaimed, like I was suggesting lunch at her favourite restaurant. Meanwhile, I had this incredibly foolish grin on my face. Naturally, my mom was a little surprised. "Sure, why don't you go visit the loo? I'll wait here for you," she suggested sensibly. I wanted to take common sense and throw it out the window. To hell with it!

"No, Ma. Why don't you walk with me? It'll be so much fun!" I tried again. My mother narrowed her eyes at me suspiciously. "Since when do we have picnics in the bathroom?" she asked. "Are you sure you're feeling okay? Are you feeling sick or something?" My witty self was itching to scream, "Or something!" Instead, I held my tongue and began to push her in the direction of the bathroom. "Me? Hahaha! No, I'm fine. Nothing wrong. I just urgently need to use the bathroom. And I think you should too." What was I saying? I couldn't believe I had just said that last sentence! Even my mom was staring at me blankly. "It's a long way to the restaurant where you're meeting your friends and I thought you might need to go," I continued lamely. Thankfully, I was rescued.

Unfortunately, my rescuer turned out to be Naina! "Hey! Lame-brain! Wassup?" she shouted across the little distance separating us. My mom turned to stare at her in shock. I hoped Naina would take one look at my mom's face and realise she wasn't welcome here. Vijay stopped in his tracks. But Naina only had eyes for me. At any other time, I would have loved it. But this was a crisis!

Naina walked straight past my mom and began to stretch out her arms to hug me. I realised what she meant to do, grabbed her right hand in both of mine and shook it vigorously. Naina stared at me. My mom stared at me. Vijay stared at me. As usual, I was at a loss for words, when inspiration struck! "Hey, Anushka! Never thought I'd see you here!" I said, winking furiously. "Pranav, do you have something in your eye?" my mom asked after an uncomfortable silence. Naina just looked puzzled, while my mom looked definitely suspicious. "I'm feeling so sad about the movie that I feel like crying," I improvised. "But the movie had a happy ending," said Naina, while my mom nodded silently. Both of them looked at me like I was crazy. To be honest, even I felt like an idiot, trying to talk my way out of trouble. "No! I'm not really sad. These are just...tears of joy!" I finished with a pathetic excuse.

"Aren't you going to introduce me to your friend?" my mom asked. To my horror, Naina began to introduce herself to my mom! "Hi, Auntie! I'm N—" I quickly interrupted her and said, "—not Naina! This is Anushka, a college friend. She's in our batch." Turning quickly to Naina, I said, "Anushka, remember how much I told you about my mom? Remember *everything*?" Her eyes widened with comprehension. "Right. Yup, I'm Anushka!" she said. Both of us stood beaming stupidly at my mom. "So nice to meet you, Anushka. You must come over sometime. Funny, Pranav's never talked about you. But you must know how useless he is!" Naina agreed heartily, "Oh, yes, Auntie. All of us in college know!" Both of them laughed.

Finally, I decided to step in so that I wouldn't be mocked simultaneously by both my mom and my girlfriend. "Ma, also meet Vijay. He's—" but Naina interrupted me. "Yes, Auntie. Please let me introduce you to my b—" I cut in again, "—boyfriend!" My mom had extended her hand to shake Vijay's and Vijay was smiling at her until he heard what I said. At that point, he pulled his hand away and looked at me oddly.

Thankfully, Naina kicked him in the shin at that moment. Unfortunately, he made a big deal of it, "Ow! Hey, what did you kick me for?" I was glad to have Naina on my side. She quickly replied, "You don't have to assume I've told everyone about our break-up. I haven't told my batchmates yet. The truth is Vijay isn't my boyfriend..." I have to admit, I think my heart stopped for a moment. I wondered if Naina was going to admit everything. But she went on, "...he's my ex-boyfriend. We broke up during the holidays. Sorry for not letting you know, Pranav. But Auntie, the 2 of us are still good friends. Now, shake Auntie's hand politely!" she ordered Vijay. Obediently, Vijay shook hands with my mom.

Vijay continued chatting politely with my mom, while Naina and I both slipped away, claiming we had to visit the washroom. The moment we turned the corner and were out of sight, we headed for the emergency stairwell. We had hardly reached it before we were in each other's arms. We held each other close. The risk factor added to the thrill. We kissed for what felt like an eternity. Then Naina gave me a coy smile and walked away, saying, "See you at lunch..."

CHAPTER 39

Only my college insisted on starting classes on the first of January! Apparently, it was meant to show how dedicated and committed we were. Yeah, right! My guess is the professors never got invited to any good New Year's Eve parties and took out their frustration on us. Anyway, everyone in class looked like they were on the verge of falling asleep.

Last night, I had been partying with Naina. After a protracted lunch, we had again met for dinner. She had looked so happy when she had kissed me to wish me a Happy New Year. It was with these rosy images of Naina in mind that I arrived at college. The guards didn't even bother to check my ID card. I guess that made sense. Only students, faculty and administrative staff would be dedicated enough to show up on the first day of the new year! Anyway, we were quickly herded from our regular classroom to the seminar hall by Professor Swaminathan, our coordinator. I wondered what this was about. I decided to head straight to the most reliable source of intel in my batch.

I sat down next to Amrish and asked him, "Hey, man! What's going on?" He was sitting next to Soorya and Ramesh. All 3 of them stared at me as if I had just asked the most ridiculous question in the world! "Didn't you get the mail?" asked Amrish. "Um...maybe. But I haven't checked it lately. Why? Are we in trouble?" I questioned.

Amrish was about to reply when the Dean of Academics walked into the room.

She was a smart-looking lady, probably in her mid-forties. She had extremely fair skin and brown hair which fell down to her shoulders. She was dressed casually in a pair of jeans and a baggy shirt. "Who's that *macha*?" I whispered to Amrish. "That's Professor Poornima. She's the one who will present us with the certificates," Amrish replied. I tried to ask him some more questions, but he shushed me. Certificates? I had no clue what was going on. That's when the idea struck me – this must be some kind of award ceremony for those who had done well throughout the semester.

I settled back in my seat, content to clap for Soorya, Amrish, Venugopal and Dhanush. I was fairly certain that Soorya had got the highest total number of marks across all subjects. But I wasn't sure if they were awarding a certificate to just the batch topper, or one to each of the top 3 students. In any case, I decided to clap for those poor nerds whose only satisfaction came from little certificates. With a hot girlfriend, I was above such things.

Then the show began. Professor Swaminathan stepped up to the podium and started speaking, "Today we are gathered here to announce the names of those who have qualified to be on the Dean's Merit List. Professor Poornima will present certificates to those who have a GPA of 3.6/4 or more. We will begin with the IMTechs. As I have explained earlier, if a student scores 'A' in all subjects, he/she will be awarded a GPA of 4/4. I'm sure all of you have already computed your GPAs using the calculator tool available on our website. I invite Professor Poornima, our Dean of Academics, to begin the ceremony."

At this point, I have to admit, I was desperately checking my grades. I figured I hadn't got an 'F' in anything, since I hadn't been asked to repeat a semester. As long as I had passed, I was happy. I was staring at my grades in shock when Professor Swaminathan announced, "Folks, let me start by welcoming the first 4-pointer in the first semester of the first batch of the IMTechs. None other than...the one and only...Pranav Dasgupta!" I was still staring at my phone. I hadn't even heard what Professor Swaminathan had just said. I had developed an ability to tune out his voice, which made my life so much nicer.

Finally, I looked up blankly at the stage. Everyone was clapping and cheering. But I was stuck to my seat. When Amrish shoved me out of my seat, I rolled up to the stage and hesitantly shook hands with Professor Poornima, before accepting the certificate and walking back.

"Dude, why didn't you say you got an 'A' in everything?!" Amrish demanded. He continued, "All of us got screwed by Professor Nayar. He kept talking about making Biology fun, so none of us prepared for his final exam!" "Well, it just goes to show...never trust a teacher of any kind when it comes to marks!" I retorted. Amrish, Soorya, Dhanush and a girl called Shruti also got certificates, but no one else had managed a GPA of 4/4. I felt on top of the world as we headed to class!

After the ceremony, we came back to Professor Mukherjee's class. Thankfully, he was no longer teaching us Real Analysis. *Unfortunately*, he was teaching us

Differential Equations. Now, I don't know about you, but I'm the type of guy who likes it when your solution is something like 'x=2'. I *didn't* like it when the solution was a sine curve (or something even more awful)!

Professor Mukherjee kept going on and on about how his marking scheme would be much stricter this semester (just what we needed!) and how he would be teaching us Ordinary and Partial Differential Equations. Don't let the names fool you. I felt relieved the first time I heard them. I thought the 'Ordinary' part meant that it would be simple. Plus, I thought 'Partial' meant that we would have to get only partial solutions (and hopefully, full marks!) and leave the remainder of the question unsolved. What a joke! It actually had to do with derivatives from calculus. Don't worry, even I don't understand what that really means!

In any case, I spent an hour and a half in a class whose introductory session put me to sleep. I didn't even want to think about future classes. However, I managed to evade being caught by one of Professor Mukherjee's questions by sitting right in front and looking at him with an expression of interest. At least, that was what I was trying for. My guess is that I ended up looking like a confused baboon. Anyway, it seemed to work. Professor Mukherjee didn't ask me any tricky questions during the entire class, though he did pull my leg a bit at the end.

As I was daydreaming about Naina, he said, "I'm hoping all of you will catch me if I say something wrong. You should keep asking questions like my friend Pranav here. However, he seems to be daydreaming today!" The class laughed and I blushed.

Our next class was Signals and Systems, taught by Professor Tyagi. My first impression of Professor Tyagi was that he was a very stylish guy, who looked like he was cut out to be a movie star. I had seen him sometimes in the corridors. But this was the first time we were being taught by him. He was wearing a mauve, full-sleeved, silk shirt. He was also wearing leather shoes, which looked like they were imported. To top it off, he was wearing a shiny pair of black pants. He looked like he was ready to burst into song at any minute. Imagine Rajnikanth (the stylish Tamil superstar!) as a college professor and you would get Professor Tyagi.

At first, he talked a little about himself. He told us about how he had got his PhD from EPFL in Switzerland. Then he talked about the structure of the course. We were going to do signal processing. That meant looking at a radio wave (or a light pulse, or sound from an instrument) and trying to extract something useful from it. He talked about time and frequency and some theorems.

The only frequency I knew was the frequency of my favourite radio stations. In fact, I didn't even know what AM and FM stood for. I just enjoyed the music. He went on for a while, talking about Fourier transforms and z-transforms and how we'd be using them.

I tuned back in when I realised that he had stopped talking and was glancing at his watch. "Since today's your first day of the new semester, how about we break early?" he asked as everyone cheered. "But before leaving, I want each of you to stand up, introduce yourself and tell us what your area of interest is," he finished. I had no idea what to say. Thankfully, he started from the other end of the class. When my turn finally came, I got up and said, “My name is Pranav Dasgupta, I’m from Bangalore and my interest is in passing this course!”

Like every comedian knows, there’s always a moment of tension when you’re not sure if your audience is going to laugh or not. Thankfully, Professor Tyagi and the rest of the class started laughing. “I’m fairly lenient, so don’t worry!” he exclaimed. With that, everyone began to head towards the door. As I was walking, my phone pinged with a WhatsApp message. I checked it out. I felt a shiver run down my spine as I read the words – “Please save me. I’m scared. Come to my college alone. I need help.”

CHAPTER 40

I raced towards my college's main gate. By now, I could tell when Naina was joking or being serious. And the message she had sent sounded very serious. Perhaps, she would finally tell me what her mysterious 'illness' was. None of it made any sense. She claimed that she "needed help". But surely someone at her college would be better equipped to handle an emergency than me? There was also the matter of telling me to "come alone". Why didn't she want her brother to help out? Had she been keeping a secret from her family all this time? Nightmarish scenarios ran through my mind as I waited impatiently for the guard to interrupt his lunch and open our college gate.

It was while I was running that the thought occurred to me – what if she wasn't facing a physical threat? Was she on the verge of committing suicide? Was this a cry for help? I dismissed the thought immediately – Naina was a perfectly sensible, ordinary girl. I was just imagining things. But from the little I had read about mental illnesses, I knew that they could affect anyone. Even so-called 'ordinary' people could suffer from them. Then, a horrible scene flashed before my eyes – Naina getting abused and raped in some shady corner of her college. I knew I would never forgive myself if something like that happened to Naina.

Throwing caution to the wind, I ran as fast as I could towards her college. It took me about 5 minutes till I saw the front gate (yes, I was *really* out of shape!). I ran till the gate and stopped as the guard looked at me suspiciously. This time, I didn't have Preetish to translate for me. How to get in? That's when it hit me! I said the one word that every college guard responds to – "Admissions." Immediately, he opened the gate and signed me in. He then looked at his lunchbox and again at me. He was obviously debating whether I was worth interrupting his lunch for. I said, "You eat. I go." I then repeated the statement in Hindi. Finally, I mimed me walking and him eating. He looked at me like I was nuts, then went back to his lunch.

Meanwhile, I ran as fast as I could towards the main building. There I paused, unsure which way to go. Panting for air, I reached the main reception area. I was about to head to the help desk and ask the people there to check on Naina, when someone crashed into me from behind. I was about to yell at that person when I saw that it was Naina!

I almost failed to recognise her. She looked like something the cat had dragged in. Her hair was a confused mess. Her clothes were dirty and crumpled. But the most striking change was in her eyes. They had a hunted, haunted look to them – as if she was being chased by monsters. We slowly got to our feet.

"Naina, are you –" I began to ask, when she ran into my arms and hugged me. "Save me from them! They are right around the corner! We have to run, Pranav!" Saying that, she ran through another exit. I had to make a choice. Should I follow Naina? Or should I try and stop the people she was running from? I had a split second to decide. So, I decided to follow Naina. I often wonder what would have happened if I hadn't chased her that day.

In any case, there I was running flat out from whoever Naina was so afraid of. After some time, we both stopped, gulping in sweet air. I felt like I had run a marathon with a 100m sprint at the end! Romik would have been proud. Amazing – even in the most extreme situation, my brain could still conjure up images of Romik. I gradually approached Naina. "Naina?" I said gently with a question mark at the end. "They're gone. It's just me and you." She looked at me with eyes that begged for help. Then she looked past my shoulder. She pointed a shaky finger and exclaimed, "They're everywhere! Save me from the Purple Gang!"

I turned around, not sure what to expect. I saw... nothing! There was no one there. Certainly no Purple Gang. That was when I realised that Naina needed medical help. Just then, I heard a girl cry out and come running towards us. I recognised her as Nisha – the girl I'd met at the debate. "Oh my gosh! Naina, are you okay?" she asked quickly. I was about to tell her everything when I saw Naina subtly shake her head. I said, "She was being chased by some people. But she's okay now. I'm Pranav Dasgupta, her boyfriend." Nisha's eyes widened in recognition. "Oh, yeah! We met at the debate! I'm Nisha, in case you've forgotten!" she laughed slightly – a soft tinkling sound, though her eyes were worried. "In any case, I'm Naina's roommate. Take my number and call me if this ever happens again. Naina is a schizophrenic." With that revelation, she gently guided Naina into the hostel.

***

I couldn't go back to my college and face the prospect of sitting in class while Naina was in such bad shape. So, I wandered up and down the maze of streets near the auto stand. I didn't waste all my time though. I spent a good deal of time learning about schizophrenia. I don't know about you, but to me it was just a vague medical term. The only time I had heard it mentioned was in the movie, *A Beautiful Mind*.

I learnt that schizophrenics are out of touch with reality. Most have hallucinations. The hallucinations can be purely auditory, purely visual or a combination of both. From Naina's description of the Purple Gang, I'm guessing she had both. I kept reading. Apparently, schizophrenics sometimes have panic attacks. They can injure themselves or others during these episodes, which are marked by pupil dilation, increased heart rate and (sometimes) palpitations. Another problem schizophrenics suffer from is paranoia. They sometimes feel scared of some (or all) people. I also read how schizophrenia is the 'king' of all mental diseases – patients are not just beset by hallucinations and panic attacks, they also suffer from delusions, obsessions and depression. I walked around as I absorbed all this information. Once a suitable period of time had elapsed, I took an auto home.

After a hurried dinner, I retreated to my room. Just then, my phone pinged. I opened up WhatsApp. It was Naina. I quickly opened the message and scanned it. "Hi. Thanks for coming today. It really helped me. I'm sorry I didn't tell you everything earlier. I just didn't want to spoil all the fun we've been having. I understand if you want to break it off now. But...thanks for everything!" I replied as fast as I could (which was not very fast!).

My message read, "You have nothing to apologise for. I should have guessed something was up when you were uncomfortable talking about your illness. All I ask is that you tell me the truth. Did you go to the hospital because you were in an accident or because you were seeing and hearing things?"

I was drifting off to sleep when my phone chimed. "Do you trust me? Or do you think I'm crazy too? Just like everyone else?" she wanted to know. I wanted her to confide in me, but didn't want to encourage her delusions. I was about to give a vague response when she messaged me again: "Do you remember you asked me about the scar on my arm? Well, it was because someone had injected me with poison. I needed to get it out of my bloodstream. That's why I cut myself. That's when they took me to hospital. They thought I was imagining things. But I wasn't! Only I could see those men who wanted to kidnap me! You believe me, right?"

I sighed and rubbed my forehead. I wanted to believe her. But the whole thing sounded too fantastic to be true. I decided I would keep an open mind. "I'll tell you what. Why don't you and I try and track down this Purple Gang or whatever of yours? But if we don't find any evidence of its existence, then you and I will go to see a doctor. Together. Is that okay with you?" I messaged.

She instantly responded, "Please don't tell Vijay about the Purple Gang. He'll just panic and give me a huge dose of sedatives. As it is, I feel like a zombie most of the time. I know you'll help me. But even if we don't find any evidence, don't let him know. I don't want my college and family to worry unnecessarily. Will you promise me that?"

Like a fool, I replied, "Of course, I promise. And you don't have to do anything you aren't comfortable with. Okay?" In retrospect, this was my single biggest mistake. I knew that I ought to tell Vijay what was going on with Naina. However, I didn't want to just dismiss Naina's fears. What if she was right? Some part of me (a stupid, blind part) still felt like she didn't need her head examined. I couldn't believe Naina would act like this without some external stimulus. I didn't want to accept that schizophrenia was just a chemical imbalance in the brain and nothing more! Finally, Naina replied, "Okay, deal. Thanks!" Then she sent me another message – "By the way, I think someone at my college is trying to kill me. But I have no idea who. Please help me solve this mystery..." I was getting more and more worried. As I was about to reply, I got another WhatsApp message – this time from an unknown number.

The message read – "Hey, sorry to bother you. Can I call you now? It's Nisha here." I replied tentatively, "Sure. Go ahead." Seconds later my phone buzzed and I answered Nisha's call. "Hi. I know you were probably asleep. Didn't mean to disturb you. By the way, I got your number from Naina," she whispered in a husky voice. I rushed to reassure her, "Don't worry. The night is young and so am I!" "Oooh...so you're a creature of the night? Interesting..." she whispered, laughing softly. "So, what was so urgent, it couldn't wait till tomorrow?" I asked.

"Well, I guess you didn't know the truth about Naina. Now that you do, I want you to let me know if Naina talks about being chased by people in purple or something. I'm the one who gives her all the pills she needs every day and night. So, if anything happens, please tell me. Did she say anything today which sounded weird or paranoid?" asked Nisha.

I hesitated. I didn't want to let Naina's secret out, but I didn't want to lie outright either. I decided to unveil a little more of the truth by probing Nisha. "No. Naina messaged, but we talked about regular stuff."

Then Nisha spoke, "A couple of weird things have happened. Her phone was stolen, but her SIM card was left behind. Then one night, she claimed someone was trying to smother her. I thought she was hallucinating, but I did hear the sound of footsteps that night. I never told her that because I didn't want her to worry even more. I'm afraid this is someone's sick idea of a joke. But it's gone too far. Can you promise me you won't repeat any of this to Naina?"

I promised and added, "Do you need my help to try and figure out who's behind this?" She paused a moment and then said, "Fantastic! Looking forward to spending some time with you! Good night." I was now involved in 2 investigations which seemed to be completely independent. What had I gotten myself into?

CHAPTER 41

The next morning, I set out for college earlier than normal. Naina had messaged me again late last night, asking if I would have breakfast with her at my college canteen. I wondered why she would ditch her own college canteen to come eat at mine. Then I assumed that she was probably so paranoid that she thought the caterers were trying to poison her. To be fair, I did have similar thoughts about my own college caterers, but I knew it was a joke – mostly.

I reached college with half an hour to spare. In the morning, we had Professor Rajendra's class. He was teaching us Data Structures and Algorithms and was taking a lab session as well.

Anyway, I spotted Naina right away. She was standing near the canteen. Despite the blazing sun, Naina was not sweating at all. She was glowing like a beacon. Listen to me going on like a poet. With Naina as my inspiration, maybe I should go write a poetry book. As I drew nearer, she saw me and smiled.

We each grabbed an *idli* and a *vada* and sat down. But before we began eating, she began to peer around. "Did you see them?" she asked, just as I was about to take a bite. "Um, of course," I replied. I wanted her to keep relying on me. "Are they still behind me?" she demanded. "Uh... no. They're walking away now. Also, they're not wearing purple," I replied as soothingly as I could. "But-but..." she stammered. "I-I'm sure they were in purple! Did you at least see the gun?" she cried. "No, but I might have missed it," I quickly said, when I realised a simple "No" would stop her from trusting me. I soothed Naina a little more, talked to her for about 20 minutes and promised we would meet for lunch. I even made some jokes about my professors. Amazing how that always makes people laugh. Finally, she left.

I gobbled down my breakfast and left the canteen. I was nearly the last to leave, but I noticed that a man who had been eating when Naina and I arrived was still there. He had a smug, self-satisfied look about him, like a well-fed cat. He had a paunch, but wore it proudly. It was more the emblem of a man who was rich and prosperous, rather than old and overweight. He had slick hair, a thin moustache and a great sense of style. If Professor Tyagi looked like a movie star, this man looked like he was the producer. The canteen in my college is of the self-service kind. But this man obviously had the right connections. He just waved a hand and caterers came rushing over with freshly-made *dosas*. He had already eaten 3 *dosas* by the time I was leaving the canteen. He waved at me and continued to gobble down *dosas*. I waved back and smiled. As I rushed to class, I wondered who the man was and if I would ever see him again.

I made it to class with minutes to spare. I asked Amrish what he had heard about Professor Rajendra. Amrish said, "I'm not sure, *macha*. Some MTechs have failed a few of his courses. But everybody seems to agree that he's a pretty cool professor. He is a little strict, but he doesn't give too many assignments and has a great sense of humour. But then again, they all do in the beginning."

I wondered whether I would be among the unlucky few who failed his course. Half an hour after class was supposed to start, there was still no sign of Professor Rajendra. By now, we were making quite a bit of noise. I think we had all just assumed that Professor Rajendra was sick and we had a free period. Some of us began to slowly drift out of the room. Preetish and Romik were among the first to leave. Amrish and I were about to get up and go when all of a sudden, the door was slammed open and Professor Rajendra walked into class. As you've probably guessed by now (if you've ever watched a B-grade Bollywood movie), Professor Rajendra was the man gobbling *dosas* in the canteen.

My heart skipped a beat. I wasn't sure whether he would be glad I had waved back at him or upset because I hadn't bothered to go and wish him good morning. Then he began talking, "Welcome to my course on Data Structures and Algorithms. I like to call it DSA. There's only one lesson that really needs to be learned here. You must always ask yourself, 'Can I do better?'. For example, today I could have wasted an extra half hour in class or eaten hot *dosas*. So, I chose to do better. Both you and I are happier now. Don't worry about attendance and all. I give everyone full attendance. You can either take this really fat textbook – which is honestly better used as a pillow – and learn it very well. Or you can come to class and see if we can do better!"

None of us knew how to respond, so we sat quietly. "No questions? Good! Then let's get started," continued Professor Rajendra. He explained that we would start things slowly. Today, we would focus on something called sorting. Sorting basically involves arranging numbers in ascending or descending order.

Professor Rajendra was talking about something called computational complexity. I had no desire to even try and understand this. Amrish and Soorya were taking down notes furiously. One of them would explain it to me later. All this time, Professor Rajendra kept discussing different techniques to sort. I wasn't sure who came up with the names. It seemed as if someone had asked a bunch of random people what they would like a new technique to be called. We covered Bubble, Insertion and Quick Sort. Funnily enough, Quick Sort is not the quickest sort! There is a sort called Merge Sort which is faster than the other 3, just to complicate life!

After studying Merge Sort, Professor Rajendra asked us if we could do better and went out to grab a cup of coffee. For the next 10 minutes, there was no sound in the classroom, except the scratching of pen on paper. Finally, Professor Rajendra returned and sat down in a swivel chair in front of the class. He then asked, "Has anyone come up with a better approach?" I watched Venugopal, Dhanush and even Soorya have their approaches shot down. Finally, Professor Rajendra asked, "Can no one do better?" Feeling irritated, I decided to act a little cocky and said, "No, Sir. No one can do better." He smiled at me and said, "Finally! Somebody gets it! You can actually prove that you can't do better. Now come on. It's time for lab!"

In the lab session, we were expected to implement all the different types of sorting techniques that we had learned. That was the easy part. The hard part was that we had to do it in C. Professor Rajendra sat down in front of the class. After about an hour had passed, Professor Rajendra got up. We assumed he was going to make his rounds like Professor Kumar or Professor Scindia. So far, he hadn't been at all involved in checking our progress. In fact, I had used the opportunity to check up on Nisha a little. I didn't really know anything about her. Plus, I wasn't sure how close to Naina she really was. I checked her Facebook and Instagram accounts. She was posing next to Naina in a lot of pictures. I quickly went back to my program screen as Professor Rajendra came close. But he walked straight past me and left the room.

At first, we thought he might have gone to the toilet or for more coffee. But when he didn't return in 10 minutes, a few people began to murmur. When 20 minutes were up, some people began to drift out. Finally, after 30 minutes, even I left. The only people left after me were Dhanush, Venugopal and Soorya. We headed to the canteen for lunch. That's where we spotted him...again! Professor Rajendra was sitting at a table with a plate full of tomato rice. "Why did all of you take so long? You should fix your priorities. Next time, code less and eat more. Or you'll never do better!" he exclaimed smilingly.

Before Naina had left in the morning, we had agreed that she would come to my college for lunch. So, I was stuck in the canteen with a plate of rapidly-cooling food, waiting for her. I was seated at a table for 2. A girl suddenly appeared from behind me and sat down at my table. I was thinking of ways to tell this girl that I was waiting for someone else. Then, the girl abruptly said, "Naina's not coming. She got one of her panic attacks. So, I had to give her a mild sedative. Nice campus, by the way." That's when I realised that she was actually Nisha (Naina's roommate)! "Thanks, I guess...whoa, whoa, whoa! Naina asked *you* to come here? I thought she didn't want anyone else to know!" I exclaimed, surprised.

I continued, "Also, who put you in charge of her medication?" She threw up both hands, shrugged and smiled. She had a nice smile. Not as cute as Naina's, but it was accompanied by a light in her eyes. Eyes which beckoned with promises of mystery. "Roommates know everything about each other. I've known about you ever since Naina first started messaging you. As for her medication, her brother asked me if I would make sure she takes her antipsychotics and sedatives. I agreed. So, Vijay and Naina both trust me. Will you?" she asked and smiled that mysterious smile.

I guess I had no choice. I had seen for myself how this girl seemed able to calm Naina down. Plus, Vijay and the rest of Naina's family obviously trusted her. "Sure," I replied with something of a forced smile.

"Before we get started, I need to know what Naina said or did the last few times you saw her," said Nisha, beginning to grill me. "Well..." I paused, unsure of how much to reveal. Then I figured I'd just tell Nisha the kind of stuff she already knew. "Um, she seemed scared. Hunted, almost. Like there was someone after her," I finally answered. "Did she mention a name or anything about a Purple Gang?" asked Nisha. I replied as forcefully as I could, "No!" But Nisha wasn't satisfied. "Has she sent you any scared or sad messages lately?" she asked. I tried to stick to the truth. "Well, yeah. She did seem a little worried about college and stuff. But nothing major." Nisha looked down at the table, took a few deep breaths and said, "I'd like you to come to our college. If you really care, there's something you should see."

CHAPTER 42

There was still a good half hour of lunchtime left by the time we reached Synergy. Thankfully, Nisha was able to dismiss the guard's objections in fluent Kannada. After signing me in, Nisha guided me towards the girls' hostel. "What now?" I asked, wondering if this was a complete waste of time.

"Now, we just have to smuggle you in," said Nisha mischievously. "Whoa! I'm sure you can show me whatever it is right here," I said in a fearful voice. I had no intention of getting caught inside a girls' hostel in a college that wasn't even mine! My main concern was that my mother would hear about it. Don't get me wrong – I love my mom and I know she loves me a lot. But if any son of hers gets caught in a girls' hostel...well, let's just say I'd rather cover myself with honey and run into a beehive!

Nisha's voice brought me back. "It's still a little crowded, so I can't sneak you in through the front door. But there's always plan B!" exclaimed Nisha, seeming a little too happy. "Why does that not fill me with confidence?" I asked dubiously. "Hahaha! Don't worry. I'll take care of you," she teased me. I chuckled nervously, hoping she had an actual plan in mind. I was growing to like Nisha too. As a friend.

"So...what *is* the plan?" I finally asked. "We're going to hide you in the girls' bathroom. When the coast is clear,

I'll come and fetch you. Okay?" Nisha confided. I did not see that one coming! "What?! Bad enough you want me to enter the girls' hostel, now you want me to go into the ladies' toilet too?! Look, I don't want to end up in jail! So thanks, but no thanks!" I said, putting my foot down.

Of course, no one ever listens to me. So, 5 minutes later, I was standing near the ladies' toilet at the back of the girls' hostel. Nisha had told the guard that she had seen someone trying to scale the back wall and had pointed somewhere in the distance. I had to admit, she was a pretty good actress. The guard had predictably gone off to chase some imaginary scoundrels. That was my cue. I ran to the washroom and quickly pulled the door open. I was about to enter when my first nightmare came true!

A girl was just leaving the washroom. She was looking at her phone, but she'd look up and see me any minute. I froze, unsure of what to do. Then, just as she glanced up, someone spun me around and kissed me full on the lips. It took a few seconds for my brain to register that Nisha was kissing me! I wasn't really sure how this would end and was on the verge of kissing her back, when she broke off the kiss.

Nisha winked at the other girl, who smiled slyly, nodded and walked away, peeking back once to see Nisha shoving me into the washroom. I supposed Nisha was just acting like we were a couple, so that the other girl wouldn't ask embarrassing questions. At the same time, there had been a part of me that wanted that kiss to last a little longer. I know, I know. I was a disgraceful, dirty dog who didn't deserve Naina. But I couldn't help my feelings.

But Nisha was being business-like once more. "Go lock yourself in one of the cubicles. I'll come fetch you when there's no one on the stairs. I shouldn't be long." She turned to go and then stopped. "Oh, I almost forgot." She gave me a quick peck on the cheek. "For luck," she whispered in my ear and was gone.

I stood still. Thankfully, no one else entered the bathroom. After 5 minutes, Nisha returned. "All clear. Let's go!" she exclaimed. "We have to take the stairs. Just stay behind me and don't say a word!" I was about to protest that she never really gave me an opportunity to say a word, when she took off.

We raced up the stairs to the second floor. We soon reached a door with a lock on the outside. Nisha quickly unlocked the door and pushed me into the room. She then entered the room and shut the door behind her. I glanced around the room. It wasn't as fancy as ICSI's rooms, but it was comfortable. There were 2 beds placed side by side with small bedside tables on either side. The room came with an attached bathroom. Nisha walked over to one of the beds.

"That is Naina's bed," she said, pointing to the one farther away. "And this is what I found this morning," she continued. She grabbed the mattress and lifted it up slightly to reveal a packet underneath. I grabbed the packet and she let the mattress drop. The packet was filled with cigarettes. Nisha lit one of the cigarettes. Immediately, the room filled with the smell of marijuana (weed). Naina's problems were due to drugs!

CHAPTER 43

Naina was a drug addict! I still couldn't believe it. I had never smelt smoke on her. I wondered whether she only smoked weed. Weed is a relatively mild drug. Could weed cause delusions and hallucinations of the sort she was suffering from? Of course, it was possible she was taking something worse. It was all too complex. I wondered whether Vijay knew about this. Definitely not! Naina's parents and he would probably have her locked up in some drug rehab centre for years if they knew the truth. As far as I knew, only Nisha and I knew about this addiction. I decided I would call Naina and Nisha tonight and resolve the issue. But right now, I was 15 minutes late for class!

The class just after lunch was Economics. It was being taught by a Professor Gopal. I knew absolutely nothing about him, except for the fact that I was probably making a terrible first impression on him! Thankfully though, before leaving the campus, I had made contingency plans. This was to ensure that I didn't miss too much of what was being taught. My great plan consisted of telling Amrish to badger Professor Gopal with questions so that he would barely be able to get a sentence out! Okay, it wasn't a great plan, but I had had like 30 seconds to come up with it.

The rest of what followed was later narrated to me by Amrish and a bunch of other guys, who confirmed the story. Of course, since it involved Amrish, I'm pretty sure there was a good deal of exaggeration involved. I owed him big time...which in turn led to another problem later in the semester! But let me tell the story following the timeline as closely as possible.

Professor Gopal entered the room and the class grew silent. He was an elderly gentleman with a head that was mostly bald, but had a few stray white hairs thrown in for good measure! He looked strict and serious. Apparently, in the beginning, everyone felt a little wary of him. The first thing he started talking about was the Economics textbook we would be using. After that, he spoke a little about himself. That frightened everyone, especially when he mentioned that he had done his MBA from an IIM. He went on to add that he expected the same standards from us.

Professor Gopal began. "Today, we'll be discussing one of the founding fathers of microeconomics – Adam Smith. He laid emphasis on 3 critical elements for any private company – land, labour and capital. Yes, what is it?" Amrish had quickly Googled Adam Smith and found an article criticising some of his views. "Sir, do you think that Adam Smith's theory of an efficient market holds good in today's world? After all, he didn't set much store by international trade, but that is what controls even local markets today."

Professor Gopal looked a little surprised that anyone had actually asked a valid question. "Well, um, yes. Adam Smith's theories have received much criticism of late. But the fact remains that this is an introductory course on

Economics. So, we must first investigate Smith's theories in more detail...Yes, what is it now?!" he asked as Amrish continued to keep his hand in the air.

"Sir, how does this relate to our everyday life? In a world, where even the theories of John Maynard Keynes have been found wanting after the global recession, perhaps we should be looking at other approaches – like Nassim Nicholas Taleb's Black Swan?" asked Amrish, having quickly glanced at an *Economic Times* article. "Perhaps in future classes we could..." began Professor Gopal. But Amrish was unstoppable. "Also, what do you think Smith would think of demonetisation and cryptocurrencies?" Professor Gopal looked like he was about to cry. "Perhaps you should take this class!" he finally snapped, just as I entered. Amrish sat back happily. "No, Sir. Please continue. No more questions," said Amrish, looking like a lawyer who had successfully dealt with a troublesome witness.

I may have seemed calm on the outside, but my mind was still reeling from the surprising discovery at Naina's hostel. I was not worried about the course, but about Naina. At first, I have to admit that I was sort of relieved it was *just* a drug problem. It somehow seemed easier to handle than a mental disorder. It's only looking back that I realise how insensitive my attitude was. Now I realise that people with mental illnesses are genuinely sick. There's nothing to be ashamed of in admitting it. Seeking a doctor is not a sign of weakness, it's a sign of courage.

Drugs seemed like a more practical problem. It was something I felt I could help Naina deal with. But my discovery today had revealed more questions than it had resolved. If Naina's problems were because of drugs, how come the doctors had given her antipsychotics for schizophrenia? Had they just not detected her addiction or had Naina developed the habit later? I was also curious about Nisha's role in all of this. How did she fit in? She obviously knew all of Naina's problems. Yet, she had shared her knowledge with me rather than Naina's family. That didn't make any sense.

But now, I had to work with her to ensure 2 things – that Naina's access to the drugs was blocked and that Naina was able to cope with the drug withdrawal symptoms. And finally (if I were being really honest with myself), I couldn't help thinking of how close I had come to kissing Nisha back. Was I worthy of these amazing girls? As soon as class ended, I decided to bunk maths and head home.

I arrived home early, much to my mom's surprise. As I was leaving college, I ran into Professor Mukherjee (whose class I was bunking). I gave both him and my mom the same story. I told them I felt nauseous and needed to rest! Actually, I just wanted to message Naina.

In the meantime, my mom decided that I needed some medicines for my stomach trouble. I had the medicines and lay down. I messaged Naina, saying hi. To my delight and surprise, she replied, "Hey, lame-brain. How's it going?" She seemed a lot chirpier than she had in the morning. "So, did you enjoy our amazing canteen food?" I asked sarcastically. "Huh? What do you mean? I've never eaten at your college canteen!" she answered. I responded, "Have you forgotten? We had breakfast together this morning!" I could see the screen flashing with the word 'typing' beneath her name. Finally, I got her message: "Is this a joke? Because I'm not getting it. I'm pretty sure I know what I was doing today. And I definitely wasn't at ICSI. Are you confusing me with Nisha?" I messaged back, "No, I'm positive it was you. Why would you think it was Nisha?" However, Naina had gone offline and showed no signs of returning. While waiting for her to respond, I dozed off.

I woke up a few hours later and spent the evening finishing a couple of pending assignments. I was debating whether or not to message Naina, when my phone suddenly pinged. I picked it up, hoping it was Naina and that she'd remembered having breakfast with me. I was surprised to see it was from Nisha instead. "Hi. Just wanted to say thanks for taking all those risks today. Naina's lucky to have you," the message read. I couldn't help but think of the kiss. I wrote back, "Thanks! She's lucky to have you too." She sent me a thumbs-up. We were both silent for a while, but still online. Finally, I asked, "What exactly are the symptoms Naina has as a result of her schizophrenia?" There was a long pause, then Nisha wrote back, "I'm not sure Naina would be comfortable with me telling you that..." I felt angry and betrayed. "Well, I doubt she'd be thrilled to discover that both of us know about her drug addiction, right?" I messaged Nisha.

She soon replied, "You're right. It was stupid of me to write that. I know I can trust you. Give me a minute." She was typing for a long time after this. Just as I was about to message her again, she sent me an essay! I'm not going to reproduce the whole thing here, but I'll tell you the gist of it. The most prominent symptom was her hallucinations. She saw and heard things which were not really there. She also had delusions, such as a severe dislike of the colour purple. She feared people wearing purple clothes and even ran away if someone offered her a chocolate in a purple wrapper. The hallucinations and delusions sometimes combined. She saw and heard people in purple-coloured outfits chasing her. She felt like they were out to get her. When she was first admitted to hospital, it was because she had stabbed herself and Nisha with a broken glass bottle. That was the cause of the scars on their arms. I have to admit that I was feeling closer to Nisha as I read this. She had been directly hurt and attacked by Naina, but she still cared so much for her friend. It was incredible.

As if she were reading my mind, Nisha added, "I think it's best if the 2 of us work together to help Naina out. What do you say?" I told myself that I didn't have to reveal all of Naina's secrets. But I would get extra info from Nisha. "Sure!" I replied. I added, "I think you should tell me the next time Naina leaves the campus alone. We can follow her and try to find the source of the drugs. We need to stop that as soon as we can." Nisha replied, "I totally agree. Also, let's not tell anyone else right now. You can keep a secret, right?" I smiled to myself. Again, as if reading my mind, Nisha continued, "I can keep a secret too! Naina doesn't have to know about that kiss! Anyway, let's meet up and share some more info?" I hated myself, but I kind of liked how this was going. "Sure...it's a date!" I wrote back.

CHAPTER 44

I began chatting less with Naina and more with Nisha as the semester wore on. Nisha and I discussed Naina's bouts of amnesia. Nisha wondered whether she ought to increase Naina's dosage of antipsychotics. Strangely, Nisha wanted to do so without consulting a doctor. I had been reading up on both schizophrenia and drug abuse, and all the articles I had read were of the same opinion – be in constant touch with your psychiatrist. I didn't want to risk pushing her away. I had feelings for Nisha. There, I admitted it. Judge me all you like, but I couldn't help the way I felt. Nevertheless, I was determined not to actually cheat on Naina in any way.

It was in the midst of this inner struggle that I suddenly received a message from Naina one night: "Hey, lame-brain! How are you?" We chatted casually for a while. No references to her hallucinations or schizophrenia. I had never directly raised the topic of drugs with Naina. I still felt uncomfortable doing so. "By the way, can I ask you something about Nisha?" asked Naina. Oh boy! I was in trouble now. "Go ahead!" I shot back.

But Naina's question surprised me. "Do you think Nisha's taking drugs?" "Well, she seems normal enough. Why? Anything suspicious happen lately?" I asked as innocently as I could. "I know it's a pretty serious accusation. But..." Naina messaged back. The word 'typing' flashed underneath her WhatsApp picture. Then the rest of the message arrived. "Remember, you can't tell Nisha anything about this, okay? Before I tell you anything else, I need to know if I can trust you. You have to answer my next question honestly, okay?" This was dangerous territory. I was beginning to wonder just how much Naina and Nisha trusted each other. "Have you ever kissed her?" came the dreaded question.

At first, I thought of admitting that I had and giving her the context. But that was no excuse. I had to lie. "No. I promise," I messaged back, hating myself for the lie. "Thanks lame-brain! I should never have doubted you!" she exclaimed. She then went on to tell me how she had found a packet of weed under her mattress. She wasn't sure how it had gotten there and was worried it was tied up with Nisha. What in the world was going on? Somebody had to be lying. But who? I was seeing 2 girls – one an honest victim, the other a vicious, scheming liar. But to tell the truth, I had fallen for both of them. I wasn't sure I wanted to find out the truth.

The next day, I found Nisha loafing near the ICSI gate. She looked as surprised to see me as I was to see her! "Hey! Wassup?" I asked casually. "Hi! Nice to see you again!" Nisha said. "So, how's everything going with you? Did you come to meet someone or are you just bunking class?" I asked, smiling and hoping to get a laugh from her.

But she just said, "Follow me," and began to walk away from the college gate towards an abandoned plot of land near the ICSI campus. We walked together in silence for a while. Finally, we stopped when there was no one in sight. Nisha looked distracted and glanced nervously around, before asking me, "Can you keep a secret?" The question clearly wasn't meant to be answered because she replied, "Duh! Of course you can. You could have told Naina about that kiss, but you didn't. Thanks for that." I probably looked as confused as I felt. Nisha promptly clarified, "She told me about your messages last night. That's how I know. Thank you so much for lying about that. I know you probably feel like you're cheating on her...but I honestly didn't mean it as anything but a distraction at the time..." her voice trailed off, leaving the obvious question.

I asked it, "And how do you feel about it now?" She looked at me and as I gazed into her eyes, I was struck by how much she resembled Naina. Then, she gave me that cute little smile and said, "Well, let's just say you're not a bad kisser." Both of us then simultaneously blurted out: "I have feelings for you!" We stared at each other for a moment which seemed like forever. Then we were in each other's arms, kissing each other tenderly. Thankfully (though it doesn't seem obvious now), I have a conscience. I broke the embrace and pushed Nisha away. She looked surprised, then annoyed. "Listen to me...this is wrong. Naina needs us both right now. Once she's okay, we can decide...well, whatever it is. But I'm not going to be a cheating boyfriend," I declared, regretting the words as soon as I said them. Nisha looked offended. Then she replied, "Is that what you think of me? That I'm trying to get you to cheat? I like you, but I don't want to upset Naina either. I'm sorry for that...that outpouring, but I'm human too!"

She wiped away the tears that had gathered at the corners of her eyes. "Hey, I'm sorry. I didn't mean to sound like a jerk. But whatever I do now, I will end up looking like the villain!" I exclaimed. She looked at me as if she could see through me all too clearly. "Anyway, now you know my secret. But Naina cannot find out about this! Like you said, it'll break her heart. The best thing we can do for her right now is just be friends. Cool?" she finally asked. I nodded. I didn't entirely trust myself.

"But there's something else I need your help with. Take a look at this..." her voice trailed off as she pulled out a poster. It read, "Buy 'pot' from the 'crackpot'!" It had a picture of Naina and her phone number. Nisha continued, "These were put up a long time ago, all over the campus. Naina and I thought they were just a mean joke. But then I got to wondering...what if *Naina* was the one who put them up? She never smells of weed, but maybe she sells it on the campus?" I have to admit this theory fit a lot of what I had seen. But I couldn't help wondering if *Nisha* was the one selling the drugs! "Okay. Let's investigate. We need to find someone who Naina has close contact with and who might have weed or smell of it," I replied. Nisha responded, "Great! Let's get started. I'll spread the word on campus and you ask Naina. Simple, right?" Sure. But I had no idea how all this was going to turn out!

I was sitting comfortably in class. We had a class in Signal Processing with Professor Tyagi. He was covering the board with all sorts of equations, none of which made sense to me. The only interesting thing about the class was its ending. As Professor Tyagi wound up, he announced that we would be placed in teams of 2 for a project. The project would involve implementing a technical paper. He had already decided the pairings and would soon allot the project topics. I waited patiently as he read out the list of teams. I was hoping against hope that I would be paired up with Soorya, Amrish, Venugopal or even Dhanush! But I ended up with Romik!

I caught hold of Romik before he could escape to the washroom. "Hey, listen! Can you let me know the topic we get as soon as Professor Tyagi posts it online?" I asked him. He looked as clueless as ever. "Mmmm...what topic?" he asked confusedly. "The topic for the project he wants us to finish in 2 weeks. You and I are in the same team, remember?" I asked. "Oh, yeah! That. Sure, I'll let you know. But you should know about my disease," he said in a very serious voice. "Okay. What is it?" I asked. "See, the thing is I can't stare at a computer screen for too long. It gives me a headache!" he clarified.

If he got a headache looking at computers, why was he studying IT?! "Okay, so what do you want me to do?" I asked, slightly exasperated. "Well, I can help you with the mathematical part of it...and any other hardware stuff. But can you do the coding?" he asked casually. This was the same Romik who couldn't even explain the (rubbish) maths we had used for our C-programming project. All he wanted to avoid was the software implementation of a mathematical paper – which was basically what the project was. "Don't worry. I have a great feeling about this!" he said happily and swaggered off towards the washroom. "Well, I don't..." I muttered to myself, before turning and walking away.

That day, I was eating lunch by myself. I wanted to think about how everything seemed to be going topsy-turvy with Naina and Nisha. I was a big Agatha Christie fan and loved murder mysteries. Okay, okay. So, there was no murder. But this was definitely a mystery. I tried to sort through everything I knew. I had seen a packet of weed under Naina's mattress. But it was Nisha who had discovered it and had insisted I witness the evidence for myself. It was almost as if she was being careful about not contaminating a crime scene. But that was odd in itself. Maybe she didn't want to get her fingerprints on the weed. That made sense. Who'd want to get involved in a drug racket? But she had to have touched it to pull it out and look at it the first time. Clearly, this train of thought led nowhere!

The other problem was Naina herself. She obviously had mental health issues. How much of what she was saying was actually true? By now, I was fairly convinced that she was suffering from schizophrenia. My everyday chats with Nisha and Naina's delusions and hallucinations seemed to confirm this. What was most alarming was her latest symptom – her paranoia about Nisha taking drugs. Had Naina (at some point in time) taken those drugs herself and forgotten all about it? Was she deliberately trying to frame Nisha or did she simply not know who to trust any longer? Who should I believe – Naina or Nisha? Again, it came down to a question of trust.

But the weirdest thing was that Nisha seemed really devoted to Naina. Not only did she seem to want to protect her, but also gave Naina her medicines. According to Nisha, they were roommates. But this was more than simple friendship. My parents were concerned about me spending a night at a friend's place. Only family could deal with my diabetes, they felt. Wait a second! Only family! That's when it struck me, almost like a physical blow. What if Naina and Nisha weren't just roommates? What if they were also *sisters*? They looked alike. But why had neither girl mentioned this to me? It almost seemed like they wanted to keep it a secret...but why?

CHAPTER 45

The rest of the day passed in a blur. I wondered whom I should confront first – Naina or Nisha. I decided to go with Naina. Technically, she was still my girlfriend. Yes, I had lied to her and kissed Nisha twice (once involuntarily!), but I still treasured my relationship with Naina. The thing with Nisha was just...hormones. Of course, that was no excuse. I decided then and there that I would do the right thing for a change. I would tell Naina the truth about Nisha and me. If she left me...well, it was only fair.

But I had my own mystery to solve. Were Naina and Nisha related? And if they were, why did neither of them talk about it? My mind toyed with the idea that Naina had a split personality. Were the personalities so distinct that she wouldn't remember something done by the other personality? If life was a murder mystery, that would definitely be the solution. Should I talk to Nisha about my theory? No! Whatever happened, I was determined not to rely on Nisha. She was a portion of my life that I didn't want to think about right now. Even if I was attracted to her, I would ignore my feelings.

That night, I lay tossing and turning – wondering how to proceed. I knew this conversation was likely to end with Naina slamming the phone down and ending the call. But I wanted to know the answers to a lot of questions before that. I could only figure things out as

Naina's boyfriend. Not as a liar and cheat. Thoughts bounced around my head as I picked up the phone and called Naina.

My call ended up being a bit of an anti-climax. The line was busy. I tried again after half an hour. Still no luck. I checked the time. It was pretty late, but Naina often messaged me at this time of the night. I was just about to nod off, when my phone rang. I was so startled that I nearly dropped the phone in the process! It was Naina – she was finally calling back. I shook off my sleepiness and tried to remember why I had been calling her in the first place. My mind was a little muddled, but I wasn't about to let go of the chance to chat.

"Hey, lame-brain! What's up? I was talking to my brother and parents. That's why I missed your call. Sorry. Hope you weren't falling asleep while waiting?" she exclaimed, not sounding apologetic in the least. I replied, "No, no. Not at all. No worries. How's your family?" I asked lamely. Naina said, before I could continue, "They're fine. My bro's busy with his internship this semester. He's hoping to get placed at Cisco. He wants to stay in Bangalore and work here. But my parents want him to live with them in Chennai. They think he should stay with them till his marriage has been arranged. So, yeah...it's pretty complicated!"

Before I could stop myself, I asked another completely irrelevant question. My question was, "Don't your parents believe in love marriages?" Even Naina seemed a little surprised by the question. "In the middle of the night, you want to chat about whether my parents prefer arranged marriages to love marriages?!" she said laughing. I captured that laugh in my memory forever.

"Hahaha! No. This isn't about your parents. But it does involve your family. Funny, I've told you so much about mine, but we never discuss yours. Why is that I wonder?" I remarked. She responded casually, as if it was no big deal, "What's to discuss? You have so many interesting stories to tell. My parents just aren't that interesting and you probably meet Vijay at the ICSI canteen more often than I do!" She laughed again, but this time the laughter sounded forced. "Ah...but we're missing one very important member, aren't we?" I continued, feeling like a jerk. But I had to know the truth one way or another. "You're starting to freak me out a little bit. Are you also going to make a big joke about my schizophrenia?! Is that what this is all about?" she now cried into the phone. I had to calm her down, "Relax, Naina. I'm not the one who's been hiding the truth. Why didn't you tell me that Nisha is your twin sister?" There was pin-drop silence on the other end of the line.

I was about to continue when I heard Naina's voice again. She sounded completely different. It was the voice of someone who didn't care about anyone or anything in the world. There was a hollow ring to it. It was almost like the voice of someone who had nothing to lose and was still gambling. "So, I guess you're not such a lame-brain after all! Ha!" The words could have been said in jest, but they sounded hard and bitter. It was almost like she had been storing up all this bitterness inside her. Now, she was letting it all out. She continued talking, "Oh, well! I'm sure you have a whole lot of questions to ask. So, fire away!"

I had thought she'd deny it or claim we weren't close enough to tell me about her sister. That was why my first question was – "Why didn't you tell me earlier?" Naina mocked me, saying, "Wow! I let you ask me anything and that's the best you can come up with? How about I give your stupid question an equally stupid answer – I didn't feel like it!" She began to laugh again. But it wasn't her normal, carefree laugh. It sounded like the laugh of someone standing dangerously close to the edge of sanity. "But why not? Were you worried how I would react if I met her?" I continued, wanting a proper answer. "You really are pathetic! You're obviously a total moron. I didn't want you to find out about my secrets, like the schizophrenia. I knew that stupid cow would reveal everything to you!" she screamed and laughed at the same time. I had never seen this side of Naina before. Was this another personality?

"Naina, you need to calm down," I said cautiously. "Calm down?!" she spat the words at me. "What would happen as a result? I'd get your pity and sympathy too? I know exactly how Nisha manipulates people to get what she wants!" "Naina, I wouldn't ever make you feel uncomfortable. I thought we were close enough that you would trust me!" I exclaimed, taken aback by what Naina was saying. She clearly needed therapy, if nothing else. Nisha loved her sister, of that I was sure. But obviously, Naina had some major issues with Nisha. I still couldn't quite bring myself to believe it. If it was an act, it deserved an Oscar.

I continued in my fumbling manner to try and understand the weird relationship between the 2 siblings. "But-but, she gives you your medication every day. If you hate her so much, why do you trust her with something so important?" I wondered aloud. There was a sharp intake of breath on the other side of the phone. "Who told you that? Vijay?" she demanded angrily. Why was she so bothered about a thing like that? "No, actually it was Nisha. She really loves you. Don't you know that?" I asked. Naina was silent for a long time. Then, she suddenly said, "But she doesn't." I wasn't about to let Nisha's name be dragged through the mud over this. "Of course she loves you!" I said. "That's not what I meant, lame-brain!" Naina clarified. For a moment, she was the Naina I loved once more. But then she withdrew back into her shell. "She doesn't give me the medication. I take it myself," Naina finished.

Now, I was thrown again. Why had Nisha lied to me like that? With each answer, I was getting more and more confused! Suddenly, Naina started questioning me: "How did you know we were twins? She told you that, didn't she?" For once, I could answer honestly, "No. She didn't tell me anything. I guessed, and thought you might admit it if I pushed you." I could almost see Naina smile through the phone. "So, not such a lame-brain. But how many times have you met her?" she demanded. Before I could answer the question, she stopped me. "Don't bother answering. You lied, didn't you? You've kissed her, haven't you?" asked Naina as her voice broke. "Yes," I answered simply. "No pathetic excuses? No justifications?" Naina asked. "Would you believe me?" I asked simply. Naina screeched, "I HATE YOU! You're nothing but a lying, scheming ass! You 2 are made for each other! I wish I had never met you in the first place! I wish I was *dead*!"

That night, I couldn't sleep. I could still remember Naina's last sentence – "I wish I was *dead*!" I had a nasty feeling that she had meant what she said. I messaged Nisha, telling her to make sure that Naina was okay. I told her the gist of what had happened between Naina and me. I warned her that Naina might try to do something foolish tonight. At some point in time, I must have fallen asleep. The next thing I knew, sunlight was filtering in through my window. I quickly checked my phone. Nisha had replied in the middle of the night. The message just read: "Will look after her."

I began to get ready for the day ahead. I felt like I had failed the most basic of tests. The test of being a good person. I knew that if anything happened to Naina, I'd never forgive myself. Even my mom seemed to have picked up on my mood. While I ate breakfast, she sat at the table beside me. Normally, she'd be in the kitchen, making breakfast for my dad. I was so surprised that I asked her, "Ma, are you feeling okay?" She smiled at me, stroked my hand and said, "You tell me, baby. Is it girl trouble?" she asked, almost as if she were psychic. I must have been looking at her in awe because she continued with a smile, "I wasn't born yesterday. Plus, I might look like a dinosaur, but I was once young too, you know!"

I have to admit, I had never had such a free and frank conversation with my mom before. "Is it to do with that girl we met outside the movie hall? What's her name...? Anushka?" my mom asked. I nodded dumbly. She held my hand in hers and squeezed it gently. Then she said, "Pranav, look at me..." I gazed into her deep brown eyes. "Did she break your heart?" my mom asked. I gave a ghost of a smile and said, "No, Ma. It's much worse. I broke hers..." My voice choked up and I fought hard to hold back the tears.

"Oh, baby...come here and tell me everything," she whispered softly, embracing me. My tears splashed onto my mom's clothes. I was so tempted to admit everything – starting from the fact that Anushka was actually Naina. But I wasn't sure I'd get the same sympathy if my mom found out that I'd lied to her. However, I told her the relevant details. "We were a couple. But then I kissed her sister twice behind her back and I lied to Anushka. I told her everything last night...and she said she wished she was dead. If anything happens to her, I'll never forgive myself!" I concluded my speech.

My mom looked at me sympathetically. Then she asked, "Do you still love her?" I examined my innermost feelings before replying, "Yes." My mom carried on, "Then tell her that. Whether or not she takes you back is another story. But you'll know that you've done the right thing in trying to correct a mistake. Most importantly, forgive yourself. You can't control everything. So don't try, okay?" I nodded, worried that if I tried to speak, I'd start sobbing. "Good. Now, go and get ready for college. I still have to give your father his breakfast!" said the mom I knew and loved.

CHAPTER 46

As I sat in class, I daydreamed about Naina. At the edge of my vision, I could see different alternate realities. Each of them involved Naina killing herself in more and more creative ways. Precisely at that time, I thought of the old proverb – "If you love something, set it free. If it comes back, it's yours. If it doesn't, it never was." If my love for Naina ended up poisoning her life, I ought to ignore my feelings and let her go. On the other hand, if she was willing to take me back, I would never so much as look at another girl. This I promised myself.

Unfortunately, classrooms are not the best places to make resolutions and discover philosophical truths! Our first class was Economics. Professor Gopal split the class into 2 groups and organised a debate about whether or not Adam Smith's theories were valid in today's world. I was supposed to defend Adam Smith. Since there wasn't time for everyone to speak, 2 main speakers were supposed to give the opening arguments for each side. After that, the 2 sides would question each other. Most of my teammates wanted me to give the opening speech, but I refused. So, we ended up sending Amrish and Venugopal. As you can imagine, it was a disaster! My team ended up losing, since Preetish was on the other side and had obviously been chosen to speak.

The next class was even worse. We had Differential Equations with Professor Mukherjee. It wasn't long before I dozed off – not once, but twice! “My friend, Pranav, seems to have been up all night studying,” joked Professor Mukherjee. “Or maybe he was with his girlfriend!” I winced a little at that. “Maybe, for the sake of my friend, we’ll stop here today and break for lunch now!” Professor Mukherjee declared. Everyone cheered as he left the class. They all slapped me on the back and thanked me. That’s when Romik caught me.

“Hey, I found out about our project topic. We’re supposed to take a fisheye camera and map the image to rectangular coordinates,” he said like a puppy who had brought his master a ball to play with. “Huh?” was about all I could manage. “A fisheye camera, dude. Like the type they use in CCTV,” he said as if that explained everything. I tried to remember what Professor Tyagi had taught us. Oh, yeah! Now I remembered what a fisheye camera was. It had a bulging sort of lens. The lens bulged outwards looking like a fish’s eye. The advantage was it gave a wider angle of view. The problem was that the image from such a lens looked distorted. Our project involved figuring out how to get a proper image from a fisheye camera.

“So, do you have the camera? Will you please set it up?” I asked hopefully. “Mmmm...I got the camera, but there’s a problem,” he replied. “What now?” I asked in a dejected voice. “Actually, I have a cold. So, I was hoping you’d take the camera from me and set it up by yourself. I’ll help once I’m better,” said Romik. Just then, my phone pinged. It was a message from *Naina*! It just read, “Meet me at your college gate.” I was about to run off, when I remembered Romik. “Okay. I’ll take care of it,” I told him.

I reached the college gate, not knowing what to expect. Suddenly, I stopped in my tracks. I had just seen a vision of breathtaking beauty. It was Naina. She looked exactly the way she had the day we first met. She was tapping her foot impatiently. She was dressed in the same clothes. That's when she saw me. I looked into her eyes trying to guess what lay behind them. But her face was a mask. She nodded, as I stepped out to meet her.

I nodded back, trying to keep a neutral expression on my face. But I couldn't help rewinding to the day we met – "So, are you waiting for someone or do you just like tapping your foot?" She smiled at that, but the smile didn't reach her eyes. "Nice to see you too, lame-brain," she replied. "I just—" I began, while Naina said, "I wanted—". Both of us laughed nervously. Then Naina said, "You go first." I took a deep breath and began, "I broke your heart and betrayed you. There is no excuse for what I've done. I know I hurt you and I'm sorry. I want you to know that I truly, deeply love you..." my voice cracked with emotion and I felt a tear trace itself down my cheek. "...and if you take me back, I will never betray you again. I promise."

She gave me an odd look after I finished my speech. Then, she started laughing and this time, the laugh lit up her whole face. "Stupid, stupid lame-brain! Why didn't you just tell me the truth?! Nisha told me about how she kissed you both times...but you didn't kiss her back. She even told me how she admitted she liked you, but you said you only wanted me as your girlfriend!" Naina said happily. I felt a little surprised. Why had Nisha made herself the villain? I had kissed her back the second time. Plus, she didn't seem to have mentioned my feelings for her. But as Naina pulled my head down to kiss me and her tears fell on my shoulders, I didn't care. I kissed her back with passion. All was right with the universe!

That night, I was surprised to get a WhatsApp message from *Nisha*! It just read, "Call me." Seemed innocent enough, right? But I still hesitated. Was this some sort of final test Naina had set for me or was Nisha angry with me for telling Naina the truth? Whatever it was, I didn't really want to hear it.

In that instant, I realised that I didn't really know either of the sisters. Nisha had sacrificed her bond with her sister to save my relationship with Naina. But if I ignored her, she could easily tell Naina the truth. It would be Nisha's word against mine and I wasn't entirely sure whom Naina would believe.

Heaving a sigh, I called her. After half a second, she answered. "Hey. You wanted to talk—" I began. But she stopped me. In a voice choked with emotion, she blurted out, "I'd do anything for you. I love you so much..." Then, she began sobbing. I wasn't sure what to say. In a teary tone, she continued, "I lied to *her* to make you happy. I'll keep our secret forever. But I want to warn you...she's pure evil!" With that, the line went silent. I was confused and a little scared. It felt as if a shadow had fallen over my perfect day...

CHAPTER 47

The Tigress had waited for the tumultuous events of the last few days to settle. Now, it was time to strike again! She knew that what she was planning to do might be regarded as wrong. But she was only protecting herself. She had hoped for more of a reaction from her target. But she wasn't entirely disappointed. She had planted a seed of doubt in his mind. In time, that seed would bear fruit. Till that day, however, she needed to be regarded as innocent. She had taken a gamble and it seemed to have paid off. But she wanted to get rid of all the evidence, so that her brother or someone in authority couldn't stop her.

She checked her watch. He was late. Of course, he *had* been through a lot lately. College authorities had talked of suspending and even expelling him. She supposed it was his fault. Though she had hoped for and ensured strict disciplinary action against him, she also felt sorry for him in a weird way. That was the way she was made. She was a mixture of opposites. She hid behind a pillar as guards passed by. She knew few students ventured this side of the campus so late in the evening. This shady corner of her college was supposed to be haunted. Apparently, a construction worker had been buried here and a garage had been built over his grave. Most of the nearby parking lots were empty. That made this the perfect spot to meet.

Just then, she heard a noise behind her and spun around. It was him. He had arrived at last. "What took you so long?" she whispered angrily. He approached her warily. Before the incident, he had always been very careful about how he looked. Not anymore. She had cut him down to size. "What do *you* want?" he demanded.

"I'm here to get you out of this mess," she hissed at him. He was obviously surprised. He had probably come to meet her out of curiosity. Nevertheless, wisely, he didn't trust her. He looked suspiciously at her. "You know who got me into this mess in the first place! Why would you want to help me?" She replied coolly, "I didn't know at the time how badly you'd be affected. Honest. Besides you're a big boy...I figured you could handle yourself." He persisted, "What's your real motive?" She sighed and then laughed, "Let's just say I need a favour. You do this and I'll start dating you. How does that sound?" He stared at her in surprise, then said, "Let me think about it."

***

She explained the plan to him. It was pretty simple. He had taken the packet from her. Now, he just had to present it to the college authorities. It was crucial that she got him to trust her. It was only natural for him to be suspicious of her motives. But she hadn't expected this much resistance. "All I have is your word...and I don't exactly trust that!" he had muttered rebelliously, when she broached the plan. She tried to stay cool. "You also have my heart..." she whispered seductively in his ear. "Fine, but I want to hear you say it out loud. Look me in the eye and promise that you'll help me out," he insisted. She sighed inwardly. Then she went through the entire plan with him again. She was a little surprised to see how smug he looked after that.

That's when it hit her. She cursed herself for being so stupid. He must have recorded her making the promise! Sure enough, he produced his phone and replayed everything she had just said. "A little insurance...in case you decide to ditch me!" he exclaimed and walked away, holding the packet. This was always the problem – some people thought that they could get away with double-crossing or blackmailing her. Till now, the Tigress had kept her claws hidden. Now, it was time to bring them out. She needed that phone. She had to destroy it. At first, she thought of resorting to violence. But there were more subtle and effective methods. She put a smile on her face.

"Hey, stranger! Don't leave me here alone..." she drawled. He spun around and looked at her surprised. "Since I made you a promise and gave you what you wanted, you owe me, right?" she asked, walking slowly over to him and pushing herself against him. "I guess..." he laughed nervously. She had trapped him. "So, you have to give me what I want, right? And I want...you!" she said, blowing gently into his ear to tickle him. "But you can't enter the boys' hostel," he protested. "I know a place. Just follow me. They rent rooms by the hour. Let's have some fun..." she replied.

They left via the back gate and walked south for a few kilometres. There were a bunch of buildings crowded together. One of them was a sleazy-looking hotel. She led him inside and to her usual room. She undressed slowly, as his eyes widened in awe. Then she began to undress him. They made love for a long time. She had forgotten how nice it was to have a body beside her. As he dozed, she slipped out of bed and began to dress herself. She held up his jeans and slipped the phone out of his pocket. His phone was the same colour and model as the one she had. Luck was on her side. She swapped the 2 phones. She put on her jeans and left his in a crumpled heap on the floor. Then she shook him awake. He reluctantly got out of bed and pulled on his own jeans. He slipped a hand into his pocket, half took out the planted phone and slipped it back in, satisfied. As they got ready to leave, she smiled inwardly, knowing she had struck again!

CHAPTER 48

It had been nearly a week since Naina had taken me back. During that time, we had messaged each other late into the nights. I had been afraid that Naina would blame me for her strained relationship with Nisha. Surprisingly, though, she had acted like nothing had happened between us. Now, we talked to each other about pretty much everything in our lives. The only topic that was off-limits was Nisha. I kept telling myself that Nisha was just mean and a bit of a drama queen. But her words still haunted me. Why had she described her sister as "pure evil"? Such words belonged in an Agatha Christie novel. Who spoke like that in today's day and age? Anyway, I ignored what Nisha had said.

In the meantime, college went on. My marks were beginning to drop, but I didn't really care. To quote Professor Rajendra, I was "doing better"! During class, I felt so sleepy that I survived on tons of coffee. I was up all night messaging Naina – with barely enough time to complete assignments and stay up-to-date with the weekly tests. My mom had started making dangerous noises. But frankly, I didn't care. As long as I had Naina, my happiness was complete.

As regards Naina, she had had 2 more panic attacks. But both of these times, she later remembered everything about the incidents – which was a significant improvement. She told me she had decreased her dose of antipsychotics. I didn't think it was a good idea...but, then again, when am I right about anything? One thing was certain, though. She was definitely more alive and alert. When she was on a higher dose of medication, she sometimes seemed a little sleepy. Everything on the horizon seemed perfect. There was only one problem that I hadn't even tried to solve – Professor Tyagi's project!

I had tried a few days ago to get Romik to help out. I had reminded him of how he'd promised to help with the hardware part. So far, his only contribution had been to take the camera from Professor Tyagi and give it to me. The paper we were implementing had suggested taking a picture of a black chart paper (against a white background) and mapping the corners from a photo with the fisheye camera to the regular camera's photo. We were then supposed to take a random photo with the fisheye camera and make it look as normal as possible, while preserving the details.

"I'd love to help, but I have a soccer tournament tomorrow. It's a college thing. Why don't you take the photos and I'll tell you later whether they're okay or not?" He made it sound like he was going out of his way to help me! He was the one who had promised to set the camera up – I was the one doing him a favour by trying to understand the paper all by myself! Still, I couldn't stay mad at him. When he said "college thing", I assumed it was an inter-college tournament. I wanted him to stay in shape for it. So, I agreed.

The next day, I was sitting next to Amrish at lunch. I asked him if he was going to watch the tournament. He asked me, "What tournament?" I told him what Romik had told me. He started laughing. "*Macha*, I can't believe you fell for such a stupid trick. These are football matches organised by the Student Council. The teams are made up of ICSI students only. It's called Sports Week. Every day, a different sport gets played. Most people don't attend!" The last bit I could believe! I swore to myself Romik was going to pay.

The very next day, I caught hold of Romik after classes were over. "You told me you had a tournament! That it was 'a college thing'! It's just some random matches within ICSI!" I exclaimed, poking a finger into his chest. I was annoyed and I wanted him to know it. He didn't seem bothered in the least. He just nodded and said, "Well, yeah. This time it was intra-college. But you have to stay in shape for inter-college matches, you know." No, I did not know. The only thing I knew for sure was that I was not doing his work for him any longer.

But curiosity got the better of me. "So, how did your team do?" I asked, despite my irritation. "We didn't do too badly. We didn't win, but we put up a decent fight," he replied coolly. Okay, I guess I was a little impressed. I assumed they had lost in the finals. But second place was still impressive. "So, you guys were second in the league table?" I asked, a little in awe of him. "Mmmm...not exactly...we actually came last..." his voice trailed off. At first, I thought he was kidding. "No, seriously. How did you do?" I asked smiling. "Well, we lost the first match 10-0, so we ended up last. But losing is a part of learning," he said like he was some new-age *guru*.

I had had it with Romik and his philosophical *gyaan* (knowledge). I don't know whether he thought he was a cross between Cristiano Ronaldo and Baba Ramdev, but he had pushed my patience to its limits. He was still talking, but I was through listening. "Shut up!" I snapped at him. For once, he actually did what I told him to do and stopped talking. I went on, "I want you to implement the mapping part of the paper, in code, by tomorrow! I don't want any complaints or excuses, understood?" He nodded meekly and I left him to his work.

The next day, I skipped breakfast at home and arrived early to see how Romik had progressed. I felt a bit bad for having yelled at him the previous day. I told myself I'd apologise and we'd collaborate properly from here on out. I entered Romik's hostel room (which wasn't locked) and saw a couple of his notebooks lying around... but no sign of Romik. While wondering where he could be, I flipped through some of his notes. I was amazed! He had incredibly neat handwriting. Not only that, he had written down every word the professors had said. It was seriously incredible! If only I could get my hands on these notes, I could bunk class and spend more time with Naina.

Just as these thoughts occurred to me, Romik entered, carrying his laptop. He was grinning at me. I was glad he wasn't mad at me. "Hey, man. Sorry about yesterday—" I began, but he cut me off. "Don't worry, bro. I've pretty much solved the problem. Just some final tweaking is needed." I was thrilled. My yelling had paid off!

That was when he turned the laptop screen around and showed me the photos. He had done more than I expected. Not only had he done the corner matching for the black on white, he had also tried to apply the transformation on a random photo. The issue was what had happened because of his efforts. It looked like a caricature of the college gate. The fisheye photo was naturally distorted, but the so-called 'straight one' looked like something in a fun-house mirror. It was *way* more distorted than the fisheye photo. On top of everything else, his 'corrected' photo had a giant diagonal black stripe across it.

I remembered something Professor Tyagi had once told us about image processing. He had said that there were no right or wrong photos. There were just photos that looked good and photos that looked bad. Finally, Romik asked, "Well, what do you think?" I could only come up with, "Dude, I think you just invented the concept of a 'wrong' photo!" He pouted a little. Then he said, "Like I said, it needs some tweaking. But the overall idea is solid..." I cut him off. "Dude, forget it. I'll tell you what. I'll finish this project if you let me borrow your notes and study them. You attend every class and jot down every word said. Do we have a deal?"

Romik was so surprised that he just stood there, stunned. That was when my phone rang. I checked the caller ID. It was Naina! I answered immediately. "Lame-brain, come to my college *right now*!" she panted, then cut the line. I pushed past Romik and raced towards Naina.

CHAPTER 49

Well, perhaps 'raced' was an exaggeration. I huffed and puffed to the ICSI main gate. Then I bent over double in desperate need of oxygen. After that, I managed a brisk walk towards Synergy College's main gate. My brisk walk had reduced to a casual stroll by the time I reached. Don't get me wrong. I was very anxious about Naina. But my body didn't seem to appreciate the need for urgency. My mind had a little Romik in it, telling me to stay in shape and take part in football tournaments. Thankfully, I was able to ignore it (much like the real Romik!).

While I waited for the guard to open the Synergy gate, my mind was racing. What could have been the source of such urgency in Naina's voice? My first concern was that she was getting a panic attack. But usually she didn't call me at such times. The last couple of times Naina had had such attacks, she had madly run around her campus without telling anyone. She had run till the panic subsided. Of course, it was possible that this attack was worse than the previous episodes and that she needed help.

Yet, somehow, my mind told me there was something different going on. Her voice hadn't sounded haunted or hunted by her usual delusions. She hadn't sounded scared. She sounded like she had run a long way. I went over her exact words and intonation again. Yeah, she wasn't scared. She didn't sound worried, just tired. Anyway, I was getting nowhere thinking about it. I had to meet Naina.

That's when I saw her. Her back was to me. I called out to her. She spun around to face me. And then she did the strangest thing – she smiled. "See? Notice anything peculiar?" she asked. Maybe I was meant to see someone in purple. But from her carefree smile...I took a gamble and said, "No. Not really. Everything is peaceful." She nodded as if I had proved her point. "This just proves that there weren't people following me. A bunch of really mean students were mocking me. Now, hurry up!" she said, racing ahead.

I followed in a slow, breathless fashion. She finally stopped in front of the main administrative building. "So, are you going to tell me why you had me come puffing and panting all the way here?" I asked in mock irritation. She turned to me, smiling mischievously. "There's still one person missing. Only when she arrives will you and I learn the truth!" she promised. When who arrived? Was this a weird game?

That's when I saw Nisha walk out of the building. My first thought was that Nisha had told Naina the truth about us. Despite that, Naina was happy because she had found a new boyfriend. However, I couldn't quite bring myself to believe that Nisha had broken her promise to me. Naina looked towards Nisha as she approached. She said nothing till Nisha was standing next to us. Then, the sisters hugged.

They hugged for what must have been about 30 seconds. But it felt like forever! I don't know if you've ever had to stand next to 2 people sharing a tender moment...

and wondered whether it would be rude to remind them of your existence! After a while, I cleared my throat. No effect. I coughed a little loudly. Still no effect. Finally, I ran out of patience. "Will somebody please tell me what is going on here?" I asked. Both sisters turned to face me. They had huge grins on their faces. Naina reached up and ruffled my hair. It was such a sudden, spontaneous gesture that I actually wondered for a few seconds if Naina was seeing me or a dog! It was so unlike her. But everything seemed different today.

"Don't worry, lame-brain. We'll explain everything... over breakfast," she laughed as my stomach gurgled. "Hey, aren't you curious about how that packet of weed ended up under my mattress, but neither of us smelled of weed, ever?" Naina asked. "Well, today you'll find out the answer. We are both innocent...now, hurry up, or the food will get cold!" exclaimed Nisha. Both sisters walked hand-in-hand towards the canteen with not a care in the world.

Once everyone had eaten enough, we picked up our coffees and sat down at a relatively empty spot in the canteen. "See...I told you that someone was trying to set me up!" Naina told Nisha. Nisha grinned and threw up her hands in surrender. "Hey, you have to admit you were suspicious of me too! Can you blame me for being suspicious of you? I just wanted you to be safe, sis," Nisha replied. Okay, now I was officially lost. Nisha had called Naina "pure evil", yet here they were now – both acting like proper sisters. Naina said, "I guess everything was a prank by some weirdo or the other. It sure is a relief to know I'm not nuts!" She sounded so convincing that even I practically forgot about her 2 recent panic attacks. What did she mean by "prank"?

Okay, I'd been patient enough. Now, I deserved some answers. "Um...do you girls plan on filling in the blanks for me at some point in time?" I asked at last. Again, both of them laughed. But then they grew serious. "Why don't you tell him?" suggested Nisha. Naina then opened up, "Well, after you and I made up, I confronted Nisha with the packet and demanded to know how it had gotten under my mattress. Nisha claimed she had nothing to do with it. At first, both of us suspected each other of being an addict or a dealer. Then we realised, we were being unnecessarily suspicious. After all, we're twins and we've known each other our whole lives." Naina paused for breath.

Nisha immediately took over. "Anyway, we put our heads together and made a list of people who might be trying to frame us or play some kind of prank on us." I guessed the twins had been through hell before they had come together as a team. They must have really hated each other's guts to say such nasty things about the other to me. I still had trouble believing that all that pent-up frustration and anger had been replaced by a spirit of camaraderie and cooperation. But, hey, who was I to make trouble?

"So, what then?" I asked. Naina picked up the narrative again, "It was pretty obvious that whoever was behind the prank wanted to frame me. Then we drew up a list of people who hated me. Trust me, that took a *long* time!" Again, I was surprised by how calmly Naina could now talk about this. Earlier, she'd have felt bad due to her lack of friends.

Nisha stepped in again. "On top of the list was the same ass Naina had kissed and told you about – Ram!"

Whoa! I hadn't seen that one coming! Nisha continued with the story, "He had been nearly suspended for bruising Naina. She had smelled weed on him the night he had hurt her. Plus, Naina's phone had been stolen. So, we convinced the college authorities to search his room. No guesses for what they found! A whole stash of weed and Naina's phone – the one that had gone missing!" exclaimed Nisha, beaming widely. So...it had been Ram all along. I should have guessed from the start. For the first time that morning, I smiled. It felt like a shadow had lifted. Looked like it was going to be a beautiful day!

CHAPTER 50

It had been 5 days since the 'Ram incident'. Naina had seemed far happier in these 5 days than she had in all the time I had known her. We had been messaging each other regularly at night. We had also started seriously dating during the day and happily bunking classes. For once, I wasn't worried that I would fall behind if I bunked too many classes. I knew that I would have a word-perfect recording of everything said, thanks to Romik and his notes! Life seemed pretty much perfect. Of course, it was too good to last. I had been running out of time to finish Professor Tyagi's project. So, I did what I always do when I find myself stuck – I went to Amrish and Soorya.

Thankfully, the horrible maths was easy for Soorya to understand. As for Amrish, he pretty much coded the whole thing by himself. But then again, that's what friends are for – exploitation! With their help, I managed to implement the project. Now, my only problem was explaining it all to Romik! If you're feeling sorry for Soorya and Amrish, let me stop you right there. They had it easy, compared to what I had to go through! It was honestly a nightmare to explain anything to Romik. For one thing, he kept stopping me midway through my speech and saying, "No, no, no, no!" (Disclaimer: I'm not entirely sure about the number of "no's".) He would then add, "Explain to me why we need to do this." It would eventually boil down to me snapping at him and saying something like "So that we'll get a good grade for the assignment!"

That's when really bad news arrived. Professor Rajendra announced an assignment – and gave us *one day* to finish it! He spent the class giving us details of the assignment. I was worried about Professor Tyagi's presentation in 2 days. Now, I had another assignment on top of that!

I convinced Soorya, Amrish, Venugopal, Sachin, Romik and Preetish to form a delegation and come with me to beg Professor Rajendra for an extension. Professor Rajendra was unreliable. Sometimes, he would load us with work. Other times, he would bunk class, while everyone else showed up. So, we weren't sure how he would react. Thankfully, they all agreed to accompany me. Now, all I could do was hope for the best.

It was 6 o'clock by the time we finished our classes, got together and visited Professor Rajendra's office. Unlike a lot of other faculty members, he lived on campus. As a result, he could normally be found in his office till 7 o'clock or later. There we were in our jeans, torn T-shirts and *chappals* (slippers). Amrish had accidentally broken one of the arms of his chair a while ago. So, he was carrying a black metal rod with him. He was swinging it around like a weapon. He seemed like a local gang member. The pack of us looked more like a bunch of *goondas* (hooligans) than a delegation of earnest students with an honest request. We had agreed earlier that Amrish and I would do most of the talking. If Professor Rajendra got into the details of the project, Soorya would take over. Under no circumstances were Sachin, Romik and Preetish to open their mouths. I just hoped he'd be like Professor Kumar and let us get away with postponing the assignment.

In any case, this time we had a valid reason! We had to finish our presentations for Professor Tyagi and that deadline was only 2 days away. Although Soorya had grumbled that he could manage both, yet we had persuaded him (with a little help from Amrish's chair handle) that he had better join our cause. My greatest fear was that Professor Rajendra would send us off by claiming we should have "done better" by coming to see him earlier. By now, we had reached the office. We could see Professor Rajendra sitting in his swivel chair with his eyes closed and his hands behind his head. I hoped he wasn't sleeping.

We knocked on the door and entered. Professor Rajendra opened his eyes. "Hey guys. What's up?" he asked before we had a chance to say anything. I think both Amrish and I hesitated a second too long. We should have come to the point directly. Professor Rajendra would probably have preferred that. Instead, before anyone with any sense could say anything, I said the first thing that came into my head: "Were you sleeping, Sir?" Professor Rajendra smiled like a Tamil movie villain and said, "Did you guys all show up at 6 p.m. just to ask me if I'm sleeping? I thought you would be hard at work on the assignment. Clearly, I didn't give all of you enough credit. I'm guessing you all finished it?"

This was the perfect opening. I should have corrected my mistake and asked him about an extension. But Amrish butted in. Before I could open my mouth, Amrish said, "We thought we'd ask you if we could 'do better'?" Amrish grinned at Professor Rajendra, who looked serious. I thought we were going to be turned away. I was afraid we had offended Professor Rajendra by using his own catchphrase against him. But Professor Rajendra just asked coolly, "What did you have in mind?" This time I piped up, "Friendly persuasion, Sir?" hoping to lighten the mood. Unfortunately, Amrish chose that very moment to smack the iron rod against his palm. I should have known better than to let Amrish carry the rod with him!

There was a moment of intense tension in the room. Then Professor Rajendra asked in an angry voice, "Are you threatening an ICSI professor?" To my horror, Amrish (still grinning, like it was all a big joke) replied, "Yes, Sir!" I was ready for screaming and shouting. But all Professor Rajendra did was lift up the intercom and say, "Security..." For an awful moment, I thought he was serious. Then, he burst out laughing. All of us broke into nervous laughter at the same time. Professor Rajendra kept laughing for a long time. He finally stopped and said, "I've seen the movie *3 Idiots*, but this is the first time I am seeing 7 of them in my office!" I had to admit that was a pretty good joke. All of us laughed at ourselves for a while.

Finally, Professor Rajendra asked, "So, I guess you guys want a deadline extension for the assignment? Fine. You 7 get an extra week. But the rest of the class has the earlier deadline. I'm happy to see that at least a few of you are doing better!"

Today was the make-or-break day. It was time for us to present our projects to Professor Tyagi. I still hadn't taken Romik through the entire paper. I had covered the basic problem statement with him. I had also discussed the results obtained in the paper and our results. Then he had waved me off, as though I was keeping him from important things (like sleep and football!). So, I was really stressed about the whole thing. To top it all, Professor Tyagi had decided that we would be the first team to present.

Anyway, I had a big speech prepared in my head. But as I stood in front of the class...I froze (yes, again!). Thankfully, Romik seemed to be right in his element. He connected his laptop to the projector and began talking. "So, our problem basically involved..." I stared at him, mildly panicking. He knew nothing! What on earth was he going to say? But that was when I realised his remarkable gift. He could sound very convincing and read very well. He basically read out what was written on the slides. But he said it in a slightly different way. He demonstrated how our code ran in real-time. So, he took a picture of the class with the fisheye camera and showed the corresponding straightened-out image. Some people actually clapped!

Then, being a showman, he handed the rest of the paper over to me. He said, "Just so that Professor Tyagi doesn't think I did all the work, why don't you talk about the rest of the paper?" I went through a bunch of horrible equations and explained everything. Nobody even bothered to look interested in what I was saying. At the end of our joint presentation, Professor Tyagi clapped long and hard. Then he said, "I'm really impressed with your work, Romik. Oh...and Pranav too, of course! I heard you guys did a project last semester on reinforcement learning. Could you tell me a little about that? I'm interested." That was what I needed. "Oh, Romik did most of the work, Sir. He'd best talk about it!" So saying, I headed off to lunch, having got my revenge!

CHAPTER 51

About a week had passed since our demonstration for Professor Tyagi. Most of that time had been spent in Naina's company. She and I had spent hours roaming around each other's campuses. It was an incredible time for us (well, at least for me!) and every day seemed to bring more joy. But it couldn't last forever. Looking back now, I wonder if things would have turned out differently had I acted some other way or said some other things. But then, I think not. Sometimes, our destiny is predetermined.

My grades weren't slipping anymore, thanks to Romik's notes. I don't think he ever fully forgave me for his humiliation at the end of our presentation for Professor Tyagi. The quality of his notes went down, but he still stuck to his end of the bargain and I managed to submit all the assignments on time and not fail any test. That's when Electronics returned!

I had bunked most of our Electronics classes this semester. The only reason Professor Scindia hadn't hauled me up was because he didn't care much about attendance. What *really* bothered him was copying (or in his fancy language, "plagiarism"). That was one thing I wasn't worried about. Sure, I would keep Soorya or Venugopal up all night to explain things to me. But I wasn't stupid enough to blindly copy something which I hadn't written.

Anyway, Professor Scindia announced one morning that he wanted us to write a report in "IEEE format with all references" for the experiment we needed to perform the next day. How I came to hate that horrible IEEE format! It was like writing a scientific paper! That is something I hope to avoid for the rest of my life. And the worst part was the References section. We had to put a scientific paper (*not* Wikipedia) as the source of virtually every word in our report. Even if it was something we had thought of by ourselves, we still had to check all of human knowledge to make sure no one had ever said something vaguely similar.

The experiment was difficult to perform. But with the help of Ramesh, I managed to get decent results. I spent the next 3-4 days putting the final touches to my report. By the time I finished typing it on my desktop at home, it was a masterpiece. Well, clearly, I'm the only one saying so, but I had spent more time on this report than I had on the rest of this course. I submitted the report 2 days early and forgot about it. But my troubles were just beginning.

Before I continue, I should explain what was going on in Amrish's life. The momentous event was that he had found a girlfriend. Yes, I know. It was hard for me to believe too. The girl's name was Sudeshna. She was the best-looking girl in our batch. Like me, she too was Bengali. We had chatted a few times, but I was too taken with Naina to pay her much attention. Sudeshna was slim and very pretty. She had grown fond of Amrish, despite his eccentricities. They made a cute couple. I was happy for my friend. Strangely, it was Sudeshna who had first asked him out, while he was busy playing video games! They were a match made in ICSI.

Now, after that (not so) brief intermission, back to our story. The Amrish who was dating Sudeshna was a very different person from the one whom I had known at school. He was lagging so far behind in some subjects that he even asked *me* for help! I helped him however much I could (which really wasn't all that much!). I was concerned that if this carried on for much longer, Amrish would get into serious trouble. As a matter of fact, he had tried to copy Soorya's answers in a quiz, got caught and flunked it.

One day, things came to a head. "Hey *macha*!" he exclaimed, spotting me at the water-cooler the day after I had submitted my report. "Can you please mail me your report? I'll go through it and then write mine," he continued. I was about to say, "Of course!" But then I looked at him carefully. Call it being psychic, but I just knew it was a bad idea. "Um...no, sorry," I muttered. "Are you seriously saying no to me? After all the years we've been friends?" he demanded. He turned and walked away, leaving me wondering if I had lost my best friend for no good reason.

CHAPTER 52

A few days after Amrish walked off in a huff, Naina and I were lounging on one of the benches scattered around the ICSI campus. We had Vijay's laptop (since I didn't have one of my own) and I was showing Naina my masterpiece of a report. Yeah, you're probably thinking this was the most unromantic thing ever. But the whole thing was actually Naina's idea. I had been whining to Naina about the irritating task of writing a report for days on end. She had been as supportive as ever. "Hahaha! I love it when you feel like complaining about your life. Puts my problems in perspective!" she had messaged me. Of course, I had felt guilty immediately and thought she was being serious. I had replied, "Oh my gosh! I'm so sorry. I didn't mean to offend you. Just ignore my whining." She had responded, "Oh, lame-brain! Are you still so gullible? I was just kidding. Don't take me so seriously. Now tell me, do you need Vijay's help? I'll tell him to help you out if you want."

I hadn't actually needed help to finish the report. I had thanked Naina for the offer, but politely refused. I guess I wanted to prove that I was capable of looking after my own business. Maybe it was my ego talking. After all, I wasn't exactly top of the class this semester, but I still wanted to do the things I could on my own steam. At least, that's what I told myself.

Anyway, after I had finally submitted the report, I had messaged Naina saying, "Over at last! I have to say, even I'm impressed with the result! If only you could see it." Naina had replied, "Don't you have a laptop or something?" I had to admit I was a little surprised. "No, I don't. But why do you want to know?" She had instantly messaged, "I figured you could show me your report. I'd love to see it." I had asked, "Why are you suddenly so interested in this paper?" In response to my question, she had replied, "Well, it's a paper that broke a long-standing friendship. I just want to see what you didn't want to show Amrish."

I had responded to Naina's curiosity by saying I had typed it on my desktop back home. So, unless she could come over, she couldn't see it. The alternative had been for me to show her the report on my phone, but she had insisted that she wanted a big screen. She had said, "You must have a copy saved in your outbox; the one you sent to your professor. I can come over to ICSI, borrow Vijay's laptop and then you show me the paper from your email. Okay?" She was clearly determined to see the paper. So I had agreed. That's how I had ended up on a bench with my girlfriend, going through a boring report which she seemed to love.

Just then, Nisha showed up. "Sorry to bother you 2 love-birds, but Naina has a quiz now!" she said by way of greeting. Naina quickly said goodbye and hurried off with the laptop. It didn't occur to me till much later that night to check if she'd signed out of my account before returning the laptop to Vijay. When I messaged her, she said she hadn't returned it yet, but had signed out of my account. I checked my inbox that night. Everything seemed normal. I fell asleep, not knowing that my whole world was about to be turned upside-down...

***

The next day, I checked my mail on my phone during the ride to college. I was taken aback to see a mail from Professor Scindia sent late last night. He had told us he would be heading back to his hometown for a few days due to a family crisis. So, I was more than a little surprised to see a mail from him in my inbox. Maybe he was happy to see that I had submitted the report early.

His mail to me had 2 attachments. One was my report. The other was Amrish's. And the weird part was... they were identical. Professor Scindia's mail read, "I've excused your absences this semester. I have overlooked the decline in the quality of your assignments. But as I've said in class multiple times, the one thing I will not tolerate is plagiarism. I don't care who copied from whom. All I want to know is how Amrish and you thought that you could get away with this! I will return in 5 days. When I'm back, I will call you both before the ICSI Board for a disciplinary meeting. I'm sure you understand that this means both of you may be expelled. I hope you have a story explaining how this was all a great big misunderstanding. Don't worry, you'll get a chance to tell your story. But just remember, make it good. You have 5 days to prepare."

My first reaction on seeing the mail wasn't fear of being pulled up and possibly even expelled. I just wanted to know how Amrish had got hold of my report. I had said no to him every time he asked, even at the cost of our friendship! Yet someone had clearly sent him the report. But I had only ever worked on it at home. And Amrish hadn't come over in ages. The only other way he could have got it was from my mail. No sooner had the thought occurred to me, than I checked my outbox. There, at the very top, was a mail from me to Amrish with no subject or body, but with the report attached. Was it possible that I had accidentally sent Amrish the report? No, there was no way. It had to be from Vijay's laptop.

Before I knew what I was doing, I called Naina. After 3 rings, she answered. "Hi, lame-brain. Why did you want to talk to me so early in the morning?" she asked, stifling a yawn. I had no time for chit-chat. "Do you still have Vijay's laptop with you?" I demanded. "Um...yeah, why?" she asked, sounding confused. "Did you send Amrish a mail yesterday with my report as an attachment?" I shouted. "No. Of course not! Listen, calm down..." she said soothingly. That's when I snapped. "You don't get to tell me when to calm down, you psycho-freak! I might be expelled from college because someone mailed Amrish my report!" I regretted the words as soon as they were out of my mouth.

There was a long pause. Then Naina said in a steely voice, "Psycho-freak, huh? That's a new one! We are officially *done*! By the way, I technically didn't log out of your account. Nisha did. I was using the washroom and asked her to do it for me. So, why don't you stop picking on the 'psycho-freak' and check out ordinary people instead, huh?!" With that, she cut the call. I couldn't believe I had broken up with Naina...again! I wanted to cry. But I didn't have time. Naina clearly wanted to pin this on Nisha. The only question was...did I believe her?

CHAPTER 53

That day, I met up with Amrish before classes began. "Dude, I'm so sorry—" he began. I cut him off. "I don't want to hear your apologies! I just want us to get out of this mess." At these words, Amrish did something I'd never expected. He began to cry. "I'm sorry, bro. I was just being lazy. Don't worry. I'll tell them that I tricked you into mailing me the report. I'll say that I told you that I just wanted your report as a reference. Later, I decided to copy yours. If I get expelled, so be it!" he concluded. I felt sorry for the guy.

In response, I said, "Don't worry, bro. We'll face the problem together. We've been friends through so much. I'm sure we can see this through till the end." He stopped crying and we grinned at each other. Then I continued, "But the funny thing is I never sent you that mail." Amrish looked at me in confusion. "Are you saying someone hacked your account?" he asked. "No... I was working on my account with Naina and asked her to sign out. She claims she did so, but I still have my doubts..." my voice trailed off, as Amrish exclaimed, "Dude, then you're completely innocent!" I was glad he still had a firm grasp of the obvious!

We headed to class as Professor Gopal arrived. I didn't want to discuss the whole Nisha angle with Amrish. Amrish and I didn't chat for the rest of the day.

But as I left college that day, I decided to conduct my own investigation.

I called Nisha and wondered if she would pick up. Just when I was about to cut the call, she answered, "What do *you* want?" she demanded angrily. I didn't expect her to be so mad at me. Then, with my (pathetic) powers of deduction, I figured Naina must have told her about our fight. "Listen, I'm really sorry for what I said to Naina..." I began. "Well, apologise to Naina then!" she snapped. Okay, it was time for me to play my trump card. "I know you lied about the fact that you give Naina her medicines. I also know a few secrets about Naina that her family should learn. Just give me 5 minutes of your time, okay?" I begged. There was pin-drop silence on the other end of the line. Then Nisha replied, "Meet me in my college canteen. Just 5 minutes, that's all. Got it?" I confirmed and hung up.

Nisha was waiting for me by the time I got there. She looked like she wanted to murder me. I hoped she'd see some point in what I was saying. I tried smiling at her. "Hey!" I said, raising an arm in greeting. She continued to glare at me as I took a seat opposite her. "What do you want, Pranav?" she asked, sounding surprisingly tired. "I just want to know the truth," I replied cautiously. She immediately hissed in an angry whisper, "The truth about what?! Naina? She's not a 'psycho-freak' as you put it. I thought you would understand. That's why I covered up for you and gave you a second chance. Guess I put my faith in the wrong guy!"

She stood up and was about to walk away, when I said, "She's cut her medication you know." Nisha spun around to look at me, suddenly confused. "She's also been seeing people in purple lately. The hallucinations and delusions still haven't stopped." I continued. Nisha sat down, looking lost for the first time since I had known her. "If this is some kind of trick..." she warned me. I shook my head impatiently. "It's not," I replied. "She's still seriously sick. She and you may not believe me, but I love your twin sister. I want what's best for her. I'll tell you everything I know. But, in return, I want your help in getting to the truth. Are we clear?"

Nisha nodded uncertainly. Then she seemed to shake off her anger. "Fine. You tell me what the real deal is with Naina. In return, you want to know the truth about what exactly?" she wondered. I asked, "Did you send an email from my account to someone named Amrish?" Nisha looked surprised. "Why would I do that? No, of course not!" I tried to check for some indication that she was lying. But either she was a really good actress or I was a really bad detective. "Naina wanted me to think so," I replied softly. "I think Naina probably sent the mail which might get me expelled," I continued. "I need your help to prove it, though," I concluded. Nisha was silent for a while. Then she smiled and said, "This is going to take more than 5 minutes. So, I'm going to need a coffee..."

Finally, Nisha returned with a glass of filter coffee. "Took you long enough," I grumbled under my breath. "Let's start with the thing about you getting expelled. What kind of mail are we talking about exactly?" Nisha asked.

I told Nisha the condensed version of the entire story. She was silent for a long time. Then she let out a whoosh of air. "Wow. Now I get why you lost your cool and snapped at Naina. You really are in big trouble," she said, smiling sympathetically. I couldn't help but smile back. I decided it was my turn to take charge of the conversation. "So, what exactly happened to Vijay's laptop?" I asked. "Well, Naina was carrying it with her. She left it in our room when we went for the quiz. I came back to the room much after Naina. She returned as soon as the quiz got over. When I came back, I was surprised to see that she still had the laptop. I asked her when she meant to return it. She said in a couple of days. Then she went to the bathroom and asked me to log out of your account. So I did what she had asked me to do. I didn't check if she had sent any mail. That's all I know," concluded Nisha.

She tapped one finger on the table and bit her bottom lip. "What time did you say the mail was sent?" she suddenly asked. In my brilliance, I had never thought of checking the time. I checked my phone and said, "Um... it says here at 7:47 p.m. What time did you sign out?" She looked surprised. "That's roughly the time I logged out of your account. So, I guess either Naina or I *could* have done it. I suppose the real question now is whom you suspect." She threw it out into the open casually. She could be in a lot of trouble, yet she seemed so laid-back. I don't know why, but she suddenly reminded me of a cat playing with its food.

"Well, I might be wrong, but I'm choosing to put my faith in you!" I exclaimed, smiling. Nisha winked at me. "Don't worry. I'm not hiding anything," she replied. She held my hand suddenly. "Don't worry, we'll work this out together," she said, squeezing my hand. I suddenly felt more confident. "First, let me get hold of Vijay's laptop. We'll take it from there," she continued. She pulled out her phone and called Naina. After a whispered conversation with her sister, she hung up and looked at me oddly. I knew something was wrong. She said wonderingly, "You're not going to believe this, but Vijay's laptop is missing..."

***

Back home that evening, I kept running through everything that had happened in that one crazy day! I hadn't told my parents about the copying issue. But, oblivious as they usually are, even they noticed that something was wrong with me. "Are you sick?" my mom asked me gently that evening. "No, Ma. Just busy," I replied. "Busy doing *what* exactly?" she asked. She had a point. All that I had done the entire evening was walk around the living room. I decided to avoid any more well-meaning questions by heading to my room. Once inside, I continued my pacing.

How could I sit down and study when I had only 4 days left to prove my innocence? Naina had tried to pin the blame on Nisha when I had initially accused her. But later, she had claimed that the laptop was missing. The only person with access to the laptop had been her. That only made her behaviour more suspicious. First, she had tried to deflect attention by suggesting an unlikely suspect. Second, she had reported a key piece of evidence as missing. Everything pointed to her being the culprit. But somehow, I couldn't bring myself to believe she had sent the mail. I mean, what was her motive? She had shared some deep secrets with me and had seemed happy as my girlfriend. While it was true that I wasn't exactly God's gift to women, I didn't think I was such a terrible boyfriend. So, why would Naina suddenly want to try and get me expelled? What could have made her change her mind about me all of a sudden?

Of course, there was the other angle to consider. Why should I trust Nisha? The thing is Nisha had lied and covered up for me when she didn't have to. I could tell she still had feelings for me, but she hid them so that her sister would be happy. She never seemed to get exasperated or annoyed with her sister. Except, of course, for the *small* matter of calling Naina "pure evil"! Why had she done that? Another thing I didn't understand was why she had lied to me about who was responsible for Naina's medication. Tomorrow, I would get answers. But first, I had to talk to another person. And that person was Vijay. I had a feeling he knew Naina and Nisha better than anyone else and only he could help me solve this mystery...

CHAPTER 54

The next day, I tried to be as attentive as possible. But the truth was I couldn't wait to meet Vijay and figure out what the deal was with his laptop. After what seemed like forever, it was time for lunch. I quickly loaded my plate and searched for Vijay. I spotted him almost at once. He was sitting all alone at a table and looked lost in his own thoughts. He hadn't yet noticed me, but I knew it was now or never. "This seat taken?" I asked casually as I sat down opposite him. He smiled at me and seemed to cheer up (which helped calm my racing heart!). "It is now!" he said, still smiling. "So, how are my sisters treating you?" he asked.

"Fine," I replied, trying to keep a neutral tone. "Have you heard anything from Naina or Nisha lately?" I asked, trying to figure out if Naina had decided to tell him about our break-up. "You'd probably know before me!" he said laughing. "So, what is Naina up to lately?" he asked. I took a deep breath and dived in, "Did she borrow your laptop? And has she returned it?" I asked quickly. Vijay frowned and replied, "No, as a matter of fact, she hasn't. She did borrow the laptop. I'm surprised she told you about it. What was the context?"

I answered, "I think she wanted to send a mail from my account using the laptop. Look...I know I'm asking a lot. But will you trust me? I think Naina might not be okay. But I promise I will help." Vijay looked at me for a long time. Then, he let out his breath and said, "Okay, sure." I was so happy that I almost forgot what I wanted to ask him! "Has Naina asked you to do anything strange recently?" I asked. "Well...she did ask me to get rid of a phone, not too long ago. She said that I shouldn't leave any trace of it and get rid of it quickly. I was a little surprised, honestly," he answered.

"How long ago was this?" I asked. "Around the time that Ram fellow was expelled. Why?" he queried. I looked him straight in the eye and answered, "Just trust me." He shrugged and said, "Okay." It was clear he thought that Naina and I were still a couple. Maybe she did too. Had she forgotten about the fight? Also, Vijay obviously didn't know that his sisters couldn't find his laptop either. Something stopped me from saying anything more. I guess I wanted to solve the mystery first. "Did Nisha ever determine the dose of Naina's medication?" I asked, continuing to grill Vijay. "No. Where did you get that idea from?" he answered with a question of his own. "Forget it. No other recent weird stuff, right?" I continued. "Nothing I can remember right now," he responded. I nodded as if things were beginning to make some sort of sense.

In fact, the opposite was true. Whose phone did Naina want to get rid of and why? And why was Vijay so clueless about what was going on in his sisters' lives? Had Naina chosen to forgive me, after all? I felt I was missing something in this complicated web of lies. Only one thing was certain...my time was running out!

The same day, I called Nisha after classes were done. "Should I come over to your college?" I asked her. "No!"

she exclaimed loudly. Then, she seemed to calm down, "I mean, that's not a good idea." She carried on, "Naina might see us here and get suspicious. I'll come over to your campus. We can talk at your canteen." That was not the response I was expecting. "What's there to be suspicious about? I mean it isn't like I'm cheating on Naina. And why haven't you told Vijay that his laptop is missing?" I asked. Nisha sighed and said, "I'll explain everything when we meet. I promise, okay?" It wasn't like I had a lot of options. "Sure," I answered and cut the line.

Nisha arrived 10 minutes later. "Hey, don't worry. You're going to be just fine," she reassured me. I smiled, but I didn't quite share her confidence. "So, what did you want to ask me?" she prompted. "Why did you lie about who was responsible for Naina's medication? I raised it yesterday too, but you dodged the question," I grilled Nisha. There was a sharp intake of breath which she slowly released. "I'm sorry I lied to you. I just wanted you to trust meeting and tell me the truth about Naina. I had a feeling she was still hallucinating, but didn't want to tell us – her family. I should have just told you the truth from the start. Sorry," she finished with a sigh and a bittersweet smile.

"Why didn't you tell Vijay that his laptop is missing?" I asked. Nisha said, "Vijay has a really bad temper, though he doesn't show it most of the time. Plus, like our parents, he feels that Naina should have stayed longer in the hospital. But I'm her twin sister. I understand her better than anyone. If she were confined to a hospital, she would be destroyed. That's why I have a request. Please don't tell Vijay anything. Can you keep the fact that Naina's still hallucinating a secret?" I thought for a while. Then I nodded. This was a family issue which needed to be resolved by all of them. "Thanks!" Nisha said, sounding relieved.

I had 2 final questions for her. "Can you recall any instance of Naina not remembering things correctly?" I asked. Nisha thought for a while and then said, "Yes. She once insisted that there had been 2 people in the room with her and she had recorded their conversation on her phone. But in the morning, the phone was gone. The same phone later turned up in Ram's room. But neither of us has a clue how it got there. I suppose Ram stole the phone because I forgot to lock the door that night. But it was still weird because we never found the recording on Naina's phone after recovering it from Ram's room. Then, another time, she had been talking about how someone had tried to smother her with a pillow. But it had been the middle of the night and there had been no one else in the room."

Finally, only one question remained: "Why didn't you tell Vijay that I'm no longer Naina's boyfriend?" Nisha replied, "I think if you reached out to her, she would forgive you." I sarcastically said, "Well, the fact that I'm suggesting she deliberately tried to have me expelled might not help!" Nisha gave me a wry smile in return, "Fair enough. You and Naina sort out stuff later. Right now, I'll get you off the hook. And don't worry, I'll swear to anything that will help get you out of trouble!"

That night, I wondered whether to try and make up with Naina or not. The truth is I wanted to. But I also needed her to admit she had sent that mail to Amrish. Another thing struck me as odd about the whole affair. Why not just delete the mail from my outbox? If Naina wanted to get me into trouble and not be discovered, she would have been smarter about this. On the other hand, Naina might have sent the mail and forgotten all about it. But if that was actually true, Naina positively disliked (or rather, hated!) me. Maybe I was being blind, but I had trouble believing someone I loved so much, hated me so intensely!

Nisha had assured me that she would swear that Naina had sent the mail and explain her sister's condition. But it still felt like I was missing a piece of the puzzle. Just then, my phone began to ring. I checked the caller ID – it was Nisha! "What's up?" I asked quickly, wanting to get straight to the point.

Nisha replied, "I think Naina might be sicker than we imagined. During the first semester, there were 2 really horrible things which happened at college. The first involved a dog, which was thought to be rabid. It was beaten to death by our security guards, since it was attacking them. But, later on, a plate filled with acid was found near the scene. Traces of acid were also found inside the dog. And..." her voice broke off as she began sobbing. "And what?" I prompted, cautiously. She pulled herself together and said, "And I found a bottle of acid in Naina's cupboard yesterday!"

I felt sick to my stomach. "That's not all," continued Nisha. "The day of the debate, a rat was found sliced up by the exhaust fan in our bathroom. I was the last one to leave the room in the morning. The only other person with access to the room was Naina. I assumed the rat had just crawled in and been cut up by the fan's blades. But what if she left it there on purpose?" Nisha finished. "Hello, Pranav? Are you there?" she asked, but I cut the line. Now, I was really scared. I knew Naina was a schizophrenic...but was she a psychopath too?

CHAPTER 55

The next afternoon, after classes were done, I waited for Nisha in her college canteen. She had tried to convince me to meet her at the ICSI canteen. But I had said no quite firmly. I didn't want Vijay to see me with Nisha.

I was lost in my thoughts at the Synergy canteen when I noticed someone sit down opposite me. I looked up and was surprised to see that it wasn't Nisha! In fact, I had no idea who she was. She looked vaguely familiar, but I couldn't recall where I had seen her before. "Hi!" she said, before I could get my thoughts sorted. "How have you been?" she continued. Okay, I was obviously expected to come up with something. "Hey, it's been forever!" I replied as enthusiastically as I could. "So, what brings you back here?" she asked, smiling. She was distractingly attractive. What was it with all the girls in this college?!

That's when it hit me! I had thought exactly the same thing when I had seen this girl at the debate. The problem was I didn't remember when and where I had met her on the day of the debate. Was she an audience member whom I'd spoken to later? The fact that I couldn't quite place her must have shown on my face. She immediately asked, "You don't remember me, do you?" She was still smiling when I finally admitted, "Um...no. No clue at all! Sorry!" Her smile widened at my discomfort and she said, "You promised me a cup of coffee when you won. Ring any bells?"

I was gradually starting to remember something... Then it hit me! "It's you – the girl at the reception on the day of the debate!" I exclaimed. She pouted, but then went back to smiling. "That's the best you can do? 'Girl at the reception'? Oh, well! Guess I shouldn't be too disappointed. After all, Naina pretty much owns you now, right?" I smiled back.

"Sorry. I'm terrible with names. But since we're both free, why don't I fulfill my promise of buying you a coffee? You tell me how you know about Naina and me," I suggested, hoping that she'd agree. She gave me a knowing wink and said, "You think I'll spill all my secrets over a cup of coffee?" I retorted, "Well, there's always tea!" Both of us laughed and the tension eased. "My name's Meghna..." she began. I opened my mouth to introduce myself, but she held up a hand and continued, "...and you're Pranav Dasgupta. Don't worry. You and Naina aren't exactly common knowledge here. It's just that I am, or rather *was*, a good friend of hers. Now, I'm friends with her sister. Both of them have told me a lot about you." I was curious. Here was an outsider who could help me understand the complex dynamic between the sisters.

"Don't look so worried. I've only heard good things. Before Naina fell ill, she was fun to hang out with. She mentioned there was a desperate guy from ICSI trying to impress her. Plus, she told me to give you her number at the debate because there was a terrible accident in her room involving a rat," Meghna said and shuddered. "Yeah, Nisha told me all about it," I replied, immediately realising my mistake. "Wait a sec, *Nisha* told you about it? Why not Naina? After all, she's your girlfriend, right?" asked Meghna, putting me on the back foot. "Well, to be honest, she sort of broke it off. So we're no longer together," I answered glumly. "Oh my gosh! I'm so sorry! Was this recent? I met Nisha yesterday and she didn't say a thing," remarked Meghna. That was odd. But before I could say anything, Meghna continued, "If you ask me, it's all for the best. What with her weird mental issues, she's become a total whack job!" shrugged Meghna casually.

That was enough for me. The way she was so dismissive about Naina made me angry. "She's not a 'whack job', okay? She's a patient suffering from a disease. It's just like having diabetes. With the right medication, she'll be perfectly normal!" I raged at Meghna. She was obviously surprised by how angry I was. "Fine, sheesh. I'm not the one who needs convincing. You're better off telling Nisha your romantic sob story!" She stood up to go.

But I had to ask one question – "Why do you think I should try to convince *Nisha* that her sister is sick? She cares so much about Naina. So, why did you say that?" I asked puzzled. Meghna began to laugh. It was a harsh, caustic laugh. Meghna looked at me and said, "I don't know what kind of con Nisha has going on. But I'll tell you the truth...assuming you want it?"

I didn't trust myself to speak, so I nodded. Meghna began to speak, "Nisha *hates* Naina. She told us that Naina was having delusions of being chased by people in purple. So, she wanted to play a prank on her sister. She asked my roommate and me to wear purple T-shirts and appear in their room one night, just to freak Naina out. I didn't want to do it at first. But Nisha convinced us that it was all a joke. According to her, Naina would later forgive us. So, we went ahead with the plan. The next day, my phone went missing and I suddenly came upon Naina about to drop it in the dustbin. I caught her just in time. She put on her typical clueless act. Anyway, I figured Nisha later told Naina the whole story. However, Nisha insisted that she had no idea how Naina stole my phone...but I've been a bit wary of Naina since then. Anyway, I don't know why I'm wasting my breath talking to you. I'm outta here." Meghna began walking and turned the corner.

I was rooted to the spot, not sure what to do. I wanted to ask her some more questions. But I also wanted answers from Nisha. Just then, Nisha appeared around the corner, smiling with not a care in the world, and waved at me. I sank back into my seat and greeted her with a half-smile. This was going to be messy.

Nisha could obviously tell that I wasn't exactly thrilled to see her. She looked puzzled as she approached my table. She had stopped smiling by the time she sat down. I silently gazed at her as I processed what Meghna had said. My continued silence and confused expression prompted her to say, "If you want to ask me something, go ahead." I wanted to know the truth, but I didn't want to lose the one witness who was on my side. But I couldn't resist her offer. I had to know. "Why did you call Naina 'pure evil'?" I asked hesitantly. Nisha looked at me in confusion. To be fair, I hadn't given her any context. "When you fixed things between Naina and me," I continued, "you said you would do anything for me. But you also said that your sister was 'pure evil'. Why would you use a phrase like that?"

She gazed directly into my eyes. Then she said in an irritated fashion, "Seriously?! You're making such a big deal out of that? I was angry and upset and still in love with you – stupidly, as it turns out! Haven't you ever said something to someone and then wanted to take the words back? It's the same." I knew Nisha was referring to my calling Naina a "psycho-freak". But somehow, Nisha's words didn't sound convincing. It seemed like a well-prepared script.

In any case, I decided to drop the issue. "Something else on your mind?" she asked as if reading my thoughts. "Well, yeah. I wanted to clear up something with you," I said. Then I stopped. I took a deep breath and decided to come straight to the point. "Did you play a practical joke on Naina and get some people to dress up in purple and enter your bedroom, while Naina was asleep?" At that, she slapped me across the face. Okay, I probably deserved that slap. But once again, it felt more like she was putting on a show.

She got up from the table with a jerk and her chair fell to the ground. The entire canteen went silent, as all eyes turned to us. "How dare you?!" she whispered coldly. "How did you come up with this stupid idea?" I kept sitting, but before Nisha could walk away, I said, "I didn't come up with the idea. Meghna told me about it. She claims you knew all along that Naina was still seeing people in purple. So...looks like you lied to me about that. In fact, that's why you planned to play a trick on her. Just tell me the truth."

Nisha stared at me for a long time. Then she began to laugh. It was a hysterical laugh, bordering on the verge of insanity. "Meghna?!" she asked disbelievingly. "You believe Meghna rather than me? She reminds me a little of you. Both of you are cruel to Naina for the fun of it. But I love my sister and will protect her from monsters like you 2!" she finished in a voice choked with tears. "I suggest you stay away from solving mysteries and stick to Computer Science. Meghna has only ever stabbed my sister in the back. If you believe her, you might as well believe Ram and his lies. Are you going to ask me if I smoke weed now? I'll tell you what...I'll message you Meghna's number. Oh, and you might want to convince her to defend you fast. You've only got 3 more days, counting today, right? And memory can be such an unreliable thing. Just like witnesses..." saying this, Nisha walked away.

CHAPTER 56

Sure enough, Nisha sent me Meghna's number that night. I tried to call her multiple times, but she refused to pick up the phone. I messaged her on WhatsApp, but she didn't reply to a single message. I was desperate, but I was also sleepy. Somewhere in the midst of all that scrambling to reach Meghna, I fell asleep. I woke up late the next morning.

It was Saturday. I had today and tomorrow left. Then, I would have to meet the ICSI Board on Monday. It looked like all my efforts to unearth the truth would be useless. I figured I ought to tell my parents that I might be expelled on Monday. As you can imagine, this was not something I was looking forward to. I was sure there would be a lot of lecturing and shouting; and maybe some Bollywood-style crying to spice up the mixture. But it had to be done – even if I was going to get thrown out of the house. So, I quickly showered and left my room.

"Mom, Dad, I've got something to tell you. I might be expelled on Monday," I mumbled softly. I was hoping they wouldn't hear me. However, they both perked up the moment they heard the word "expelled". I waited for the inevitable barrage of questions. My mom promptly obliged. "Expelled?! What? By whom? Why—" Usually, at times like this, my dad runs to his bedroom and locks the door till the shouting has subsided. But today, he raised a hand and cut off my mother. He asked sternly,

"Why are you going to be expelled?" I told them about Professor Scindia and Amrish. It was such a relief to get it off my chest that the story poured out in a flood. I told them how Amrish had been pestering me to send him my report and someone had sent him the report on the day I opened my account on Vijay's laptop.

At this, my dad interrupted me, "Who is this Vijay?" My mom answered the question for me – "He's Pranav's girlfriend's ex-boyfriend, isn't that right?" She turned to look at me and waited for me to confirm what she had just said. I paused for a heartbeat. Then I said, "No. I lied." After that, I told them the truth about Naina, Nisha and Vijay. I waited for my mom to slap me for lying to her. But the slap never came. She only asked in a deadly serious voice, "Are you lying to us now?" Tears sprang to my eyes. Even if they hated me for it, I wanted them to believe me – "No! Everything I'm saying right now is the truth! I know I haven't given you much reason to believe me, but trust me now. Please, I'm begging you!" They both nodded seriously.

"So, did you send Amrish the report?" my dad asked. "No way! I'm being totally honest with both of you now. I never sent that report. Someone sent it from Vijay's laptop. I think it's Naina." I told them how Naina was a schizophrenic and often didn't remember things she had done or said. Finally, I told them about Nisha and how we had tried to pin the blame on Naina. But then came my discovery that Nisha was hiding her own secrets. I told them how I had been trying to get hold of Meghna since then. Finally, I said, "I understand if you want to kick me out of the house. But I just thought you should know the truth."

For a long time, they stood there looking at me. Then (to my great surprise!) my mom came forward and hugged me. My dad came and wrapped us in a bear hug. "I'm so sorry, my baby," my mom whispered. "But I want you to know that we are always there for you. No matter what happens, you can count on us!" she exclaimed. Then we were laughing and hugging and crying and kissing all at once. For a moment, I forgot all about Monday and the Board meeting.

It was my dad who brought us back to reality. "We will fight this every step of the way," he said supportively. "If you're innocent and this is someone's idea of a joke, then your mom and I will be present at the Board meeting to explain our position. Let's see how much ICSI values its IMTech program. I'll speak to some of my media contacts. They'll love the possibility of a scandal. After all, is ICSI going to expel a student on the evidence provided by a family of liars? Not if we have anything to say about it!" he finished. I felt a rush of adrenaline course through my veins and (after a long time) I began to hope again. "If this professor gives you trouble, then he better be ready for some trouble from us!" my mom added.

Just then, my phone began to ring. My parents took a step back. "You better check who that is. Let's hope it's Meghna with some nasty secrets about Naina and/or Nisha!" said my dad with a mischievous twinkle in his eye. "I too hope it's Meghna. But I have a strong feeling that she's not going to be the one spilling the last of their secrets. But don't worry. I have a plan," I said to my parents, before rushing off to answer the phone.

It was Meghna after all. I quickly answered, before she could cut the call! "Hey! How are you?" The words popped out of my mouth before I had a chance to think of how daft the question sounded. "I'm feeling pretty lousy, considering I found out yesterday that Nisha – whom I thought was a friend – hates me and makes up lies about me to tell her sister's ex-boyfriend. So, yeah. Pretty lousy. But thanks for reminding me!" Meghna replied, sarcastically.

I cringed. Okay, I probably deserved that. But before I could say something apologetic, another question popped into my head and out of my mouth: "How did you find out what Nisha said to me?" She replied instantly, "Well, quite a few people heard Nisha shouting at you in the canteen. Some of them are my friends and told me all about it." I couldn't resist asking, "Did you speak to Nisha after finding out?" Her answer was short and to the point: "Yup." I was done with the suspense! "And...?" I asked pointedly. Meghna sighed and said, "She called me a liar in front of half the college. Then she acted like I had done something terrible and left for her room." Meghna heaved another sigh, then said, "So, if you need any help bringing that backstabber down, just let me know." Looked like I had a reliable witness at last.

I told her all about the report, Amrish, Vijay's laptop, me opening my account and Nisha logging out around the time the mail was sent. Meghna was quiet for a long time. Finally, she spoke. "I think you're chasing the wrong person." I was a little surprised. "Well, don't tell me Nisha sent it," I joked, grinning at how dumb the idea was. "Why not?" Meghna replied innocently. "But she told me all about it. Why would she be so stupid as to admit that she logged out of my account around the time the mail was sent?!" I asked. Meghna quickly answered, "Don't you see? It's reverse psychology. She admitted to being a possible suspect. Didn't she virtually say that? She asked whether you trusted her or Naina. She knows Naina is suffering from delusions and is a schizophrenic. Naina was the obvious suspect right from the start. All the evidence points directly at her. Nisha knows all this. So, she admits she might be guilty. You chuck the possibility out of the window. Everything else she told you is her version of the story. I'm not saying you're wrong. I'm just saying you need strong evidence that Naina is the one in the wrong."

Unfortunately, Meghna was right. I had no solid proof that Naina had sent the mail, except for the fact that Nisha had told me as much. And time and again, Nisha had lied. Nisha had claimed that Naina hadn't mentioned anything about the delusions to her. She'd said that she regulated the dosage of Naina's medication. She was the one who had suggested the possibility of Naina killing that mouse and the dog. She had known exactly where to find (what seemed to be) Naina's stash of weed. In fact, she'd even offered to lie for me as a witness. But I had no solid evidence against Nisha either. It was a lot of guesswork and leaps of faith (or rather, disbelief).

"Would you be willing to tell the truth about your involvement in the practical joke? I need a witness to prove that Nisha is a liar. Maybe if I can convince the ICSI Board that Nisha lied about one thing, I can convince them that she might also be lying about other stuff. What do you say?" I asked. To my surprise, Meghna started laughing. Once she was done, she said, "No problem. I'll swear to having seen her mail the report if you want. After the way she embarrassed me yesterday, she deserves some payback!" I wasn't exactly sure how to react. Part of me wanted to leap for joy. I had a witness on my side. But I was also scared. There was a certain 'feel' about her. I don't know how to describe it. Meghna seemed like a sweet girl. But there was a hard, steely edge to her as well. It was as if she had a bitter, sarcastic core which she covered up with fake sweetness. She honestly freaked me out more than Naina or Nisha. Maybe it was simple. Maybe she was ordinary...and sometimes being ordinary makes you less sensitive to life.

"Hello? You still there?" asked Meghna. I focused on the problem at hand. Now wasn't the time for my *gyaan* on love and life. "Awesome. Thanks a lot. Keep Monday free in case I need your help," I responded. "Sure. See you," she said and cut the call. I was about to put the phone away, when I thought of something. It was a long shot, but I had to try. I messaged Meghna and asked her for a favour – I needed someone's phone number. In a minute or so, my phone pinged with her response. I smiled and dialled the number she had sent me. As the line continued to ring, I became more and more convinced that this was a bad idea. Then a voice answered and asked, "Who's this?" I replied as coolly as I could, "Hey Ram..."

"Hey Ram, you probably don't know me. Meghna gave me your number. My name is Pranav—" I was cut off midway. "Dasgupta, right? You're that pathetic puppy Naina keeps on a chain. I know all about you. You're a total loser. I've got nothing to say to you or your psycho girlfriend!" Okay, I clearly didn't know how to handle this guy. I desperately needed to find out a vital piece of information from Ram. But no one called Naina "psycho", except me! Okay, that came out wrong. But you get the idea. I would have happily cut the line.

Instead, I bit back my initial reaction and said, "Actually, this was Meghna's idea." I hoped that he would take the bait. Sure enough, he did. "Huh? What does Meghna have to do with all this?" asked Ram. "She seems to think you can help me out of a fix. She said you'd love a chance for some payback or something like that." "What do you think I can offer? Relationship advice? I'm a 'stalker', according to Naina. What kind of dating tips do you want from me?" Ram snapped.

"Why were you stalking her anyway? And why did you molest her?" I asked, before I could think of a more diplomatic way of framing the question. I still loved Naina and didn't want to have to talk about anything with this jerk. Ram got defensive and replied, "I didn't do anything! Anyway, I don't have to explain myself to you. I'm done talking to you." I couldn't let that happen. "Hang on. I think Naina might get me expelled. I don't want that to happen. I just want to hear your version of events," I said and paused for breath.

I could hear his heavy breathing on the other end of the line. Then he spoke, "The trouble started when we kissed. Suddenly, she started screaming and trying to run away from me. I thought she was scared of me. But she was obviously seeing things – or, at least, pretending to. I thought it best not to let her run off, so I grabbed her hands and tried to hold her back. When other people arrived, she pretended I had harassed her. The professors saw me clinging on to a screaming girl. That nearly got me suspended."

I tried to absorb what he was saying. It sounded like one of those episodes Naina suffered from. But no one had paid any attention to Ram's version of the story. Still...Nisha must have figured it out. "Why didn't you ask Nisha to explain her sister's problems to the college authorities?" I asked. There was a long pause at the other end of the line. Then Ram hissed in a vicious whisper, "This is another one of her schemes, isn't it? She wants to land me in jail or something. When will she think I've been punished enough?! And for what sin?!" Ram was shouting by now. But he wasn't making any sense. "What are you talking about?" I asked, honestly confused. "Naina's phone was found on you. You stole it. Why would you think that Naina had put me up to this anyway? You're hardly innocent yourself!" I shouted, losing my own temper. He started laughing again. It seemed as if he had figured something out. "Are you really that stupid?" he laughed.

I decided not to say anything. Suddenly, he began yelling at me: "You think *you* have problems? Why should I care if you are expelled?! You must have known about Naina's delusions. Yet, when Naina told you, you did nothing to help me out. Why? Because you wanted a hot girlfriend and I was a random stranger. It's exactly the same situation here. I only bothered listening to you because you mentioned Meghna. But I'm guessing you lied about that too, right?" I took a moment to figure out what to say and decided to stick with the truth. "Okay, you're right. This wasn't Meghna's idea. It was mine. Meghna just gave me your number. I was Naina's boyfriend. But we've broken up now. Actually, she broke it off. The reason I'm in trouble is because I think she sent a mail from my account. So I'm asking, no begging, for your help. Can you come to ICSI on Monday?"

I figured there would be a long pause on the other end of the line. But his answer came immediately: "No!" Wow! Talk about being unhelpful. I asked, as gently as I could, "Why?" His reply didn't really surprise me. "I don't intend to fly down from Delhi just to fix your life." Ram answered. Well, I couldn't really blame him. Still, it had been worth a try. He added, "For what it's worth, I doubt ICSI would have much faith in the words of an expelled drug user!" he exclaimed and I smiled. Oh, well! I guess some things just couldn't be helped. At least, I still had my parents and Meghna on my side. I took what little comfort I could from that.

Then a thought struck me. "Hey, listen. I don't mean to pry, but what exactly were you expelled for?" I asked as casually as I could. "That is prying and you can ask your ex-girlfriend for the details," he retorted. "Come on, man. Please! I just want to figure out the truth. Tell me." He exhaled forcefully and said, "For possession of weed." I was getting a little confused again. "Was this the first time or have been doing drugs for a while?" I asked. "What if I have?" he demanded aggressively. "How come you were stupid enough to get caught *this* time?" I asked point-blank. "I wasn't caught! I was framed...by her," he muttered. "Her? Whom? Naina?" I asked. "Of course not, you moron! By *Nisha*!"

"*Nisha*?!" I repeated, sounding like an echo. "She was the one who supplied me with drugs. Never touched the stuff herself, but that's how dealers work I guess. She was also the one who claimed her sister had a crush on me and suggested I make a move. But when I got into trouble, she didn't say a word in my defence. After disciplinary action had been taken, she suggested I hide some weed in my room for one night. She claimed she would take it from me the next day and plant it among Naina's things when Naina wasn't in the room. I didn't trust her. So, I recorded her saying it. She seduced me and swapped my phone with Naina's at some point. That same night, she told the authorities I had weed in my room. They found it stashed among my clothes. I told them about my conversation with Nisha and pulled out the phone to play the recording. That's when Nisha accused me of stealing Naina's phone. So...now you know the full story. Hope you're satisfied. Never call this number again and I hope the lot of you get what you deserve!"

CHAPTER 57

Ram cut the line. My mind was still reeling from what he had just said. I had had my suspicions about Nisha after speaking to Meghna. But I had never imagined she would go so far to harm her sister. I *wanted* Nisha to be innocent. But why would Ram or Meghna lie to me? I don't know how most guys feel when they've loved a girl and lost her. But I knew that I still liked Nisha as more than a friend and I had difficulty believing she could be so utterly "*evil*"!

Of course, I should have realised that Nisha had been lying all along. The evidence of her having been the one to harm her sister had been staring me in the face. I could probably have saved everyone a lot of trouble (and a lot of pages for you, my dear reader!) if I had not been so stupid and blinded by love. Actually, I wasn't really sure what that word meant. I had "loved" Nisha once upon a time. And I considered myself to be "in love" with Naina. Anyway, now wasn't the time to think about how I had messed up my love life. Now was the time for quick, decisive action.

Once I was thinking clearly again, my first thought was (surprisingly) not about my pending expulsion. No, I was worried about Naina. Nisha didn't know that I had spoken to Ram, but she knew I no longer trusted her. There was no telling what she might do to her sister if she realised that I had figured out what she had been up to. I messaged Naina on WhatsApp, hoping that she had not blocked me from her contacts. My message read: "Hey. I'm truly sorry for what I said earlier. You are a wonderful, beautiful girl and I will understand if you don't reply. But you might be in more danger than you think. Can we meet one last time?" I felt I had to warn her. I was surprised when the phone pinged immediately. Naina's message read: "I'm so glad you reached out. I've been meaning to do the same thing. I'm sorry about what I said to you too. I think we both regret stuff we've said and done. But we survived one break-up. I think we can get through another one, right?" I have to admit that I thought I was dreaming. I wrote back, "You don't know how happy you've made me!!! But you probably don't realise what a dangerous situation you're in. Can we meet and talk today?"

There was a pause on the other end of the line, as if Naina were weighing her options. Then, she replied, "Sorry, spending the evening with Vijay. Will meet you tomorrow at ICSI, 1:30 p.m. Don't be late, lame-brain!" I just hoped that I would be in time to save Naina from Nisha, and myself from being expelled.

***

I don't really remember how I spent Saturday evening. I went out because I was extremely restless – worried about what Nisha was planning. Plus, the way my parents looked at me made me feel guilty about the whole affair. I thought some fresh air would give me a chance to sort out my thoughts and feelings. While walking, I pulled out my phone and found myself calling Amrish. Like they say, 'misery loves company'. I hoped he had some sort of half-baked plan to make sure he didn't get expelled! For all his faults (which I have to say are many!), he was still my best friend.

The phone rang several times before he picked it up. "Hey, *macha*! What's up? You need something?" he asked breathlessly, like he had just been jogging. But I know Amrish. He's too lazy to ever go jogging when an auto does the job of moving him equally well! "Is something wrong?" I asked in a concerned fashion. He said, "You won't believe this, *macha*, but the whole day feels like a nightmare! I just want to escape all the trouble I'm in." I smiled, though I felt like crying. "I know the feeling," I empathised. "I just hope you have a plan to get yourself out of trouble, bro," I added. "I'm not sure, dude. Maybe I should try not dying so frequently..." Amrish's voice trailed off.

Hearing this, I had a minor heart attack! Amrish was obviously thinking of suicide. My friend's life was worth way more than some stupid charge of plagiarism. I tried to convince him he shouldn't quit. "*Macha*, we'll get through this together. Don't quit on life. You should definitely try not dying! Have you told your parents about it?" I was trying to be helpful. But his answer left me stunned. "Huh? Why would I tell my parents about it?" I shot back, "Dude, they're going to know if you get expelled!"

Amrish began to laugh. I still wasn't sure what was so funny. "Did you think I was talking about plagiarism? I was talking about the fact that I've only got 3 kills while playing Counter-Strike today! Don't worry about Monday, *macha*. We'll figure something out. Together. Now, die, die, die!" he yelled as he went back to his game. I still wasn't sure whether to laugh or cry. I certainly picked some strange characters as friends!

CHAPTER 58

Eventually, Sunday arrived – my day of stress! I was going to tell Naina the truth about her sister. I woke up earlier than normal for a weekend. My mom was surprised to see me up so early. "Are you feeling all right?" she asked, as soon as I stepped out of my room. No, I was *not* feeling all right! But I knew my mom would just get upset if I said I was troubled. So, I reassured her, "I'm fine, Ma. Just nervous about tomorrow." She immediately came over and hugged me. "Don't worry. I promise everything will be fine. You're not going to be expelled for a crime you didn't commit!" she reassured me. Good. She was acting a little less strict than usual. Now was the perfect time to ask her.

"Hey, Ma, I want to ask you if I can go to college today...?" I asked hesitantly. She narrowed her eyes and looked at me. You know that all-knowing look that moms sometimes give? That's the one. "Are you meeting those girls again?" she asked seriously. I was about to deny it, but realised that I might as well tell her the truth. "Yes," I answered. To my surprise, my mom nodded. "You can go, but I'm coming with you." Wow! That was not what I had expected. This was going to be embarrassing. But I had no choice.

We left home after breakfast. I wondered how to tell Naina that her sister was a psychopath. It's not like I could just bring it up casually. Imagine saying something like, “Hey, do you know your sister makes dogs drink acid and cuts up rats in the bathroom? No? Well, besides that, she also hates your guts and wanted to frame you for sending the report to Amrish. Oh, one more thing, she’s a drug dealer! Just thought you should know!” While I was thinking, we reached ICSI.

I was 5 minutes early. I called Naina, but she cut the call. She messaged me a few minutes later, “Have you reached?” I messaged back, “Yeah. Where are you?” I tried calling, but she cut the call again. Then she messaged, “I’m in ICSI in the new block. Come meet me there.” I was a little surprised. What was she doing there? “On my way,” I messaged and stashed my phone in my pocket. The new block was still being built and was a little away from the main building and canteen. Since today was a Sunday, it would be deserted. I asked my mom to wait in the reception area of the main building and headed there alone. I sneaked past a couple of guards and jumped a wall. I walked on for a while till a familiar voice said, “Hello, Pranav.” I turned around slowly to face...

...Nisha! Of course, it had been Nisha all along. I felt like a fool. I should have guessed that she had stolen her sister’s phone and was using it to message me on WhatsApp. That was why she had never answered any of my calls. For all I knew, Naina didn’t have any idea that this meeting was taking place. Naina might not even have forgiven me for what I had said. Perhaps it had all been Nisha’s doing. But why did she want to meet me? To figure out how much I really knew? However I looked at it, my best option was to keep her talking. Maybe I could even get a confession out of her. I needed to record what she said. I reached for my phone and pulled it out slowly. I needed to start the app while distracting her.

"Well, you might as well record whatever happens here. Don't worry. I'm not going to stop you. In fact, it's refreshing to forget about all the lies and secrecy. But hurry up. I'm sure we both have a lot of things to say to each other and not much time to say it all. After all, it looks like it's about to start raining. And I do so hate getting wet!" said Nisha, winking at me and smiling as if this were a casual date. So much for distracting her. I took my time starting the app. Then I gradually approached her. I wanted to be close to her so that the app could pick up whatever she said. But there was a certain distance I wanted to maintain. She looked like a tigress, watching her prey. She had that look of absolute control and confidence in her eyes. She was toying with me and enjoying it.

Once I felt I was close enough, I said, "Forgive me if I don't fully trust you. When Ram tried to record a conversation with you, he ended up getting expelled! So, did you just want to chat? You could have called, you know?" She laughed and replied, "Poor Ram. He was a fool...but a sweet one. Too bad I had to get rid of him. Did he tell you the details about how I got his phone? I doubt you're stupid enough to let me seduce you. I still feel bad about Ram, you know. You could have told him that...if you were leaving here alive!" she exclaimed with a mad gleam in her eyes. I hadn't guessed how crazy she was. I didn't see any weapons on her, but I wouldn't have been surprised if she had pulled out a gun and shot me. "So, you're going to kill me like that dog and that rat?" I asked. She looked surprised, then recovered and said, "So...you figured that part out? What gave me away?" I felt like a detective announcing what piece of evidence led him to the criminal. Problem was...I didn't have any concrete proof. But I wasn't about to admit that. "You went too far. You told me about the incidents in your bid to prove Naina crazy. But I had only your word to go on. It was a little too convenient."

Suddenly, I was struck by a thought. I started speaking aloud to test my hypothesis. "The other incident which was suspicious was that attack Naina suffered, when she claimed someone had tried to smother her with a pillow. You attempted to convince both Naina and me that she had imagined it. But the truth was simpler, wasn't it? The only other person in the room was you. So, you were the one who tried to smother her!" Nisha bowed, still smiling. "Guilty, as charged," she replied. "It certainly took you long enough to figure out the truth," she continued, smirking. "So, why did you stop? You could have killed her if you hated her that much," I wondered aloud. She sighed and looked very tired. "I could have...but that would have taken all the fun out of it. I didn't want it to get boring!"

Was this girl even human? The words came pouring out of my mouth – "Do you think this whole thing is some sort of twisted game?" She kept smiling. "Of course! All of life is a game!" she responded. She added, "And I always win!" I tried to think of what else I could get her to admit. "So, you're a drug dealer too? Another one of your little schemes?" I queried. She narrowed her eyes at me and stopped smiling. "Are you and Ram really that stupid? I just wanted to keep up an act to get Naina into trouble. Unfortunately, Ram tried to beat me at my own game. So, I needed to teach him a lesson," was her answer. That meant everything Ram had said was true. It was time to figure out her motives, though.

"I'm guessing Meghna also told the truth, right? You know – about the delusions and Naina's paranoia about being chased by people in purple. Why did you pretend not to have any clue about them when I said she was still seeing people in purple?" Nisha smiled at me again. "Well, my sister seemed to genuinely like you. That's why I figured I'd let you think you knew her better than anyone else," she answered.

"So, you really did convince Meghna and her roommate to dress up in purple to scare Naina? And you're the one who stole Meghna's phone and tried to pin the blame on Naina? I guess you planted Naina's phone on Ram, right?" I asked jumping from thought to thought and question to question. She was as cool as ever. "Do you want a gold medal for having figured it out after so long?" she asked sarcastically. "Are we done with the questions?"

"Why the elaborate set-up with the report?" I continued badgering Nisha. She coolly replied, "Like I said, she was crazy about you. Imagine how tough it would have been for her if you and I had ganged up on her and sworn that she had sent that email. Naina had told me that you and Amrish had had a spat over the report. She had also mentioned that you didn't want to mail Amrish the report in case he copied it. So, I took a chance and tried to hurt both Naina and you at the same time."

"Did you ever have feelings for me? Or was that just for show?" I continued relentlessly. Nisha laughed and replied, "Of course it was for show. I thought I just had to make you betray her once at the first chance I got. To be honest, I imagined that when she found out that you had cheated on her with me, it would be enough. But she still kept longing for you and forgave you. So, I figured I'd wait for a better chance to hurt both of you."

"Just tell me one thing – why do you hate Naina so much?" I asked her, honestly curious. She was still smiling, but seemed a little uncertain. "Just tell me the truth," I requested her earnestly. "No more games. No more lies. No more playing around. Please tell me the truth." She still seemed hesitant, as if I was about to spring a trap. Then, she got a faraway look in her eyes. "I don't hate her. Everything I do is out of love. I've always loved her deeply. She's not just my sister. She's my twin. I've always felt connected to her in a way that only the 2 of us can understand. From childhood, trouble seemed to follow Naina around. She is a pure beauty which this ugly world doesn't deserve. And it's been my job to protect her from it. I've always tried to keep other people away, so they don't bother her. If that means she needs to be locked up in a hospital, then so be it!" declared Nisha, her eyes opening a window to a haunted, insane soul.

"Don't you think that Naina should decide how she wants to live her life?" I asked, disgusted and fascinated at the same time. Nisha looked straight at me and spoke, "She's too innocent. She doesn't understand the way the world works. The 'pranks' I played on her were meant to scare her and convince her to leave college. Even my so-called attempt to 'smother' her was nothing more than a way of proving to her that she didn't belong in college. I believe she should be isolated from this filthy society. I wanted her to be expelled. That's why I said that I would swear to seeing her email your report to Amrish. But I never wanted to spoil her little bits of happiness. That's why I lied to her about the 2 of us, when I saw she couldn't get over you. I wanted her to enjoy a 'real' relationship for a while." Then Nisha's voice turned bitter. "I wanted her to understand that no relationship is actually 'real' and that all her wanna-be boyfriends would eventually let her down. The only relationship that matters is the one between me and her."

Nisha paused for a moment and then carried on, "She has always been like a child who needs protection. But when she developed schizophrenia, things got even more complex. I realised she wasn't depending only on me anymore. She was relying on you to help her through this difficult period. So, I set up an elaborate scheme and mailed the report. That would prove to her that she couldn't rely on you or me. She would probably be distanced from me, but she would be safe...safe from the horror of life and the likes of you. In time, I knew she would trust me again and then everything would be okay. No matter what I do, she always forgives me. That's what it means to be a twin. After you were out of our lives, we would be happy again." Nisha sighed and closed her eyes.

I was still recording everything using my app. I had what I needed. I could now prove my innocence and walk away. I could also stop Nisha. I didn't want Naina to suffer at the hands of this lunatic. Because that's what I was convinced she was – a lunatic! Nisha was the one who needed to be locked away. I began to back away from her. Immediately, she opened her eyes. I turned my recording app off and stuffed my phone inside my pocket. There was something in Nisha's eyes which made me want to run. By the way, I should probably mention that I had my backpack on. It carried all my critical care stuff – my insulin injection, a blood glucose monitor and a bottle of Coke. I carried it pretty much everywhere all the time. There was always a chance that my blood glucose would go too high (for which I had the injection) or too low (for which I had the Coke).

I was wondering if I could use the injection as some sort of weapon if required. "You can probably hear it, can't you?" Nisha asked suddenly, startling me. I wasn't sure what she was talking about. "I mean the thunder, of course." She was right. Lightning was now crackling above us and thunder roared all around. "Do you know what that means?" she asked, coming closer. "It means it's time for you to die..."

There was something ridiculous about the entire situation. A thin, small girl was threatening to kill a tall, broad guy. But, as funny as it seemed, I wasn't laughing. She was obviously planning on physically stopping me from being able to grab my phone and play the recording. To be honest, I still wasn't sure why she had let me record everything. Also, how was she going to explain my corpse if I wound up dead? Then again, she was probably going to be long gone before my body was discovered. However, she was obviously planning to strike soon. I needed to keep her occupied, while I kept enough distance between my phone and her.

"So, you're going to kill me, huh? Why don't I delete this recording and you go back home? You don't need any more blood on your hands. Isn't torturing animals enough for you?" I prattled on as she kept coming closer with a smile fixed on her face. "If you're going to kill me, then why didn't you murder Ram too?" I was trying to buy time. I could see the wall I had jumped over. If I turned around and ran, could I jump over it before she reached me? It all came down to how she planned to kill me. If she was going to use a gun, I had no chance at all. But I was hoping she didn't have access to a gun. At the same time, she had got illegal access to drugs, so why not a gun?

Suddenly, she stopped and replied to my last question, "There was no need to kill Ram. It was more fun to watch him live and suffer. But I want you out of Naina's life. It's not difficult to kill someone with diabetes. Besides, I think I'm finally ready to kill a human being. Framing people is fun, but taking a life has a different kind of thrill!"

She had given me a hint about how she wanted to kill me. She either wanted my blood glucose level to go too high or too low. But my guess was she wanted to send it plummeting, since that would make me lose consciousness very soon. Nisha carried on while these thoughts raced through my mind, "I did you a lot of favours. I told you the truth about Naina's condition and helped you to understand her. I patched things up between you and Naina. I would even have given evidence tomorrow to stop you from getting expelled. But you went too far in your search for the truth. If you believe in rebirth, then in your next life, stay away from my sister!" She practically growled out the last few words.

Then, I was running. I just needed to get enough momentum to jump the wall. Maybe I should have listened to Romik and exercised more. I was already panting. I was conscious of Nisha running behind me, but I didn't dare look back. She obviously didn't have a gun. I still had no desire to find out how she meant to kill me. I put on a desperate burst of speed and tried to jump the wall. For a moment, I was free! Then Nisha caught hold of my legs and pulled me down. I collapsed with my upper body above the wall and my legs stretched out behind me. I covered my face with my arms as I fell. The impact still knocked the breath from my body. My upper body crashed down in slow motion till I lay in a tumbled heap at the base of the wall with Nisha standing over me.

I thought she would try to jump me and take advantage of the pain coursing through my entire body. But she didn't. She casually walked up to me and said, "Thanks for making it easy for me." Then she pulled out a stun gun (taser) and touched my arm with its 2 electrodes. If I had been in pain before, I was in agony now. It felt like every nerve in my body was on fire! I jerked around crazily as my body convulsed. I couldn't stop Nisha. I couldn't even move a finger. Meanwhile, Nisha unzipped my bag and took out my insulin pen. The maximum dose I take at a time is 30 units. But Nisha injected me with 300 units! Since I was jerking around while she injected me, there were cuts all over my injected arm. She stooped down to my ear and whispered, "Say good night!" Then, I saw a face and heard a voice I definitely hadn't expected. Naina stood behind Nisha and said, "Not quite yet, sis. I think we should have a talk first..."

CHAPTER 59

I was still jerking uncontrollably as Naina approached us. I wasn't sure whether I should be happy or sad to see her. Was she going to put a stop to Nisha's crazy plan? Or had she just come to gloat with her sister? I took one look at Nisha...and realised the truth. All the colour had drained out of Nisha's face. She looked like someone who had just seen a ghost. She kept muttering to herself, "No, no, no, no, no..." She obviously hadn't expected or wanted to see Naina here. That meant Naina probably wanted to save me.

Sure enough, just as the thought entered my head, Naina said, "You're going to kill him, sis. Are you out of your mind?" Her voice was surprisingly calm and collected. "Did you really think I wouldn't guess you were messaging Pranav when you borrowed my phone yesterday? I thought you were playing some kind of prank on me. But this...this is insane. I don't care if he broke my heart or yours. I can't stand by and watch you kill someone. There is no way I'm letting my sister become a murderer."

Nisha finally managed to whisper, "How did you find us?" That was exactly what I was wondering. "I ran into Pranav's mom at reception. She said he was here to meet me. She told me where he'd run off to. She's coming here as we speak. So, put away the insulin and the taser, and come with me," Naina said, as if she were talking to a

5-year-old. For a moment, Nisha hesitated. Then she got a determined look on her face. "You're not going to stop me. Not now. I'll kill his mother too! I'll kill everyone who tries to come between us. I'll kill anyone who tries to harm you!" shrieked Nisha, getting hysterical.

"No one's going to harm me, sis. The only one who's getting hurt is you. Please stop this," Naina said as she began to walk closer and closer to Nisha. Nisha held up the taser and Naina stopped. "Do you plan to kill me too, sis?" asked Naina softly. Tears were streaming down Nisha's cheeks now. "I just want you to be safe. Why is that so difficult to understand?" she cried. "I understand perfectly, sis. But you can't kill the whole world in the process. I'm not going to let you go to jail for murdering someone," Naina said, walking forward again. Nisha jabbed the taser in Naina's general direction. But her hand was trembling.

Speaking of trembling, it so happened that my taser tremors were coming to a stop. Neither sister had noticed, but I could now curl my fingers into a fist. I still couldn't get up and stop Nisha, but maybe I could distract her for a while. Strangely, I suddenly felt intensely hungry and started sweating. This was not good. My sugar must have been low as I had delayed lunch. On top of that, the insulin I had been injected by Nisha must have started acting. Therefore, my blood glucose level was dropping fast. As the sisters argued, my vision developed black spots in the middle. In another 5-10 minutes, I would be unconscious. I had to do what I could immediately. I looked at Nisha's legs. One was near my right hand. I moved my right hand around her ankle and grabbed it tight. Then I pulled hard!

Nisha glanced down when I gripped her ankle. Before she could react, I yanked and she began to fall. Naina was ready. She pulled the taser away from her sister and held on to it. Nisha collapsed next to me. Naina bent down and touched the taser's electrodes to Nisha's arm. Nisha began to convulse. She was down for the count. It was over. I saw black for a minute. Then I saw Naina's face above me. When I smiled, she smiled back and helped me sit up. I was still a little stiff from the effects of the taser, but with Naina's help, I got to my feet. "Your mom will be here soon. Don't die on me," said Naina with a tremulous smile, but worried eyes. "Meanwhile, you and I need to talk..."

I vaguely remember stumbling to my feet and walking shakily with a lot of help from Naina. She let me lean on her. I could see she was straining from the effort. My huge body was nearly crushing her delicate frame. By now, my sugar was probably in free fall. I felt dizzy and weak. I was scared I was going to black out any minute. "So, where exactly are we going?" I asked Naina. "Towards your mom," came Naina's prompt reply. "You want to chat while I'm still alive, or do you want to let your sister get away with murder and be holding the corpse when everyone arrives?" I joked. Naina glared at me, as if she wanted to kill me, but then grinned.

"You're still not officially forgiven. Why were you meeting Nisha, by the way?" she asked. "Well, I thought I was meeting you, but... it's a long story," I said, smiling back. Then I remembered what I had come to do. I began, "Listen, you're probably not going to believe me, but

Nisha is..." I was interrupted by Naina, "...trying to harm me and protect me at the same time. I know, Pranav. I've always known." I looked at her in shock. "You knew?! You knew the whole truth about everything? And you never told me? Why?" I asked, aware that speaking without slurring was getting difficult.

Naina stopped and looked at me with an extremely pained expression. "I'm so sorry. But she's my sister and I love her. I never thought this side of her would show itself again. When we were young, she tried to drown me in a swimming pool. Thankfully, my parents stopped her. She then began to call herself the 'Tigress' and developed another meaner side to her character. She developed a sadistic streak and began torturing animals and hurting even those she loved. My parents got her the best treatment possible. The doctors said she *didn't* have a split personality, but was obsessed with me. She was protective of me; she wanted to keep me to herself – away from the rest of the world. I knew she wasn't stable even with medication, but my parents and brother thought I was imagining things. She would often hurt me and frame others. We increased her dosage and she seemed normal in high school. But I was always afraid this would happen again."

Naina stopped and turned away from me. She cried silently and her tears mixed with the rainwater. She looked back at me and said, "I'm so sorry, lame-brain. I love you and I know you love me too. I had no right to keep this from you." She stood on tiptoes and kissed me. It felt like a nicer version of the taser. Every nerve in my body began tingling. I wanted to stay like this forever. However, my body wasn't okay with that arrangement. I fell on the ground. Naina helped me stand up again.

The wind was howling now. The rain was coming down in sheets. Clearly, my brain wasn't functioning properly, because my first thought was that Nisha was going to get wet even though she disliked it!

"It was the schizophrenia, wasn't it? That's why you weren't sure whether you were just imagining stuff or Nisha was actually trying to harm you. I'm right, aren't I?" I asked, willing myself to stay conscious. Naina nodded slowly. I pulled out my phone and handed it to her. "Here. This has all the evidence of her guilt. Tell everyone the truth of what happened here. I love you...more than life itself," I said, trying to keep my balance. Naina smiled that smile of hers I loved so much. "Sure you love a 'psycho-freak'?" she teased. I laughingly replied, "It takes one to know one!" We both kissed.

"You know, lame-brain, you have all kinds of animals on your campus. From 'Tigresses' to monkeys to ducks. And I'm not even counting the faculty and students! This place could probably be called a wildlife sanctuary!" Naina joked. I laughed, though my vision was clouding. "Where's my bag?" I slurred the words. "I need Coke," I managed to say. "It fell near Nisha. Shall I run and fetch it for you?" Naina asked. I nodded my assent.

Before going, Naina looked me straight in the eye and said, "I have one last favour to ask of you..." She paused as if unsure. I had no idea what she had in mind. "What do you want from me?" I asked, feeling totally clueless. "I want your forgiveness," she replied. I was confused. "I forgive you. I thought the fact that we're kissing on my deathbed made that obvious!" I said, trying to smile. She gave me a half-smile in return. "Not for me..." she whispered. My eyes opened wide as I realised what she meant. "You want me to forgive *Nisha*? Why?! What possible reason could I have for forgiving my would-be murderer?" I slurred. I couldn't believe what Naina was suggesting. "I know, I know. She's crazy. But so was I at one time. You didn't lose faith in me. So, I'm asking, no begging, you to let her walk free. She's my twin sister and I love her no matter what. I hope you understand. Please!" begged Naina.

For a long moment, I stood silent. Then I nodded once. Naina kissed me one last time and ran to get my bag. The clouds rumbled ominously overhead. The sky blazed with lightning. As drops of rain fell on my brow, I wondered where the hell the roof was! I tried to focus on the here and now. My mom was rushing towards me. I would pretend that it was a suicide attempt. Nisha would walk free and Naina would be happy. I heard my mother call me, but I was sinking into the black...

CHAPTER 60

Naina walked slowly over to her twin sister. They were not identical, though they might as well have been. After all, their souls were the same. Nisha was still convulsing from the taser. Naina gazed at her. She was still holding onto the taser. For once, she was angry with her sister and was tempted to use the taser again. Nisha managed to smile through her agony. She asked haltingly, "D-D-Did y-y-you do it, s-s-sis?" Naina said nothing. Her face was expressionless and her eyes were completely empty. Then she bent her face towards her sister and whispered, "You're not out of trouble yet!" Nisha's eyes widened in shock and she tried to move away from her sister. But her limbs were still dancing madly. She was stuck and she knew it. "S-s-sis, you know w-w-why I-I had to do it, r-r-right?" she begged desperately. Naina bent down and used her free hand to stroke Nisha's cheek.

Then Naina began to speak, "Don't worry about the authorities. Or about Pranav. I fed him a pack of lies about how everyone in our family knew you were crazy and how you always wanted to hurt me, since we were children." Naina's eyes began to sparkle and she continued, "I acted like you were on medication, which was the only thing keeping you from a mental asylum. I pretended that I was the only one who suspected that you still wanted to harm me. He was so stupid, he believed me. The best bit is he made up the most difficult part of the story himself. He assumed that because I had got schizophrenia, I was no longer able to tell if you were really trying to hurt me or not. He was right...to some extent. Some of your 'pranks' really freaked me out. But no one, except us, knows that you let me in on the secret later."

Naina stopped stroking Nisha's cheek and got to her feet again. There was a mischievous glint in her eyes. "You did a good job – claiming credit for my schemes to hurt Ram and send the report to Amrish. I like the way you set yourself up as the main villain. Acting comes naturally to us, I guess. Anyway, he gave me his phone. We just need to get rid of the recording and then he has no proof. In any case, he's so in love with me that he would never tell anyone his version of the truth. Everything has gone off smoothly," said Naina. Then, her voice hardened, "But as he cared for me during my delusions, I...loved him back."

By now, Nisha could control her jaw. "I had to try and kill him, sis. You were getting too attached. It was the only way," Nisha muttered, as her eyes pleaded with her sister. Naina was unmoved. She said, "No. I-I loved him. But I wasn't about to let that come in the way of our hunt. You should have been content to follow my lead. I, and I alone, decide the time to strike! I let you torture and kill animals to satisfy your urges. But when we have bigger fish to fry, I take charge. However, when the schizophrenia set in, you thought you could usurp my position, didn't you? We had already discussed how to get Ram into even more trouble, after I pretended to freak out when he kissed me. But you foolishly went ahead without my approval. In fact, you could have been spotted with Ram at the hotel and got into trouble. Next, you thought my love for Pranav would get in the way of our hunt. That's when you tried to frame me for having sent Amrish the mail. But you should have had more faith in me. After all, I am a few seconds older. I figured Pranav would try to contact me to warn me about you. But, at that time, you conveniently borrowed my phone. I guessed you had set up a meeting with him and were coming here to kill Pranav. So, I followed you and listened secretly to your conversation with Pranav. You're good, sis...but I'm better!" Naina paused for breath and noticed that her sister had stopped jerking.

"Do you need another dose of this? Or are you going to stay down and listen?" asked Naina menacingly, waving the taser in front of Nisha. Nisha immediately cringed and raised her hands defensively. "Please don't, sis. I'll do whatever you say. I promise," she replied. Naina nodded, then carried on, "When I realised you were going to kill him, I understood 2 things. One was that you need me to look after you. The second was that you complete me. That's when I knew I had to stop you from killing him. You would have been caught and locked away for good. We would never have been able to meet again. That's why I had to intervene. I'm pretty sure Pranav will survive, but he'll never tell anyone what really happened here. When I'm through with him, he won't have any evidence against us. Now come on. Rain's stopped."

Naina held out her hand and helped Nisha get shakily to her feet. "I'm sorry, sis. I should never have tried to go it alone," muttered Nisha. "Yes, you shouldn't have," Naina replied. "You know, it's funny. I told Pranav everything. Even the fact that you're the 'Tigress'. The only thing I didn't tell him is that I'm the 'Lioness'! The ultimate predator and mistress of the hunt!" finished Naina.

www.ingramcontent.com/pod-product-compliance
Lightning Source LLC
LaVergne TN
LVHW041146150826
845673LV00001B/76

* 9 7 9 8 8 8 9 7 5 9 7 7 5 *